F LEW

The Crossroad

BEVERLY LEWIS

The Crossroad

BETHANY HOUSE PUBLISHERS
MINNEAPOLIS, MINNESOTA 55438

The Crossroad
Copyright © 1999
Beverly M. Lewis

Cover by Dan Thornberg

Published by Bethany House Publishers
A Ministry of Bethany Fellowship International
11400 Hampshire Avenue South
Minneapolis, Minnesota 55438
www.bethanyhouse.com

Printed in the United States of America by
Bethany Press International, Minneapolis, Minnesota 55438

ISBN 0–7642–2212–0 (Paperback)
ISBN 0–7642–2239–2 (Hardbound)
ISBN 0–7642–2240–6 (Large Print)
ISBN 0–7642–2238–4 (Audio Book)

Library of Congress Cataloging-in-Publication Data

Lewis, Beverly, 1949–
    The crossroad / by Beverly Lewis.
        p.   cm.
    Sequel to: The postcard.
    ISBN 0–7642–2239–2
    ISBN 0–7642–2212–0 (pbk.)
    I. Title.
PS3562.E9383 C76   1999
813'.54—dc21   99–6719
                                                    CIP

This book is lovingly dedicated
to my parents,
Herb and Jane (Buchwalter) Jones,
whose zeal and devotion to God
have both inspired and encouraged me
throughout my life.

Together, they pastored
Glad Tidings Temple
in Lancaster, Pennsylvania,
during my growing-up years.

By Beverly Lewis

*with David Lewis

About the Author

❖ ❖ ❖

Beverly Lewis was born in the heart of Pennsylvania Dutch country. She fondly recalls her growing-up years, and due to a keen interest in her mother's Plain family heritage, many of Beverly's books are set in Lancaster County.

A former schoolteacher, Bev is a member of The National League of American Pen Women—the Pikes Peak branch—and the Society of Children's Book Writers and Illustrators. Her bestselling books are among the C. S. Lewis Noteworthy List Books. Bev and her husband have three children and make their home in Colorado.

Prologue: Rachel Yoder

❖ ❖ ❖

*A*ll my life I've been drawn to wooded land-
scapes—thick green groves of maple and sycamore. And
weeping willows, 'specially those growing alongside the
creek bed. As a young girl, I often crept out of the house
just as the sun's glorious first rays peeped over distant
hills, running lickety-split through dawn-tinted shadows of lofty tree umbrellas. Those early-morning ram-
blings, and the carefree way I felt in the midst of the
woodland, gave me cause for living.

Now, as a young widow and mother, I'm reasonably
content to help my parents run the Orchard Guest
House, instruct my six-year-old daughter, Annie, in the
ways of the Lord—and the Beachy Amish church—and
help out wherever I can amongst the People, doing my
best to keep up with sewing, quilting, gardening, canning, cooking, and cleaning house with *Mam*, in spite
of things being the way they are with my eyes.

Here lately, I've begun to miss my morning run more
than ever, but I daresn't mention it to Mam or *Dat*, or
they might start pressing me to pay a visit to Blue
Johnny or one of the other powwow doctors in the area.
Far as I'm concerned, that subject's settled, 'cause at
long last I know the whole story behind my great-uncle

Gabe Esh—on account of an innocent little postcard, of all things. So I know in my heart of hearts, sympathy healing and Blue Johnny's "black box" just ain't for me. Not for any of us, really.

Ach, such a time we've had here lately. On Thanksgiving Day my young nephew Joshua Beiler nearly drowned in the frigid pond back behind Bishop Glick's house, where a wedding of one of the bishop's granddaughters had just taken place. I 'spect Josh was just itchin' to crack through the ice, knowin' how Lizzie's boy carries on sometimes.

My Annie said Cousin Josh was "a-flailin' and a-squealin'," carrying on to beat the band about getting himself soaked and freezin' cold. Well, it was nothing short of divine intervention that our Mennonite neighbor was out driving past the pond 'bout the time Josh skidded out of control and slammed through the surface into the frosty water below. *Jah,* the boy's life was spared, and it's a right *gut* thing, too, this side of Christmas and all.

Back last week, we had us a time while some of the women were over at Lavina Troyer's—my father's distant cousin—butchering chickens. Honest to goodness, if one of the teenage boys—who was helping chop heads off, defeather, and char the birds—didn't cut off one of his own fingers in the process. 'Course, someone had the presence of mind to wrap the finger, along with the missing piece, and hasten him off to the Community Hospital.

Then yesterday our cocker spaniel puppy, Copper, knocked over the birdbath in the backyard, breaking several terra-cotta pots along the walkway. Mam scolded the poor thing up one side and down the other; really, 'twas a shame the way she laid into him. But that's her way of handling most any conflicting situation—take the bull by the horns and show 'um who's boss.

Other than those mishaps, we've had a real pleasant autumn, I'd say. But just the other day, Mam remarked that she hated to see the "chillin' winds come and benumb the posies."

'Course, I agreed with her, though I can't actually see the nipped blossoms any more than I can make out my own little girl's features, but I *do* remember how the early frost used to make bedding flowers turn dark and shrivel up.

Mam and I, with some help from Annie, who pushed up a kitchen chair to stand on, baked a batch of molasses cookies to serve to our B&B guests at our afternoon tea. We topped the morning off with a steamy mug of hot cocoa, and all the while Mam bemoaned the fact that snowy months were just around the corner.

My heart feels more like the onset of springtime, though I don't exactly know what's come over me. Even little Annie seems to notice the bounce in my step. Mam, on the other hand, acts as though she's downright put out with me, and if what I 'spect is true, she has it in her head that the fruit basket got upset back in September when a New York City journalist paid a visit here at the Orchard Guest House. I'll have to admit, Philip Bradley *did* raise quite a ruckus, findin' Gabe Esh's love note the way he did. But I believe God put that old postcard in Philip's hands, and, honestly, I don't care what the People say or think, or anybody else for that matter. Out-and-out timely was his discovery of Great-Uncle Gabe's story—hushed up under a covering of mystery far too long.

"Rachel," my father said to me last night at supper, "you have no idea what that New York fella did, comin' and diggin' up the past, finding Gabe's note thataway. No idea a'tall."

Oh, but I *did* know. For sure and for certain, Philip was the best thing that had happened here in Bird-in-Hand in recent years, and whether or not the journalist ever returned to do research or write more Plain articles was beside the point. Fact was, he'd changed the entire landscape of a gut many lives. 'Specially mine.

Part One

❖ ❖ ❖

'Tis the gift to be simple,
'Tis the gift to be free,
'Tis the gift to come down
Where we ought to be.
And when we find ourselves
In the place just right,
'Twill be in the valley
Of love and delight.
When true simplicity is gain'd
To bow and to bend
We shan't be asham'd,
To turn, turn will be our delight
'Til by turning, turning we come round right.

—Shaker Hymn, 1848

York photojournalists were known to be pushy and demanding. They had to be.

"Just caught your Amish piece. Keep it up, and I'll be working for *you* someday," Henning said.

"You could do worse," Philip joked.

The elevator door opened and they followed the crowd inside.

Philip turned to Henning and whispered, "So . . . you liked my Christmas feature?"

"Yeah, yeah, but the photos were weak. You didn't give 'em much to work with. That's what I wanted to talk to you about."

"Uh-oh. Here we go." Philip chuckled.

"No, this is good. Hear me out. I'm thinking about a photo essay . . . featuring the Amish."

At the mention of the Plain People, a number of heads turned. Henning dropped his voice. "I think we could get Farrar, Straus & Giroux interested if you're on board."

Philip cringed. Most likely, the young photographer had no knowledge of Plain folk and their ways, probably didn't know they would shy away from being the subject of a photograph.

The elevator doors opened at the thirty-fourth floor, and the mass of humanity poured out. He followed Henning past the law offices of Abrahms and Hampshire to the double doors of *Family Life Magazine*. They opened to an enormous room of congested cubicles housing busy writers and copy editors. The entire floor was abuzz with the low but steady hum of computers, ringing phones—cell and otherwise—and human voices, peo-

One

❖ ❖ ❖

𝓜anhattan's skyscrapers jeered down at him as he flung open the door of the cab and crossed the narrow, congested street. Behind him, yellow cabs zigzagged in and out of indefinable traffic lanes, blaring their horns. Side by side, late-model cars, shiny limousines, mud-splashed delivery trucks, and pristine tour buses waited for the light to change, exuding puffs of exhaust. Each contributing to the chaos typical of New York City's business district.

The glassed entrance to the Lafayette Building, where the editorial offices of *Family Life Magazine* were located on the thirty-fourth floor, revolved with an endless tide of humanity, ebbing and flowing.

Pulling his overcoat against his tall lean frame, Philip Bradley pushed through the crush of the crowd, leaning into the bitter December wind. At the portico, he nodded to the Salvation Army volunteer with the red velvet Santa suit, ringing a small but mighty brass bell, the *plinking* of which added to the hubbub.

"Merry Christmas," the would-be Santa called to Philip, and the young journalist stuffed a five-dollar bill—his first contribution of the season—into the donation box.

"Bless you," Santa sang out.

May the Lord bless you always. . . .

The words had echoed in Philip's brain these past months, and immediately his thoughts sped back to the unassuming and beautiful Plain woman he had met while staying at an Amish B&B in Lancaster County. A young widow with a delightful little daughter named Annie, Rachel Yoder lived in the quiet farming community of Bird-in-Hand. While on assignment for the magazine, he had gone to research Amish Christmas customs, staying—by mere chance, he'd thought at the time—at Rachel's parents' Orchard Guest House on Olde Mill Road.

"May the Lord bless you always," had been Rachel's parting words, and the impact of her blessing and gracious Christian witness had resonated unceasingly in his mind. So much so that Philip had begun to read his Bible again, after years of indifference; even attended church services with his married sister and family, the very church he had once privately sneered.

Inside the atrium-style lobby, businessmen and women bustled to and fro, their well-polished shoes clattering and scuffing against gleaming tiled corridors.

The security guard addressed Philip with a nod and "Morning, Mr. Bradley." He returned the smile and greeting, making his way toward the elevators, where a large cluster of people extended out to the atrium itself.

Though not an impatient man, Philip glanced at his watch, wondering where he *might've* been in the early-morning scheme of things if he hadn't left his apartment twenty minutes earlier than usual. He made a mental note

to give himself an extra ten tomorrow. It might help alleviate his increased feelings of stress, what with traffic surging in ever-increasing swells—weekly, it seemed.

Philip shifted his briefcase, waiting for his turn in the elevator, recalling a recent predawn stroll—a ramble, he'd called it—while in Amish country. There had been something exceptional about that particular day; the memory lingered fondly in his mind. Something about the quietude, the beauty of witnessing the sun's lustrous, silent rise over the horizon, breaking upon distant hills, spilling a rose-stained glow across the earth.

Something ever so special, he thought, recalling an Amish expression. He couldn't seem to shake the images and emotions of that singular short week, and he did not know why. Was it the tranquil, slower pace of things he longed for? The farm-fresh aroma of cows and soil?

Philip found himself thinking of Rachel, missing her—though in a non-romantic sort of way, he was absolutely certain. They were worlds apart, and both he *and* Susanna Zook—Rachel's determined mother—had recognized the all-important fact at precisely the same moment. Nevertheless, the enticing thoughts prevailed to the point that he had to shove them aside lest he not focus sufficiently on his journalistic assignments.

"Bradley!" a man called through the crowd, standing a few feet from the elevator doors.

"Hey, Henning," Philip replied with a grin. Richard Henning was a lead photographer for the magazine. Red-haired and sporting a goatee, he was a brilliant artist, if not a little overzealous at times. But most Ne ple scrambling here and there. Philip waved at several co-workers in his section, then turned to Henning and motioned to his cubicle.

Henning started off in the opposite direction. "Give me a minute!" he shouted, and then he was gone.

Philip's writing space was clogged with vital paraphernalia: newspaper clippings, snatches of notes for interviews and email addresses, and an occasional phone number. His computer stood ready, centered on his desk, a telephone off to the left, and his married sister's family portrait—framed in oak—to the right of a wide red canister of pens and pencils. The picture included Janice, her light brown hair pulled back on one side, her tall blond husband, Kenneth, sporting a jovial smile, and their perky, flaxen-haired daughter, twelve-year-old Kari.

A bespeckled brunette in a navy blue pantsuit knocked on his partition just as Philip was logging on to the computer. "Great piece, Phil."

Looking up, he smiled at Beth, a top-notch copy editor for the magazine. "Thanks . . . but *you* make me sound good."

"So, any truth to the rumor?" she asked, ignoring the kudo.

Philip scratched his chin. "Okay, I'll bite. What rumor?"

"That you're joining the Amish." She stood at attention in the doorway, as though waiting for an answer.

"My buggy permit hasn't shown up in the mail yet. Until then, all plans are on hold."

Beth laughed. "Don't ask me to ride with you." She wiggled her fingers at him, then headed across the room.

Philip turned back to his desk and thumbed through his Rolodex, locating the address for his late-afternoon interview. Congressman Thomason, New York state senator. A man who, at the age of fifty-eight, had become an adoptive father. The perfect feature for next June's Father's Day issue.

Meanwhile, Henning had returned looking like a hungry puppy. He sat in a chair in the corner of the cubicle, slurping a cup of coffee, and staring intently at Philip.

"I know that look," Philip said.

Henning's smile turned dubious. "So . . . I come up with these incredible ideas, and all you want to do is shoot them down. That's what our friendship's come to?"

Philip sighed dramatically. "Okay, let's hear it."

Henning's smile broadened, and he affected his best Ross Perot impression. "Here's the deal."

Philip groaned.

"In a nutshell—I set up the photo shoot; you write the copy. Subject matter: the Amish."

"It's been done."

"Not like *I* can do it," Henning replied. "We go more in depth, maybe find an Amish family that'll take us in for a few days. Up close and personal. None of this superficial and pretentious stuff. We'll bring more humanity to the subject."

"With pictures," Philip muttered.

"Lots," Henning replied without skipping a beat. "The way I see it, this Amish thing's a hot button. People are just plain nuts about the plain and simple." He laughed at his own word play. "Everyone's yearning for the earthy, the back-to-basics approach to things . . . to everything."

What the man said rang true. Maybe the unending emphasis on technology *had* backfired on the entire human race. Were we, all of us, craving a simpler life, a slower pace?

Philip studied Henning. "Count me out this time."

"That's it? Just like that, you dismiss it?"

Shaking his head, Philip said, "I don't feel comfortable about any of it."

Henning rubbed his pointer finger back and forth under his nose. "I don't follow, Phil. I thought you were smitten with the Plain culture. Bob says it's all you talk about . . . Amish this, horse and buggy that."

Bob Snell, their editor, had every reason to regurgitate Philip's own enthusiasm to Rick Henning. "Most Amish disapprove of photographers," Philip explained. "It wouldn't be such a good idea to sneak around with your high-powered lens, taking shots of folk who've chosen to disconnect from the outside world, which just happens to include free-lance photographers."

Henning's jaw dropped. "Are you saying I can't zoom in on the eighteenth century, standing halfway across a pasture?"

"There's a difference between *can't* and *shouldn't*." Philip inhaled, then expelled the air loudly.

"Hold on a minute. Couldn't we try to get their permission—at least make some attempt?"

Philip wasn't surprised at his friend's persistence. "Whose permission?" he asked.

"*You* met some Amish folk—some you interviewed,

right? Just get their consent. How hard can that be?"

Philip thought of little Annie Yoder and her widowed mother, Rachel; the stiff-lipped Susanna Zook and her bearded husband, Benjamin. He shook his head, staring hard at the bridge of Henning's long nose. "You really don't get it, do you, Richard? We're outsiders to the Amish world—two men they'd never be willing to trust, especially one with a camera poised and focused. Sorry, I'm not interested in exploiting their lifestyle to make some extra bucks."

"But the Amish exploit themselves. You've seen the tourist ads out in Ohio—tourism is a big part of their livelihood."

Philip stood his ground. "There are limits."

"All right, have it your way." Henning got up to leave. "But I'll be back."

Philip crumpled his coffee cup and threw it, but Henning ducked and scampered down the hallway.

Philip turned his attention to the project at hand— writing three pages of upbeat, family oriented questions for Senator Thomason. Something to engage and inspire the middle-aged politician, questions to set him at ease, make him feel altogether comfortable chatting about the toddler-aged Romanian twin girls he and his wife had recently adopted. Philip promptly set to work, putting Henning and the ridiculous proposal out of his mind.

Two

❖ ❖ ❖

*R*achel Yoder sat next to Lavina Troyer in the older woman's enclosed Amish buggy, wrapped in a woolen lap robe. She heard the gentle clatter and *clip-clop* of a passing horse as they headed south on Beechdale Road toward Lavina's house for a morning of baking. Just the two of them.

"Nothin' gut ever comes of deceit," Lavina said out of the blue.

Rachel listened intently. She had become slightly better acquainted with her father's somewhat eccentric relative recently. The discovery of an old postcard had drawn the two women together.

"Awful shame . . . the People payin' no mind to Gabe's preachin' back when."

Of course, Rachel supposed a gut many *had* given it some thought, seeing as how there was a hearty group of Amish Mennonites 'round here these days. She patted her mittened hands together against the cold, attempting to warm them under the blanket. "Uncle Gabe had a right gut heart," she said.

"Not one bit timid 'bout preachin' the gospel neither . . . long afore you was born."

Rachel thought on that. "I'm wonderin' some-

23

thing." She paused a moment, deciding if this was the right time to tell the woman 'bout the promptings inside her. Most everyone looked on Lavina with pity. Even Bishop Seth Fisher did, because she was slow in her mind, had to think right hard 'bout reading and writing, and needed more time than most to process her answers. Proof was in the fact that she failed near every school test she took all through eighth grade, be it true or false, multiple choice, or fill in the blank.

"Well . . . cat got your tongue?"

Lavina was trustworthy. Rachel knew it sure as anything, yet something kept her from speaking her heart. "You won't laugh if I tell you?"

"Never onct laughed at Gabe an' his secret prayers."

Rachel was truly glad to be able to share openly with someone 'bout her mysterious relative, the young man born as hesitant and shy as she, but who'd become mighty bold, rocking the community with his teachings against powwow doctoring and superstitions. Lavina was one of the few Plain folk around who knew the whole truth about Gabriel Esh, yet looked on past events in a sympathetic manner—in light of the spiritual, too, which wasn't all too common among the People.

Lavina had begun to attend the Beachy church, Rachel knew, turning her back on *das alt Gebrauch*—the Old Ways—though at the present time she was allowed to continue fellowship with many of the womenfolk from her former church district, even hold work frolics at her farmhouse. Some folk just assumed she'd upped and joined the Beachy group because of the way she was and didn't know any better.

But in the past weeks since Lavina had been driving her horse and buggy over to pick up Rachel and Annie for church, Rachel had begun to understand the woman more—what made her tick and all. Jah, Lavina's faith had nothin' whatever to do with her being slow. After all, the Good Book said "except ye . . . become as little children, ye shall not enter into the kingdom of heaven." So folks could flap their jaws all they wanted 'bout Lavina being backward, but when it came down to it, the gray-headed woman was the most accepting, kindest person Rachel knew. More so than her own mother, though Rachel assumed Susanna Zook was more peeved than uncaring these days.

"If'n ya ain't comfortable tellin' me, well . . . it's all right," Lavina spoke more softly now.

"That's kind of you." Rachel breathed in the frosty air, sure that Lavina would never tell a soul. Not if Rachel asked her to keep it under her bonnet, so to speak. She forged ahead, taking a deep breath. "I've been praying about seein' again . . . that the Lord might bless me with my sight."

Lavina said nary a word.

"I've been using Scripture tapes to memorize Bible verses 'bout divine healing, till it sinks in deep."

"Hate to think what some are sayin' 'bout your blindness, Rachel. Mighty distressing, 'tis."

Rachel knew. Even her own kinfolk figured she was as daft as Lavina was empty-headed. "But I truly *want* to see again," she said with boldness. "And in God's time, I believe I will."

She felt comfortable revealing this to Lavina, ever so

glad the woman wouldn't be gasping or boring a shameless hole in her. Jah, it was right gut to express her desire because a strong and nagging feeling reminded her that the path to recovery might be a long, difficult row to hoe.

"I'll be prayin' " was all Lavina said as the horse pulled them forward toward the intersection of Beechdale Road and Route 340.

Rachel felt her muscles relax now that she'd shared one of her deepest longings with a sister in the Lord. Her *other* secret desire must remain veiled, shrouded in silence forever.

❖ ❖ ❖

Several batches of whoopie pies were ready to be stacked in the freezer by close to midmorning. All the while, Rachel continued to talk to Lavina, though mostly a one-sided conversation, it was. "What wouldja think of goin' to visit Adele Herr?" she asked.

Lavina was slow to reply. "Are ya sure . . . you wanna go to . . . to Reading?"

"I thought we could hire a Mennonite driver. Make a morning of it."

"An awful long ways," Lavina said. "I . . . I just don't know."

"We don't hafta decide this minute, do we?" Rachel chuckled softly, a bit surprised at her own resolve. "Let's think on it. If the Lord sees fit for us to go, we can take some goodies along. Maybe a basketful to share with the rest of the nursing home folk. Spread 'round some Christmas cheer."

Again Lavina remained quiet for the longest time, and while Rachel washed up, she wondered if she might've pushed too hard. Maybe she'd best back off the subject of visiting her great-uncle's former English fiancée. Maybe it had been too long for Lavina since the pain of those past days, the wounds too well-healed to risk scraping open again.

Rachel set about humming awhile, drying her hands and praying that the Lord might give her wisdom to know how to ease the fear in the poor dear, though she couldn't say for sure that she herself wouldn't be right bashful about traipsing off to parts unknown, really and truly.

"Adele always did like my apple butter," Lavina said at last.

Shuffling her feet and using her cane, Rachel felt her way across the linoleum floor of the large kitchen. She knew its setup—where the table and benches were positioned; the wood stove, sink, counter space, and battery-powered refrigerator, too—as well as she knew the kitchen at home. Long about now the sun should be pouring in real strong through the east windows, near the long trestle table. Sure enough, as she perched on the wooden bench, she felt the warmth caress her back.

"Had a letter from Adele . . . a few weeks back," Lavina said.

Rachel was surely glad to hear this interesting tidbit. "Well, if it's any of my business, what did she have to say?"

"Doctor's givin' her a different medicine. Seems to be helpin' some."

Rachel was curious, though she was too hesitant to ask. Had Adele mentioned anything of Philip Bradley in her letter?

But Lavina was off on another tack. "Sometimes I wonder if'n folk who knew 'bout Adele and Gabe's affection for each other . . . ever questioned why me 'n her never visited through the years," she remarked.

"I've wondered that myself."

"Me 'n Adele didn't write all that much—mostly just Christmas cards and birthdays."

Rachel perked up her ears. The woman was talking up a blue streak!

" 'Twasn't my idea for Adele to stay put in Reading—not come to visit me none. But . . . well, we'd killed off her one and only love, so 'course she wouldn't wanna come back—not here."

"But you invited her plenty, didn'tcha?"

Lavina was quiet again, then she replied, "Adele was happiest teachin' school close to home."

Rachel could understand that. She, too, was a homebody. "Did she ever leave Reading?"

"Far as I know, never did." Lavina sighed and her breath sputtered a bit. "Doubt she ever forgave the bishop for Gabe's dyin' an' all."

"For goodness' sake, why *not?*"

"We're sharin' secrets today, ain't? So I got one of my own." Lavina drew in another deep breath. "It's been a-troublin' me for years, now."

Rachel felt herself tense up, wonderin' what was coming next.

"Adele did write me onct . . .'bout the bishop and Gabe."

"She did?"

"Jah. Guess I oughta try 'n look for it . . . so's you know for yourself what I mean," Lavina said, excusing herself.

Rachel heard the quick footsteps on the stairs, and after what seemed like a long time, the woman returned. "Listen here to this. Back in 1963—one year after Gabe's death—Adele wrote this to me."

Lavina rattled the letter and, with great effort, began to sound out the words: " 'Something tells me things were . . . horribly strained between Bishop Seth Fisher and Gabe . . . prior to the accident. You may not know it, but Gabe once told me . . . that the bishop had . . . threatened his life on more than one occasion.' "

Rachel was aghast. "Threatened his life? Whatever for?" She thought back to Adele's story. What had *she* said about any of this?

" 'Twasn't any secret . . . some of the People thought the bishop put a hex on Gabe." Lavina's voice trembled momentarily.

Rachel felt breathless all of a sudden, as though someone had knocked the air out of her. "The *bishop*? A *hex*? I hate hearin' suchlike."

"Well, I, for one, never believed it. 'Least I didn't *want* to. And now it's mighty hard to know for sure, really."

"What with most everyone who knew anything 'bout it long passed on to Glory?" asked Rachel.

"Jah."

"Bishop Fisher's still alive," Rachel offered, hoping

to draw more of the story from the one and only person who might know something 'bout her great-uncle's untimely death.

"Well's . . . there's no talkin' to *him*."

"I 'spose. The way Gabe upped and died . . . I hafta say I thought it seemed awful peculiar," Rachel replied. "Too abrupt it was, and right after he'd started preachin' so strong against powwow doctors and all. Does seem right suspicious, really."

"Best to just leave it be."

Leave it be. . . .

Lavina's words churned in Rachel's mind. Her own father had said something similar when she'd asked questions about Gabe's unjust shunning and ultimate excommunication. Rachel knew from Adele's lips the stand Dat and others had taken in their hush-hush approach to Gabe's ousting.

The women's talk eventually turned to domestic matters. "Are you comin' to Aunt Leah's for the quilting frolic next week?" Rachel asked.

"If'n I don't up and kick the ol' bucket. That, or they make the shun worse on me than 'tis already." Lavina laughed a little, making Rachel feel even more uneasy.

"I don't think we oughta talk 'bout untimely deaths or shunnings," Rachel was quick to say. "We best guard our lips."

"Well, now, I think you're right, prob'ly."

"The Lord's been showin' me some things in the Scriptures that have pricked my heart here lately."

Lavina spoke up. "Talk has it your cousin's spoon-feedin' you *her* beliefs."

"I don't have to guess who's sayin' those things." Rachel knew, sure as anything, Mam and Aunt Leah were the ones, prob'ly. "It won't be long and the People will know for sure and for certain. What I believe ain't just from Esther . . . it's deep in *my* heart, too."

"Your great-uncle would be shoutin' for joy . . . if'n he could see you now—one of his own family standin' up for Jesus right under Bishop Seth's nose. Just goes to show . . . no matter how hard the ol' enemy tries to stamp out the torch of truth, God always raises up someone to carry it along."

Rachel wished she could see the heavenly glow that surely must've settled over Lavina's long and slender face. Why, she'd never in all her days heard the backward woman express herself so easily, so sensibly.

Lavina rose and poured black coffee and served some homemade cinnamon buns. "I think you may be right 'bout spreading 'round some Christmas joy . . . up there in Reading."

Rachel's heart leaped up. "So you *do* wanna visit Adele?"

"Didn't know it before this minute, but, jah, I believe I do!"

Rachel didn't know what had come over her father's cousin, but she didn't plan to question Lavina's decision.

"I'll do some bakin' to take along, then." Lavina made a slurping sound in her coffee. "It'll be ever so nice, seein' the dear English girl again."

Dear English girl. Rachel had to smile at the remark. Of course, the older woman would remember Adele Herr as the young Baptist who'd come to fill in at the one-room school those many years ago. "Adele seemed like such a nice lady when I met her back in September. But I think it was right hard on her, tellin' the saddest story of her life."

They fell silent for a time, and Rachel relished the coffee bean aroma filling the kitchen.

It was Lavina who brought up Adele's letter again. "She's been gettin' letters—even postcards—from her friend in New York."

"Would that be . . . the journalist who came last fall?" Rachel carefully kept her tone matter-of-fact.

"That's who. Said Philip's become almost like a son. And he's goin' to church again, readin' his Bible, too."

"Well, I'll be. . . ." Rachel licked the syrup from her fingers.

"Seems them two are becoming fast friends . . . since he's the one who found Gabe's postcard, 'n all."

"I'm not surprised, really," Rachel replied. And lest she give too much away, she hushed right up. Wasn't anybody's business how often her mind traveled back to the early autumn days, when Philip Bradley had been a guest at the B&B.

After they'd finished drinking a second cup of coffee and devoured more than their share of sticky buns, Rachel rose to wash her hands. She was more than grateful she'd come to Lavina's today. Seemed to her the Lord was working in *both* their lives! Honestly, she thought it would be ever so nice if Philip Bradley would send *her* a letter. 'Course, the way Mam told him off on the phone that final day, the man would have to have nerves of steel to consider such a thing!

Three

❖ ❖ ❖

Kari opened the door nearly the instant his finger pressed the doorbell. "Uncle Phil!" she squealed, as though she hadn't seen him in years. She threw her arms around his neck, and he leaned down, hugging her.

"How's my sunshine?"

She let go, stepping back, then twirled about to model her long floral skirt, blond hair fanning out around her shoulders. "What do you think? I made it without any help from Mom."

"Wow, is *this* the sewing project you told me about?" He eyed the new skirt. "So . . . along with your *other* talents, you're a seamstress, too."

Kari beamed, still posing a few feet from the arched entrance to the dining room, where the table was set with Janice's best dishes and tall white tapers, already lit for supper. Kari had chosen the perfect backdrop to show off her newly acquired domestic skill.

"Hey, wait a minute. I think I may be underdressed for this occasion." He unbuttoned his overcoat, pulling it open slightly to gaze down comically at his own clothing—dress slacks and a sweater.

Kari giggled at his antics, her blue eyes twinkling.

"You're just fine, Phil." Janice breezed into the living room, reaching for his coat. "Let me take that for you."

Philip exchanged a glance with Kari while his sister hurriedly hung up his coat in the entryway closet. "Hope you're hungry," she called over her shoulder as she sailed back to the kitchen.

Kenneth Milburn, his brother-in-law, emerged from the hall study. "Good to see you, Phil. How long has it been?" He thrust out his hand, and Philip returned the warm handshake.

"Weeks, I'm afraid," replied Philip.

"Too long," said Kari, still spinning. "It's about time for the London trip, don't you think, Uncle Phil?"

"London?" he teased, knowing she was definitely counting on him to follow through on an earlier promise.

Ken smiled. "Give your uncle a chance to catch his breath," he admonished with a wink. Then, turning to Phil, "I've heard nothing but good reports about your Vermont vacation. Kari and Janice talked of it for days. And it was educational, which was a real plus."

Kari followed her dad to the sofa and curled up on one end, while Philip took the wing-back chair across from them. "Dad thinks most *everything* in life should be educational." Kari grinned at her dad. "We toured Robert Todd Lincoln's estate, where one of Abe Lincoln's three remaining stovepipe hats just so happens to be on display. Can you believe it? Mom and I had Uncle Phil take our picture next to it. For posterity."

Philip chuckled. "Don't forget the Norman Rockwell exhibit in Arlington," he prompted her. "That was also *educational.*"

She took the cue, describing the magazine cover illustrations for *The Saturday Evening Post* they had enjoyed. "We found lots of surprises in Vermont when we stayed at Great-Grandpap's cabin."

Philip remembered. They *had* discovered some fascinating treasures on their daily treks through the woods. Things like a rusty horseshoe, old pennies, red and yellow leaves, and aluminum cans imbedded along the trail, which they picked up and deposited into Kari's backpack to be recycled later. But it was the chatter between him and his niece that he recalled as being the most rewarding aspect of the trip. For some unknown reason, she had been curious about the Amish and their plain attire—especially the women's clothing—so he had attempted to describe the details he remembered: the length of Susanna's and Rachel's dresses, the colors—not mentioning Rachel's choice of gray for mourning—the cape-style bodice and high-necked, full-length apron, and, of course, the white head covering. "Not a sign of makeup," he'd told her. "But, it's funny, you really don't notice."

"Is that because their cheeks are naturally rosy?" Kari had asked.

He thought about that. "Well, yes, I suppose they are."

"Must be all the gardening they do."

He let his niece think the latter, though he knew for a fact that Rachel Yoder had not been one to expose her face to the sun. Yet she was beautiful—pink-cheeked—nevertheless.

Kari had been so excited upon hearing his account that while they were still in New England, she decided to look for some fabric to sew a long skirt. He'd gone with Janice and Kari to a fabric store, following them around as Kari looked for the "perfect print." The material instantly reminded Philip of another flower print dress he'd seen while in Bird-in-Hand. It was very similar to Emma's dress, the Mennonite woman who owned Emma's Antique Shop.

So here was Kari, presently modeling the finished project. "It's as pretty as you said it would be," he told her. "I'd say you could compete with any Plain woman I know!"

With that, she burst into laughter again, and he felt the heat creep into his face. "Oh, so you *do* know a lady in Lancaster County." She turned away, calling for her mother. "Mom! Guess what—Uncle Phil has a secret love in Amish country."

Secret love . . .

When no reply came from the kitchen, Philip was more than relieved. No sense exposing that part of his Pennsylvania sojourn. He preferred to keep his passing interest in Rachel Yoder under wraps. That way, there could be no misunderstanding.

"What sort of grade did your mom give you on your sewing project?" he asked, changing the subject rather naturally.

"B-plus." Kari shrugged. "Mom doesn't believe in perfection, you know."

Philip wondered how his sis was managing the home-schooling program she and Ken had chosen this year. "How're you doing in language arts?" Dramatically, he pulled out a pen and tiny note pad from his shirt pocket.

"Oh, so you're going to take notes?" Quickly, Kari fluffed her hair. "Is this an interview?"

"Just checking up, that's all."

Her face shone with delight. "Tell Uncle Phil how school's going, Dad."

Ken nodded, smiling. "Janice gives Kari plenty of writing assignments, if that's what you're concerned about."

"Glad to hear it." His niece had real writing talent, quite a surprising way of expressing herself. "Tell me about some of your essays." He knew they existed because she'd dropped hints several times on their hiking trips.

"She's written some excellent poetry, too," Ken spoke up.

"Oh, Daddy, *please*."

"No, really, hon," Ken added. "I believe you may be following in your uncle's literary footsteps."

Philip had begun his early writing career by jotting down free verse during adolescence. He preferred to think of that youthful time as purely a phase, mainly because he had felt caught up in the tension of those turbulent years. But when he emerged safely into his early twenties, it was journalism that called to him. Not poetry.

He put his pen and note pad away. "So you're going

to be a girl after my own journalistic heart."

"I'm not a girl, Uncle Phil. I'm almost a teenager!"

"Hang on to your youth, kiddo." With that, he found himself pummeled with sofa pillows. Even Ken joined in the trouncing, picking up pillows and tossing them to Kari.

It was Janice's dinner bell and "Time to wash up for supper" that brought their rambunctious play to an end.

"We're having pork chops," Kari announced after they'd taken turns washing hands.

"Really? Where'd you get the recipe?" Philip asked, nearly forgetting himself.

Janice's brown eyes shot daggers across the table. "What do you mean, *where?* It's *my* recipe . . . I've been making it for fifteen years," she jived him.

He would not reveal his thoughts—that Kari's innocent announcement and the tantalizing aroma of broiled pork chops had sent him drifting back to another supper, served with an astonishing array of colorful and tasty side dishes, freshly baked bread and real butter, various condiments, and sumptuous desserts.

It was well after supper when Philip brought up the subject he had been researching on the Internet—the treatment for various hysterical disorders. Especially blindness. He hadn't fully understood Susanna Zook's comments on the phone the day he'd called Rachel to say good-bye. But after mulling it over, pieces of the full picture were beginning to come together. He was especially curious about any information Ken might have, as he was a nurse and rubbed shoulders with doctors on a daily basis.

"Tell me what you know about conversion disorder," Philip said later as Kari helped Janice clear the table.

Ken scratched his chin, leaning back in his chair. "It's rare, but we see it on occasion at the hospital. Why do you ask?"

Philip hesitated, uncertain how to proceed. How much should he reveal? How much of Rachel's situation did he really know? "I think I may have come across a case of hysterical blindness . . . in Lancaster County."

Ken frowned, apparently concerned. "Do you know what caused it?"

"Not all the particulars, but the person *did* witness the death of two family members and her unborn child."

Janice emerged from the kitchen with dessert plates. "Was this *someone* Amish?" she asked.

Nodding, Philip hoped he wouldn't have to say much more. He wouldn't feel comfortable discussing Rachel Yoder—even with his family.

"There really isn't any treatment other than psychiatric care," Ken said, shrugging. "It would depend on the cause of the conversion disorder and the extent of denial and repression."

This sort of terminology had been used on the various Web sites Philip had located when he did his investigating late at night on forms of hysteria—the term Rachel's mother had mentioned. At the time, though, he'd just assumed she was merely flinging angry words. But the more he thought about it, the more he believed that Susanna had not misrepresented the situation to him at all.

"I don't know about the denial angle." He didn't want Ken or Janice to guess just how much time he had already spent on his net-search. Fact was, the pace with which he had kept at it—feverish at times—had cost him more than a few nights of sleep.

Yet something urged him to find a way to help Rachel Yoder. She was missing out on her daughter's life, her precocious little Annie. And as much as he loved children, he was dismayed by that fact alone. So he had worked diligently over the past months, reading accounts of patients who'd received various kinds of intervention, though he assumed Rachel would be resistant to anything involving hypnosis or other forms of New Age therapy.

So he would continue to seek out medical opinions, talk to Ken and Janice—in a vague sort of way—and most of all, to pray. At some point he would decide how he should go about contacting the Amish widow. That is, *if* he chose to reach out to her directly. He'd thought of sending information her way, though with Rachel unable to see, the data might very well fall into her parents' hands, serving no purpose whatsoever.

Recent correspondence with Adele Herr had shed some light on the fact that Adele and Lavina Troyer, Adele's longtime Amish friend, still kept in touch through letters. He had actually considered Lavina the better choice for getting the information to the Bird-in-Hand area but had yet to do anything.

Ken's comment brought him back to the conversation at hand. "I'd recommend your friend getting some group grief counseling, for starters."

Grief counseling . . .

It was almost impossible to imagine Rachel seated in a circle of chairs, surrounded by non-Amish folk, pouring out her heart amid strangers, both by way of their cultural differences and because she seemed quite shy. No, he couldn't imagine her attempting such a thing. Too, the way he perceived the Amishwomen's interconnectedness in the community, no doubt there was a close bond of candor and affection among the womenfolk. More than likely, Rachel had already talked out her memories, her sorrow, and the ongoing emotional feelings of loss.

"I've read that grief counseling can help a person know they aren't going crazy—that they are experiencing the same sort of symptoms as other members in the group," Ken added.

"That, along with a feeling of camaraderie," Janice spoke up, pulling her hair back away from her face, only to let it fall down over her shoulders again. "No one should face a grief situation entirely alone."

"Just so the person doesn't become too dependent on the group," Ken interjected, "so much so that he or she gets 'stuck,' continuing to focus on the grief event rather than growing beyond it."

"Guess I'll have to go to work with you sometime . . . so you can introduce me to your shrink friends," Philip quipped.

Ken responded to Philip's jest with a hearty laugh. "The only so-called shrinks I know are brain surgeons."

That got all three of them laughing, just in time for Kari to serve up Janice's surprise dessert of the evening—apple pie a la mode, warm from the oven. The cinnamon-rich smell tickled his memory again, buttering the Lancaster County scenes in his mind's eye with vivid sensory recollections.

❖ ❖ ❖

Philip turned the key in the lock, opening the door to his thirtieth-floor Upper Manhattan apartment. On the wall of windows, he noticed the reflection that crept up from the streetlights far below. They cast a silvery glow over the living room walls, tables, and sectional.

He double-locked the door. Then, instead of turning on the lights, he allowed his eyes to grow accustomed to the dim surroundings. Feeling his way across the wide tiled entrance and toward the living area, he was able to make out more of the furnishings—the long chalk-colored sectional and matching chair, as well as the artsy decorator touches he had scouted out at various bazaars and art exhibits over the past few years. In the absence of interior light, the longer he groped his way toward the windows, the more he was able to see.

He stood near the central window and stared down at the still busy street, ablaze with red and yellow bands of color. He thought of Rachel, blind by choice, though in no way to blame for it. And he thought of bright-eyed Annie, offering her own sight—her little-girl perspective—on their noncomplicated world. It was not his place to attempt to alter things for them, to stick his nose back into their lives on the slim premise of making things better. Besides, Rachel might not embrace the prospect of regaining her sight as something better at all, although he would certainly assume so. No doubt she had been a sighted person prior to the accident that took her husband's and son's lives. Yet she *had* seemed somewhat content with her state, though he could only speculate on the matter, due, perhaps, to the fact that he'd scarcely had time to really know her. But, surprisingly, what he had discovered about her—her lack of artifice and pretense—well . . . simply put: He missed Rachel's old-fashioned mannerisms.

In his world, where women willingly and purposefully climbed corporate ladders, it was refreshing to learn that meekness and gentleness were alive and well in the heart of Pennsylvania Dutch country.

Even despite the rousing and interactive discussion with Senator Thomason this very afternoon—thoroughly enjoyable, since he himself craved the writing life—Philip recognized that in the depths of his soul he truly longed for something fresh and new. So he had come upon an unexpected fork in the road of his journalistic career—aware of his own talents, yet desirous of a saner pace and setting in which to work. He had shared these concerns openly with Lily—Adele, as she now insisted on being called—in a recent letter, detailing his soul-searching, explaining how the aspects of life in the village of Bird-in-Hand had strongly appealed to him. He'd let her know, too—as a young man might share with his own mother or father—his purposeful return to his faith, his renewed journey to know the Lord. And he *had* mentioned this to his parents as well. But Adele . . . well, there was just something about the woman that allowed him to be completely candid with her.

Adele had replied within a few days of receiving his heartfelt letter. *All of us, at one time or another, must make a choice,* she'd written back. *I'm delighted to know that you are relying on God's help with your 'fork in the road,' as I should have, back when I lost my way spiritually.* Her comment had been a direct reference to having allowed the disappointments of life to lead her astray. Philip had read and reread the passage so many times, he'd come to memorize it.

Thankfully, he wasn't standing at such a crossroad, but when the time came for him to choose a life-mate, he would hope to make his decision based on God's will.

One thing for sure, in the next weeks he would make a conscious effort to fight off the impulse to entertain even the most subtle thoughts of a plain and simple country Christmas, possibly a few stolen hours with Rachel and her young daughter in the delightful farming village.

From his perspective—where he stood this night—Rachel Yoder and her People were light years away. . . .

At last he turned from the window, disallowing himself the luxury of the track lighting overhead to guide the way to his writing studio, even closing his eyes to experience something of what it might be like *not* to see.

Then, fumbling about, he located his office chair, desk, and the computer and monitor, permitting his fingertips to direct him. Eyes tightly shut, he felt his way to the On button, then waited for his computer to boot up. Even before opening his eyes, Philip's thoughts raced ahead to his nightly research of conversion disorder, namely blind hysteria.

Four

❖ ❖ ❖

"What're we gonna do for you on your birthday?" Susanna Zook asked her younger sister, Leah, as the two women darned socks in Leah's warm kitchen.

"Ach, ya know better'n to bring up such a thing," said Leah, flashing her brown eyes.

"Well, why not? A body only turns sixty once."

"And fifty-nine once, too!" Leah, on the round side of plump, stood up and laughed over her shoulder as she prepared to pour another cup of hot black coffee.

Susanna shook her head. "Oh, go on. You can't mean it."

"I'm sayin' what I mean, Susie. You just listen to me 'bout this birthday nonsense." Leah placed two steaming mugs on the table. "Seems to me a person oughta have a say in how she celebrates—or doesn't."

"S'pose we oughta do something *extra* special for a stubborn sort like you," Susanna shot back.

"Mark my words, if there turns out to be a party or some such thing, I'll know who's to blame." She wagged her finger in Susanna's face.

"*Himmel*, then, if ya really and truly don't want nothin'."

Leah's face broke into a broad smile. "That's what I

want. No cake, no pie . . . no nothin'."

"Well, what if we sang to you at the frolic—how 'bout that?" She knew she was pushing things past where she oughta.

Leah kept her eyes on her mending. "You just never quit, do ya?"

"So . . . if you aren't sayin' we *can't* sing to you, then I 'spose that means we *can*." She'd made her pronouncement.

Leah clammed up for a good five minutes, so Susanna figured it was time to bring up another subject. Best not to allow festering thoughts to continue. Still, she didn't see any harm in honoring her youngest sibling's sixty years on God's green earth. It wouldn't be like they were behaving like the Mennonites, partying and such 'bout a birthday. No, they'd just have a nice excuse to fix a big meal and invite everybody over.

"Well, you'll never guess what I heard Rachel a-mumblin' to herself yesterday," Susanna said as casually as she could.

Leah glanced up, grunted, then stuck her head right back down, paying close attention to her poised needle.

Susanna took the grunt as a go-ahead to talk about something unrelated to birthday dinners. So she did. "*Ich hab mich awwer verschtaunt*—Was I ever surprised! Rachel was saying, 'I will see . . . I will see!' over and over in her room. Don't quite know what to make of it, really."

"I don't see how that's so surprisin'. After all, you kept tellin' me—for the past two years or so—that she's made herself blind, didn'tcha?"

"Jah, I've said as much."

"Well, maybe then she can make herself see again, too. What do you think of that?" Leah was truly serious and looked it in the face, the way her dark eyes were so awful intent on Susanna.

"If you ask me, I think Rachel's gone *ferhoodled.*" Susanna hushed up real fast, though, realizing what she'd just said. Didn't wanna let on too much 'bout her daughter's state of mind, 'specially the way Rachel seemed so awful bouncy these days . . . like she was in love or some such thing.

"What do you mean, Sister?" Leah asked, still sending forth a powerful gaze.

Susanna was cornered—had to say something or leave it up to her sister's imagination, which, in the end, might be even worse. "Ach," she pressed onward, "you know how it is when a body gets eyes fixed on something they can't have."

Leah brightened. "Are we speakin' of romance?"

Susanna swallowed hard, worried 'bout what she'd gone and gotten herself into. "Well, I couldn't say that for sure. But"—and here she dropped her sewing in her lap and gave Leah a grim look—"Rachel's a bit perplexed, I'm a-thinkin'."

"Over a man?"

She shrugged. "Who's to know."

"Well, I think *you* know," Leah piped up. "And truth be told, you oughta make positively sure that Mr. Bradley never comes pokin' his nose 'round here anymore."

Susanna was surprised that her sister seemed to

know exactly what she herself was thinking. And it *was* true. Philip Bradley best not come looking for her daughter anytime soon. That, in fact, must *never* happen. The girl was much too vulnerable these days, what with her comin' out of mourning just now, wearing the usual Plain colors of blues and greens again. Even the purple dress had up and appeared here lately—the day Lavina came and took Rachel over to her place, just the two of them.

"Don't 'spose you'd know of a Plain widower 'round Lancaster who might be lookin' for a right gut wife . . . and stepdaughter," Susanna said.

"Well, now, if that don't beat all."

"What're ya sayin'?" Susanna wondered if she'd opened her mouth too soon.

"I think I might know of someone." Leah's face looked quite a bit rosier than Susanna had seen it in weeks. Almost as if her sister had stood outside pickin' sugar peas or tomatoes or shellin' limas for hours in the sun.

"So . . . what widower is it that's lookin' to marry a second time?" She thought it best not to hold her breath, make her face go white or whatnot; it would never do for Leah to know just how she felt 'bout losing her daughter and granddaughter to marriage. And most likely to an older man at that.

"Name's John Lapp—a right nice Amishman down in Paradise, though it might be a ways too far . . . for courtin' and all. And then again he's Old Order, so I don't know how that'd work, what with Rachel leanin' toward the Beachy group."

Paradise . . .

Susanna felt herself sighing with relief. Jah, the town was prob'ly too far away for a romantic encounter, 'specially for horse-and-buggy Amish. Still, if she hadn't brought up any of this to Leah, the word might never have had a chance to spread 'round the area. 'Course, now she couldn't go and stick her foot in her mouth and ask her sister not to say anything.

"Best just to let the Lord God set things up," she managed.

"Jah, but a little help from His children wouldn't hurt none, don'tcha 'spect?"

Leah had her but good.

The sun clouded over around the time Susanna got in her buggy and prepared to head home to Benjamin. She glanced at the sky, wondering if the weatherman's prediction would prove true 'bout the first snowstorm of the season. Wasn't that she minded the snow so much. It was the wind whipping at her face that she had to put up with when she rode horse and buggy somewhere or other. Here lately, she'd gotten more accustomed to calling a van driver to take her places—mostly for trips into Lancaster and sometimes down to Gordonville to buy quantities of fabric on sale for Benjamin's pants and shirts and little Annie's slips and things. Rachel, it seemed, had plumb wore out her gray mourning dresses. 'Twasn't any wonder, seein' as how she'd put on the same ones over and over again for the past two and a half years.

Jah, it was high time Rachel threw away her old

clothes or made rag rugs out of 'em, 'cause her mamma had been thinkin' of sneaking them dresses out of her daughter's room and making sure they disappeared. Rachel couldn't see anyway and wouldn't know the difference.

Susanna couldn't be sure, but she thought her daughter might just be getting to the place where she'd listen to some advice 'bout some of her ongoing quirks and whatnot. Folks were starting to talk here lately 'bout the amount of time Rachel was spending with Lavina, who was under the *Bann*—the shun—for breakin' her baptismal vow, goin' off to the Beachy church on account of Rachel and Annie. Susanna and Ben had never approved of Rachel and her beloved Jacob headin' off to the Beachy church, but least her Rachel hadn't broken any vows, never having been baptized in the first place. Still, all that time spent with Lavina couldn't be any gut for Rachel, really, even though she and Lavina *were* kin in a far-removed sort of way.

Truth be told, Susanna was worried that some of Lavina's peculiar ideas and ways might rub off on Rachel. The poor girl sure didn't need that.

❖ ❖ ❖

Rachel redd up the entire upstairs, cleaning bathrooms, shaking rugs, dusting and sweeping under each bed. Then she ironed every last one of her father's shirts and pants and even cooked up a pot of chicken and dumplings before she slipped the corn bread batter into the oven and hurried upstairs to make a tape-recorded "letter" to her Ohio cousin, Esther Glick.

She saw to it that Annie was occupied downstairs at the kitchen table, making her little drawings with her favorite crayons, before Rachel closed the bedroom door and turned on the recorder.

Hello, Esther!

Greetings from chilly Bird-in-Hand.

Scarcely could I wait to share with you today—you just have no idea how excited I am! Last Thursday, I spent part of the morning with Dat's relative, Lavina Troyer. Anyhow, she and I got to talking, and she agreed to go with me to visit my great-uncle Gabe's former fiancée, Adele Herr. Remember, I told you how that New York writer came to stay with us, and he took me to meet Adele? Remember, too, how she told all 'bout what happened here to Gabe when he wouldn't go along with Bishop Fisher, wouldn't accept the unholy "healing gift" the bishop wanted to pass on to him? The same way I didn't wanna have anything to do with Blue Johnny and his black box?

Well, I've been thinking long and hard 'bout what it'll take for me to get my sight back, and I hafta tell you, Esther, it's become ever so important to me here lately. Something new is happenin' inside me. I truly want to see again. Not just because it's so hard bein' blind in a sighted world—it ain't that a'tall. I want to see so I can raise Annie, and more than that, I want to see again so I can be a better witness for the Lord.

You might be thinkin' that I want to take Gabe Esh's place in ministry, and that could be what God's callin' me to do. I don't know for sure or for certain, not just yet, but I'm trusting the Lord to show me, day by day, what He would have me do for His glory.

I know you and Levi are doing your part out there in Ohio to spread the Good News. Well, I want to do the same. I believe, as you do, that we don't have much time before the Lord says, "Come on up a little higher."

Don't forget how much I enjoy hearing those sermon tapes of your pastor. Whenever you can, will you please send some more?

Wait just a minute, I believe I hear Annie callin' me. I best run down and check on her.

I'll finish this later. . . .

Pressing the Off button, Rachel left the tape recorder on the floor near her dresser and scurried out of the room and downstairs to Annie.

"I've been wonderin' where you were," the child fussed.

"Sorry, dearie. I was taping a letter to Cousin Esther."

Annie sighed. "Do ya think they'll ever come back and live here again?"

"Esther and Levi will prob'ly stay put in Holmes County. But, jah, I wish they'd move back," Rachel was quick to add.

"They like farmin', don't they?"

She nodded. "Workin' the land's the best thing for a farmer."

Annie was quiet for a moment. "Will *we* ever get to farm, Mamma?"

"Well, now, you know we live with *Dawdi* Ben and

Mammi Susanna so we can help them make a living . . . with the English guests."

"Are we gonna stay with 'em forever?"

Forever . . .

Rachel hadn't thought of that. She'd felt ever so content for the longest time, just going on the way she and Annie had been living.

Annie whispered, "Maybe someday we could farm, too, like Cousin Esther and Levi."

"Are you hopin' that we'll move to Ohio and live with your young cousins—James and Ada, Mary and Elijah?"

"Well, it *would* be lotsa fun havin' other kids my age, unless . . ." Annie grew silent again.

"Unless what?"

"Well . . . I don't mean to speak out of turn, but it would be awful nice to have some brothers and sisters someday, like my cousin Joshua has, you know?"

Lizzy, her older sister, and her husband had a good many children and another baby on the way. "In order to give you little brothers and sisters, I'd be needing a husband, and you know that's impossible," Rachel reminded her daughter.

" 'Cause Dat got killed in the car wreck?"

"That's right."

"But does that mean you can't marry somebody else?"

Annie's childish question took her off guard. "Well, I guess I *could* marry again, if the Lord saw fit."

"Why don'tcha, Mamma? Then you can have some

brothers and sisters for me—and some more cousins for Joshua, too."

Rachel had to smile at her darling girl. "It's not as easy•as just sayin' it."

"What do you mean, Mamma?"

She sighed, wondering how on earth to explain that one person couldn't just decide to up and marry. "It takes *two* people—a man and a woman—who love each other very much."

"So . . . all's we need is one more—the man— right?" Annie was giggling now. "I think I know where the other *one* can be found."

"Where's that?" Rachel asked absentmindedly.

"New York City."

Rachel's heart leaped at the mention of Philip Bradley's hometown. "What in the world gave you such an idea?"

"Mister Philip did," Annie replied.

Rachel was flustered beyond all words. "What . . . whatever do you mean?"

"Oh, I almost forgot you couldn't see what I saw, Mamma."

She wasn't clear on what her daughter was saying. And she was beginning to feel uncomfortable with her father sitting just around the corner at the end of the sunroom. "We best keep our voices down," she whispered.

"Nobody's near," Annie volunteered.

Rachel grinned at her girl's insight—another one of those traits passed down through the family. Only this wasn't a questionable one, like some of the "gifts" on her mother's side, beginning as far back as Gabe's great-grandfather, Ol' Gabriel Esh, a powerful conjurer in the area. No, God was going to use Annie for His glory and honor. Rachel honestly believed that and had begun to pray blessings over her daughter, till such time as Annie herself could give her heart and life fully to Jesus.

"I saw something in Mister Philip's eyes, Mamma . . . the way he looked at you. There was something wonderful-gut 'bout it."

Rachel felt the heat rising into her cheeks. "Well, I don't know how that could be."

"*I* do, Mamma. He must've seen in you what Dat saw a long time ago."

She leaned down and wrapped her arms around Annie. "You're sayin' the silliest things, I daresay."

"No . . . no, I ain't makin' it up. I saw what I saw!"

Sitting down, Rachel held Annie on her lap. "Listen to me, honey-pie. Mr. Bradley is an *Englischer*. So there's just no way in the world Mamma could marry him." She couldn't bring herself to speak further of romance or whatever it was her darling girl had in her little head. "I believe it's time we stopped talking 'bout this and get something to eat. What do you say?"

But Annie didn't budge. She leaned against Rachel and began to whimper into the bodice of her apron.

"What is it, little one?" She kissed the top of her daughter's head, holding her close.

"I miss him, Mamma. Mister Philip . . ."

'Course, she couldn't openly agree. She couldn't tell her precious girl that for some reason or other, she, too, felt the selfsame way about Philip Bradley of New York City.

Five

*T*he weatherman hit the nail on the head 'bout the snowstorm, turned out. Susanna was mighty glad the quilting at Leah's wasn't till tomorrow morning, 'cause the sky was awful heavy with the grayest-looking clouds she'd ever seen. And the snow! Goodness' sakes, it was comin' down!

So for today, she and Rachel would keep the kitchen cozy and warm with plenty of pie-bakin' and cookie-makin'. Rachel had asked if she could take one of the pies to a friend of hers, though she hadn't said just who or where. Fact was, her daughter was too quiet most the morning, Susanna thought, but she decided not to press for reasons. No, she'd bide her time.

Annie entertained Dawdi Ben in the not-so-sunny sunroom, where the B&B guests always took their breakfast of a morning. Now that it was deep December, the Zooks were without a speck of overnight folk. Susanna was honestly enjoying the break from her hectic schedule of cleaning up after one guest or another, making sure every room in the house was ready at all times. And they *were* ready, but it was nigh unthinkable that anybody in their right mind—especially an out-of-towner—would attempt to make his way up Gibbons

Road and on over to Olde Mill Road to their secluded property nestled along Mill Creek.

Annie came into the kitchen just then. "Dawdi Ben says he's awful thirsty," she announced.

"Well, let's get him a nice cold drink." Susanna moved to the sink and let the water run a bit.

"He's mighty hungry, too," Annie said, her blue eyes shining mischievously.

"Well, now, I wonder what he's hungry for?" Rachel chimed in. "Go ask him."

The child turned and scampered out of the kitchen.

"Aw, he's playin' with her," Susanna whispered to Rachel. "She'll come back wantin' a piece of pie, you watch."

A right curious look came over Rachel's face, and Susanna caught herself gazing in wonderment at her grown daughter. It was an honest-to-goodness glow! Susanna couldn't quite remember seeing Rachel look so radiant. Well, no she *did* recall, now that she thought 'bout it. Back when Rachel was sixteen and had first met up with Jacob Yoder. Jah, that's when it was. . . .

Annie soon returned to tell them just what Susanna had predicted. "Dawdi Ben wants to have the first taste of apple pie, if that's all right with Mammi Susanna, he says."

The two women burst out laughing.

"What's so funny?" asked Annie, eyes wide.

"Aw, honey, we're not makin' fun of you, not a'tall." Susanna waved her hand, still laughing so hard the tears were coming. "I think it's 'bout lunchtime here, perty soon."

Annie, bless her heart, looking ever so perplexed, turned and went to report to her grandfather.

Rachel stooped to pet Copper, and while she did, Susanna heard her whisper something 'bout it snowing so hard the puppy would hafta stay in the house all day. "Just like all the rest of us."

"'Tis awful cold out," Susanna ventured, hoping to draw her daughter into conversation.

"Jah, and from what Lavina says, we'll prob'ly hafta hitch up a sleigh to the horse so we can get to Leah's tomorrow."

Susanna peered out the window. "Well, if it keeps a-comin' down like it is, we'll have us a white Christmas this year."

"Would be nice, wouldn't it?"

Nodding, Susanna caught herself, realizing anew that her daughter could not see even the slightest movement. "It's *wunnerbaar*—wonderful—to see you wearing colors again," she said softly. "And green suits you right fine."

Rachel's face broke into a smile. "*Denki* . . . it's gut of you to say so."

It was then that Susanna wondered if the color of the dress had been the reason for Rachel's radiance. Or was it that she'd gotten so used to the drab grays and blacks that she'd forgotten how rosy-cheeked Rachel could be in blues and greens?

"I daresay you'll be the talk of the frolic tomorrow," she said. "The womenfolk ain't seen anything but mourning clothes on you for so long."

Rachel didn't say a word, just sat quietly at the table, still stroking Copper's back.

"This is an awful nice change for you." Pausing for a moment, she was eager to press on. "Does this mean you're movin' past your grief?"

Blinking self-consciously, Rachel replied, "I doubt anyone ever gets over the grief of losin' a beloved husband and child, Mam. I just don't see how."

So Rachel's choice of colors didn't mean what Susanna thought . . . hoped, really.

"I get ever so weary of folks starin' hard at me," Rachel blurted out. "I can *feel* their stares."

Susanna was somewhat surprised at this admission. But she needn't have been, now that she thought on it, for she herself had witnessed some of the womenfolk lookin' on Jacob Yoder's widow with eyes full of pity.

"Lavina's one of the few who doesn't," Rachel remarked. "She may not be very smart 'bout book learning, but in other ways she's wiser than us all."

Susanna was disturbed to hear that assessment of her husband's rattlebrained cousin. Just how wise Lavina was, well, that was perty obvious after all these years. "She oughta know better'n to push the bishop's hand on the probationary shunning, really. Attending the Beachy church, and all."

Rachel exhaled audibly. "Lavina wants to follow the Lord just like the rest of us. Maybe more so."

"Well, whatever does *that* mean?" Susanna was feeling a bit put out.

"She's searching for truth in the Scriptures . . . just like Esther and Levi and I. Lavina's as hungry for the gospel as Dat is for the first piece of your apple pie."

Susanna didn't quite know what to say to that. So she kept quiet, waiting—ear tuned—for the oven timer to *ding* and interrupt the flow of this nonsense talk.

❖ ❖ ❖

Rachel was happy to have a chance to finish her taped letter later in the afternoon before supper preparations. She waited till Annie fell asleep for a nap, then reached for the tape recorder, beginning where she'd left off.

> *I'm back again, Esther. I had to stop a bit and do some baking with Mam, and before that Annie and I got into quite a long conversation, but now I'll take up where I left off.*
>
> *I've been meaning to ask: Do either you or Levi know anything 'bout how Gabe Esh died? The reason I ask is Lavina said something right startling to me the other day—about Bishop Seth Fisher and Gabe's death. Don't know if I oughta say it on tape and all, but some folk 'round here evidently were suspicious of the reason for my great-uncle's death back then. If you happen to know something, will ya tell me? I'll leave it up to you if you wanna put your answer on tape or not . . . or you could tell me sometime when you're visitin' here, which just got me thinking how nice it would be if you and Levi and the children could come to Lancaster for Christmas. Will you think about it, at least?*
>
> *Well, the Lord bless and keep you and your little*

ones. *I miss you, Esther. Really, I do! I best sign off for now.*

> *Your Pennsylvania cousin,*
> *Rachel*

❖ ❖ ❖

Leah Stoltzfus found *great* pleasure in telling her youngest daughters, Molly and Sadie Mae, the news that their widowed cousin, Rachel Yoder, had "turned a corner" on her grieving.

"What's it mean, then?" Sadie Mae asked, brown eyes wide with wonder. "Surely, she won't start showin' up at the singings on Sunday nights. She's too old for such things!"

"Well, no, but it does mean you and your sister can start spreadin' the word on her behalf," Leah was quick to say, enjoying the flurry her news had caused.

"So now there's *another* woman lookin' for a husband?" Molly's mouth dropped open. "I'd say we'd best keep it quiet."

Sadie Mae pulled up a chair near the wood stove. She looked more than a mite worried, her forehead creased with concern. "Ain't even enough fellas for us girls of courtin' age. You know it's true, Mamma."

Her Sadie had a point, but that didn't stop Leah. "I heard tell of a Paradise widower eager to marry."

"How old is he?" asked Molly.

"A farmer?" asked Sadie Mae. "Most all the young women wanna marry a farmer."

"Who's got plenty of land," added Molly.

The girls burst into laughter.

"He's not so old. Not a farmer, neither." Leah sighed, wondering if she should continue. After all, the thirty-year-old blacksmith was a distant cousin to Gabriel Esh, her own uncle, though the blood lines were thinned way out, even enough for one of her own daughters to consider John for a possible husband. Thing was, John Lapp was known to have an occasional temper flare-up, wanted things done just so; Leah wouldn't have wished that type of fella on either of her darlings. Besides, he was too old for her girls, prob'ly.

But now, Rachel Yoder was another story altogether. Leah wondered if someone like the smithy Lapp might not be a gut idea for her widowed niece, the way Rachel seemed so awful unsettled and all. 'Course if it was *her*, there would've been no getting her into a courtin' buggy with the likes of one John Lapp.

"Just ain't that many widowers 'round here, Mamma," Molly spoke up again. "Rachel's twenty-six now, ain't so?"

"Close to twenty-seven . . . birthday's a-comin' in February."

"Maybe she's too old to get married again," Sadie Mae offered. "After all, look at Lavina. She never seemed to mind being an *alt Maedel*."

"Some mind more than others," she said, keeping an eye on her girls' faces.

"The older men get snatched up the minute a wife dies, you know," offered Sadie Mae. "But I'm thinkin' that maybe Rachel ain't much interested in marrying again. After all, she's blind."

Molly nodded her head. "But Rachel can perty much do what any of us can."

"And to think we used to say she was touched in the head," said Sadie.

"Seems to me a woman who's grieved so awful hard for her first husband might just not be able to let herself love another." This from Molly.

"Jah, but think of poor little Annie," said Sadie. "Can you imagine goin' through life without even *one* brother or sister?"

Molly snickered. "Bein' the only child of the family? Jah, I'd like to know what that'd be like."

The girls exchanged snooty glances. Leah was outdone with the both of them. "Now, girls, quit your bickerin', for pity's sake."

Sadie Mae rose and hurried out to the utility room off the kitchen. Molly, in turn, headed upstairs, her feet much too heavy on the steps.

"Well, now, the word's out about Rachel," Leah muttered, turning her attention to finishing a cross-stitching pattern on a pillowcase. "Won't be long till Paradise comes a-callin'."

Six

❖ ❖ ❖

Such a perty snowscape Annie had not remembered seeing in all her six years. Perched on Mamma's lap in the horse-drawn sleigh, she took it upon herself to describe every detail. "There's white everywhere. Looks just like sugar frosting!"

"Are the trees covered with white, too?" asked Mamma, both of them wrapped in woolen blankets.

"The branches look like ice cream Popsicles, without no chocolate, all coated with ice the whole way 'round each branch. Honest, they do."

"And the fields? Tell me about the wide-open spaces."

"I wish I had some black paper to draw on right now. I'd make the snow with a white crayon—so someday when you see again, you can remember this day."

Mammi Susanna snorted like the horse, but Annie kept on. "I'd make my drawing look just like the neighbor's field and their yard, too."

"Rebekah Zook's yellow spider mums are but a memory," Susanna said with an absentminded sigh.

"How do *you* see the snow today, Mammi?" Annie asked.

"Ach, snow's snow," her grandmother replied, wav-

ing her mittened hand in the air. "But I *would* say it's
the worst storm we've had in a decade or more."

"A decade?" Annie asked. "How long's that?"

"Ten years," replied her mother.

"That's a gut long time," Annie said, thinking of
Mister Philip just then. The nice man from New York
had said he'd have to "come back and visit again."

Seemed to her *that* was a decade ago.

Rachel couldn't help but worry about the tone in
Susanna's voice. Sounded to her like Mam was still
peeved 'bout something.

"Whatcha wantin' to draw the snow for? So your
mamma can look at it *if* her sight comes back?" Mam
said out of the blue.

She is still angry at me, Rachel thought. And she was
perty sure why. Susanna had sneaked Blue Johnny, the
area's conjurer/healer, into Rachel's bedroom, without
her permission, back six weeks ago. Had him chant over
her. Prob'ly used his black box, too—the one that was
supposed to tell what was wrong and cure it. Both.

She knew it was true, 'cause she'd gone to her father
to check, and Dat had told her so. It was just what she'd
expected, anyways. Blue Johnny *had* given her a glimpse
of sight that night. It hadn't been a dream at all. So now
Mamma was going to keep stewin' about it. More so
over the fact that Dat had spilled the beans than the
short-lived miracle the powwow doctor had performed.

Rachel, having refused the healing, was glad about
her bold decision. The dark and shrouded happening
had caused her to consider her healing in the light of

Scripture. And thanks to Esther, she was doing just that. Truth was, she was beginning to stand on the promises of God for her sight, which she believed might just occur any day now. Whenever the Lord saw fit to bless her with full vision once again.

"I'm gonna draw a picture of snowy cornfields for Mamma. When I get to Great-Aunt Leah's, I will," Annie said, bringing Rachel back to the matter at hand.

"That's right nice," she whispered to her little girl. "Now, just leave it be."

Susanna slapped the reins and called for the mare to move along faster. Rachel thought it foolish to make such a request of the animal in this weather. After all, the road must surely be snow-packed and ever so difficult for the horse to make passage. A *gut* thing they didn't have far to go.

The buzz at the quilting frolic was about Rachel's coming out of mourning. "She looks the picture of health," said one of her mother's cousins.

"Jah, and she's got her little one to think of, too," said another. "So . . . we know what that means, prob'ly."

Rachel was aghast—the women talking so openly about her state of singleness. Later she discovered that Mam was also upset—more vexed than surprised—though it only served to compound the problem of Susanna's sour perspective.

All the while, the women cut, sewed, and pieced, preparing to make a large quilt—the dahlia pattern—sitting twelve strong around the frame. Rachel entertained the children in the kitchen, doing her share of piecework, though it wasn't complicated.

"Mamma *ain't* gettin' married again," she heard Annie whisper to one of the other children.

"How do you know?" came the coy reply.

"I just know."

Rachel held her breath, wondering what to say or do to counter the childish exchange. But just as she was about to interfere, to distract the girls, Lavina came into the kitchen.

"All ready . . . for our trip tomorrow?" asked the older woman.

Rachel nodded toward the sound of Lavina's voice. "What do you think about going in all this snow?"

"Well's . . . if'n you'd rather not go . . ."

"Let's see what the weather's like tomorrow. I called the nursing home yesterday afternoon, and the receptionist said Adele's very excited to see you."

"And you, too . . . surely she is."

Rachel smiled, wishing she could see the look on the woman's face. "You're just as eager as I am, I'm thinkin'." She leaned forward, talking more softly. "I asked Esther if she knew anything about what you said the other day."

Lavina was silent.

"About the problems between Bishop Fisher and Gabe." She wasn't comfortable spelling things out, not with children playing at her feet.

"Best be careful . . . who you talk to," Lavina warned, and she was gone.

Her words rang in Rachel's memory for more than

an hour, till midmorning, really, when quilters broke for refreshments.

It was the continued chatter about various Plain widowers in the Lancaster area that made Rachel feel *naerfich*—nervous. No, it was worse than that. She was downright jittery. Truth was, she had no interest in marryin' again. 'Least of all to an older man, off in another township.

After lunch, while generous portions of white-as-snow cake and chocolate mocha pie were being served, Lavina observed the determined look on Susanna Zook's round face. Smack dab in the middle of the kitchen, Susanna started warbling the birthday song for Leah, encouraging everyone to join in.

Leah, quite befuddled, folded her arms over her ample bosom, trying to be polite. She didn't scowl really, the way she had on certain other occasions in the past. Her face flushed an embarrassed pink, and Leah simply avoided eye contact with her older sister. But it was all too clear the birthday girl was peeved, just not letting on too awful much, for the sake of company, prob'ly.

Keeping her peace, Lavina watched the amusing situation unfold. Slipping behind the long kitchen table, she located Rachel and stood silently behind the younger woman's bench, listening to the chatter but not entering in. She was a shunned woman amidst the Old Order. Soon her six-week probationary period would be up, and she'd have to decide whether or not to offer a kneelin' confession before old Bishop Fisher, the preachers, and the church members.

Just now, as she was thinkin' things over, she real-ized she wasn't much sorry for her actions—attending the Beachy church with Rachel and Annie. That was all her transgression had amounted to. She didn't see how she could turn her back on the prayerful atmos-phere and God-inspired sermons each and every Sun-day. Besides, she was learning new things about divine grace and love, and how to gain freedom in the Lord.

So if she *didn't* bend her knee in repentance, she'd have to put up with being shunned, though she guessed the People wouldn't treat her as harshly as Hickory Hol-low's district had one young woman, Katie Lapp. The church members here would be kinder, seeing as how she was slow in her mind. Still, she'd have to bear the shame of being the only shunned person in her entire family.

Spending time with Rachel here lately had softened some of her pain. Rachel Yoder was about as dear to her as anyone in the community, aside from a few elderly relatives and many, many nieces and nephews. 'Twasn't such a surprise that Rachel was so sweet neither. Lavina should've known it, having worked closely with many a Yoder and Zook at pea-snappin', apple-cider makin', and corn-huskin' bees over the years. Jah, she'd watched Rachel grow from a wee girl in a sheer white pinafore apron and tiny head covering, to a blushing young bride, whose light brown eyes shone at the slightest glance from Jacob Yoder. She had just never had the opportunity to get to know Rachel all that well, due to the wide age span between them.

Now that Gabe's story was more out in the open, so to speak, Lavina felt she could talk freely 'bout it with Rachel. And tomorrow she'd be visiting Adele Herr, too. Face-to-face after forty-some years.

The thought of seeing the woman Gabe had loved, after such a long time, gave her a peculiar feeling in the pit of her stomach. Still, she wanted to please Rachel by going. Sure, the visit might stir up sad feelings, but more than that, she knew it would be a chance to share the pain of another hurting woman.

She leaned down and asked Rachel, "Want another piece of pie?"

Rachel nodded. "But why are ya hiding?"

"Thought this was as gut a place as any to be . . . out of the way, ya know."

"Because of *die Meinding*?" Rachel asked softly.

"Jah, the shun."

"Wish there was no such thing," Rachel spoke up. She was quiet for a moment. Looked to be studyin' on somethin'. Then, "Come to think of it, I'd like some ice cream on my pie this time, if you don't mind."

Lavina reached for the younger woman's dessert dish. "Don't mind a'tall." She scurried off to do the favor. Honestly, she wished she could help Benjamin and Susanna's widowed daughter even more. She'd do just about anything to help Rachel get back her sight. Till such a thing was even possible, she figured her best choice was to be as gut a friend to the young woman as possible. Agreeing to ride to Reading and visit Adele was a nice start.

Lavina knew why she'd hemmed and hawed at

Rachel's initial suggestion to see Adele. Only one reason, really. She'd written few notes and letters to Adele Herr over the years. And, well, she felt embarrassed at her lack of correspondence skills, though she would've been glad to visit with the woman face-to-face on any number of occasions. Fact was, she'd suggested regular visits early on, soon after she and Adele had buried Gabe's body in the cemetery just blocks from the Herr family home. House-to-house visiting was the Amish way—what she was most used to—but Adele had said in a letter that she felt uncomfortable returning to Lancaster County, and for a gut many reasons.

Something else pricked her mind as Lavina waited for a turn at the chocolate mocha pie. Adele Herr was the woman Gabe—*her* Gabe—had loved, proposed to, and longed to marry. Not his first companion and buddy. Not the tall and lanky Plain girl in the grade above his. Still and all, Lavina knew he *had* loved her just the same. In his own, wonderful-gut way, he surely had.

As a young boy he'd displayed his quiet affection when they were in school together. Sixty years ago. And she'd saved the get-well cards he'd made for her, kept them in a treasured, yet crude, wooden box, also hand-crafted by Gabe Esh. Sick with the flu one winter, and other times, too—when she was ill with chicken pox and the croup—she welcomed his little cards, sometimes rhyming, sometimes merely signed with his boyish scribble, under a backdrop of cornfields in summer, swollen creeks in springtime, or woodlands in autumn.

Gabe had been her one and only hope for love, and just 'bout the time she thought he might actually take her for a ride in his open courting buggy, the English girl from Reading had come along, filling in as a sub-stitute teacher at the nearby one-room schoolhouse. It was Adele who'd caught Gabe's attention back then. Hadn't seemed fair either.

In the early days, she remembered trying her best to appear to be "normal" for Gabe's sake. Whatever that was she didn't know, 'cept what she observed in the folk who were of average or higher intelligence. She remem-bered practicing her speaking skills, gazing into the pond just south of her father's barn, on a day with not a stitch of a breeze in the willows that circled the shin-ing water. There, in the water, she'd seen a slight face and gray-blue eyes staring back, framed by her white netting *Kapp* atop her wheat-blond hair.

She'd gone to study her reflection—since Mamma wasn't all too happy 'bout mirror-primping and such. While she sat by the pond, she had asked herself one question after another, pretending to be her classmates, tryin' her best to think up the answers. When the ex-perience was past, she believed her practicing had paid off. 'Least *that* summer it had, 'cause Gabe asked if she wanted to go fishing, and would she help him gather worms for some bait?

She remembered having to push answers out of her mouth quick as she could that sunshiny day. "Jah, I'll go with ya," she'd said, scared he'd up and change his mind. "Betcha I can dig worms faster 'n you!"

He'd taken her comment as a challenge, like most any eleven-year-old boy. So they'd spent one whole af-ternoon digging for fish bait, her hands wrist-deep in mud, grabbing hold of one slimy earthworm after another. 'Course, every bit of the mess and mud was worthwhile, sharin' the day with the handsomest Amish boy on the face of God's earth!

A slice of chocolate pie and vanilla ice cream in hand, she scurried back to Rachel. Placing the dessert in front of her, Lavina thought how blessed she was to be getting better acquainted with a woman who resembled Gabe, not only in looks, but in temperament and deed. Why, it was downright uncanny, come to think of it. And here, with talk of Blue Johnny eager to pass his powwow doctoring gift—and the evil "black box"—to someone younger, well, it made her honestly wonder 'bout family ties, generational sins, and all. The very things Rachel's cousin Esther had been sharing with Rachel by tape. Some of the things Rachel Yoder now believed.

She touched Rachel's shoulder gently. "Want some coffee . . . to go along with that second helpin'?"

Rachel smiled her thanks. "Pie's fine for now."

Lavina, still bending over, whispered, "Leah's birthday song set me thinkin'. . . ."

"Oh?"

"Tell you tomorrow . . . on the trip to see Adele."

"I won't forget," Rachel said, finding her fork. "What 'bout the snow? Is it still comin' down hard?"

Lavina turned to look out the window. Sure enough, the snow had begun to slow a bit. "Seems like the Lord above might be smilin' down on us, come tomorrow."

"He blesses us *every* day. Snow or no snow," Rachel replied with a nod.

Just then Annie came in carrying a picture she'd made of a snow-covered field with gray clouds overhead. Three birds in one corner of the sky. "Look-ee here," the little girl said. "I drew a wintertime picture. It's for when Mamma can see."

The drawing reminded Lavina again of Gabe's third-grade artwork. Along with his homemade cards, she'd saved his drawings, too, storing them away in the hand-hewn box to be cherished all her life.

Rachel spoke up, "Jah, hang on to your drawing, Annie, dear. 'Cause I *will* see it someday. I truly believe I will."

Lavina couldn't help but smile as Annie hugged her mamma's neck. She felt the familiar twinge of sadness for all the little ones never born to her. "Come along, now, Annie," she said. "Did ya get yourself a slice of your aunt Leah's choc'late pie?"

Grinning, Annie showed a missing front tooth. "Jah, I had more than one. *Appeditlich*—delicious!"

Like mother, like daughter, Lavina thought, now more eager than ever to share Gabe's drawings with someone. Someone like the deceased man's great-grandniece—Annie Yoder.

And possibly Adele Herr. . . .

❖ ❖ ❖

The day had been long and arduous, filled with rewrites, interviews, and follow-ups, yet Philip sat in his apartment, gathering together the many snippets of information he'd found while in Pennsylvania. Each was directly related to Gabriel Esh's fascinating story, one of rejection and betrayal among his own people. It was the story he had uncovered while innocently jiggling a stubborn drawer in the recesses of an antique desk in his room at the Amish guesthouse.

He smiled to himself at the myriad of notes he'd jotted down—even on a paper napkin from the Bird-in-Hand Family Restaurant. Having gone to the Lancaster County area to do research on behalf of the magazine, he'd returned home with numerous ideas and observations on the Amish culture. That uncomplicated community of the People, where respect for each other's opinions and privacy was a daily occurrence, where a person was expected to be conscientious, civil, generous, and responsible. Where the wholesomeness of rural life abounded. Where time seemed to stand still.

Upon locating the business card from Emma's Antique Shop, he studied the address and phone number, noting there was no fax number or email address. Emma, a young Mennonite woman, had given him the card after he'd browsed there, looking for an antique rolltop desk similar to the one at the Amish B&B. Emma had informed him that the desk was one of a kind, yet he'd hoped to find something comparable. He had searched various New York antique shops and prestigious stores in and around Columbus Avenue, near Lincoln Center, on weekends, then later in Vermont, where he and his sister and niece had gone to enjoy the autumn foliage. But he had found nothing to compare with the magnificent piece in his former guest bedroom at Benjamin and Susanna Zook's B&B.

He felt the urge to pick up the phone and call the Bird-in-Hand antique shop to inquire as to other desks Emma may have procured recently.

Too late in the season, he decided, changing his mind. He recalled that stores in the Lancaster area, especially those catering to tourists, were often closed during the winter months.

Philip leaned back in his chair, his hands clasped behind his head. Sighing, he looked around the apartment-sized writing studio. Tall custom-made cabinets of white oak graced one full side of the room. Shelves lined with handcrafted contemporary pottery and wrought-iron art, purchased from juried artisans, reminded him of his travels. Behind him, a silkscreen silhouette of oval leaves, pale yellow and green, juxtaposed the unadorned wall. To his right, a bank of windows allowed daylight to flood the room, and at night reflections from a thousand windows flickered across to him. Usually, he preferred to keep the designer blinds open at all hours. Tonight, however, he rose after a time and pulled the cord, blocking out the enormity of the population, noise, and vibrations of the city that surrounded him, threatening to strangle him.

Sitting down at his desk once again, he thought of Lancaster County, where farmers talked to their cows and went to bed with the chickens. A world set apart.

And not so surprisingly, a place he missed more than he cared to admit.

He stared at the telephone, wondering if it was too late to make a phone call to Reading, Pennsylvania. He wanted to talk again with his new friend, Adele Herr.

Seven

$\mathcal{F}$or as long as she remembered, Rachel had awakened early, at the pre-rooster-crowin' hour. Bone-chilling cold no longer greeted her first thing on a winter morning, however. Not in the toasty-warm bedroom she and Annie now shared at the Orchard Guest House B&B.

Growing up in Dat's drafty old farmhouse was another story. There the wood floors were as cold as a frozen pond, and she'd discovered it firsthand. As a child she'd stuck out a brave big toe on more than one occasion. Quickly, she would retrieve her bare foot and slide it back under the warm quilts, all the while shivering at the thought of facing the morning. Pleading for one or more of her older sisters to bring her a pair of long johns—and warm socks—she waited for her requests to be granted, putting up with occasional teasing. So she dressed *before* actually emerging from bed, similar to the way she lived most of her youthful days, shy and retiring.

This December morning a bitter wind had blown about flakes of light snow, reminding her anew of those childhood days. She'd gotten up early as usual and bundled up for the trip to Reading, accepting the arm of their usual Mennonite driver—Calvin Witwer—who'd come for her at the door.

"It's not snowing as much now," he said as they made their way to the waiting van.

"Are the roads cleared off, then?"

"Plowed and sanded. Shouldn't have any trouble getting to where you wanna go." Calvin helped her inside the warm vehicle, and they were off to pick up Lavina.

Rachel's thoughts ambled back to the first time she'd ever gone anyplace with her father by herself. It, too, had been a wintry day. Mid-January. She had been 'bout eight, prob'ly, and had need of some needles and thread for a practice quilt she was making with her sisters, Lizzy and Mary.

"*Kumm mit!*" Dat had called to her, offering to stop at Beiler's Country Market on the way to Bird-in-Hand.

"All's I need is some sewin' needles and thread," she'd replied, skipping down the back porch steps to the waiting carriage.

Mamma had come to the back door, calling that it was all right to go. "Have a gut time with your pop."

Rachel, silent as always, had realized just then that none of her sisters or brothers—or Mam—were comin' this morning. Just her and Dat.

"Well, now, hop in, Rachel. I'll take-a-you along." And Dat helped her up into the enclosed gray buggy, covering her real gut with several warm lap robes.

She remembered feeling a bit more grown-up than she'd ever felt before in her young life. To think that Dat was taking her for a buggy ride to the store, and all by herself. Well, now, must he be thinkin' his little girl was ready for such an adventure on a snowy day?

The horse had trotted slower than usual, but that didn't seem to bother Dat. He was gentle and kind to the animal, letting the mare set her own pace. And, funniest thing, Dat talked a blue streak, never stoppin' once to ask her a thing, though, 'cause she was just too shy to answer him. But that day, *that* day, she had begun to change her mind 'bout having a conversation with adults. Talkin' with a grown-up didn't seem all that frightening anymore.

Maybe it was the way the snow fell quietly, like a curtain 'round them, as they made their way down the long road. Or maybe it was Dat's voice lulling her, oh so steadily, keepin' her mind off herself for once—she didn't know, really—but something stuck in her child-ish mind 'bout that wintry ride to market.

When they arrived at the little country store, al-ready there were two buggies parked out front. The folk who shopped here, her mamma had always said, liked cookin' from scratch, as if there was any other way. And the shop owner, Joe Beiler, seemed to know it, too. So after locating the exact sewin' needles she wanted and three colors of fine thread, she wandered over to the dry goods section while Dat chewed the fat with Joe.

What she discovered made her eyes pop out nearly. Why, there was an amazing amount of beans—seven kinds in all—and ten different noodles, along with six varieties of flour. All sorts of dried fruits, too, including raisins and dates. Nuts and oodles of other dry goods were on display along the long wooden counters.

Things like white, brown, and confectioners' sugar; baking powder, salt, pepper. Countless types of seasonings, grains, and cereals, too.

'Course, there were baked goods, in direct competition with Grandma Smucker's Bakery. But that didn't stop Joe Beiler from offering the ooey-gooiest cinnamon rolls this side of Ronks Road. And she found out just how tasty they were, thanks to Joe's wonderful-nice wife coming over and chattin' with Rachel.

"Well, now, look-ee here at you," the blue-eyed woman said. "You must be Ben Zook's littlest girl."

She hadn't known whether to nod her head or just blink her eyes at the pudgy Mrs. Beiler.

"Cat ain't got your tongue, has it?" she asked.

Rachel shook her head.

"I've got just the thing to make ya smile, girlie." The owner's wife motioned for Rachel to follow her. "As long as you live, you'll never taste any sticky buns better'n Nancy Beiler's."

So . . . Rachel found out her name, and she never forgot it, 'cause that day Nancy Beiler insisted that Rachel was the "pertiest little girl" she ever did see.

"And whenever you want yourself a free samplin' of my sweets, well, you just call me Auntie Nancy, and I'll come a-runnin'."

Rachel figured, without ever speakin' a word, she'd just stumbled onto the nicest person in the whole world. And she never, ever forgot the way those sticky buns melted in her little mouth. She just never did. From that day on, Auntie Nancy kept her word 'bout the free samples, too. She even came through on the day before Rachel's weddin' to Jacob Yoder, too, along with every other time she stopped in to say "hullo."

Every so often, Rachel thought 'bout Auntie Nancy, wonderin' what had become of her—'cause for the past year or so, nobody ever talked of Joe's wife. Rachel 'sposed it was none of her business, but still, she wondered.

"Do you ever hear tell of a Nancy Beiler over off Stumptown Road?" Rachel asked, finding her voice long enough to ask the driver.

"Last I heard, Joe quit stocking the bakery part of the store."

"Oh? Why's that?"

"His wife left the Old Order."

That surprised her. She hadn't heard of any shunning over in that area. "When was this?"

"Couple of years ago, if my memory serves me well. Mrs. Beiler went and joined the New Order Amish folk over near Gap."

"I wish I knew where she lived," Rachel said softly. "I miss seein' her."

"Well, I believe I could find out for you, if you want me to."

She was glad to hear it and told him so, and she couldn't help but smile 'bout that wonderful-gut *first* time at the country market. Just Dat and his little Rachel, on a cold and snowy January day.

When the two women were settled into the backseat, they got their offhand prattle all talked out—Lavina, in her slow, measured way; Rachel, prompting her when her mind took to wanderin'.

"You were going to tell me something today," Rachel reminded her after a time, keeping her voice low.

Lavina was quiet for a bit before she spoke up. "I've been thinkin' . . . 'bout Bishop Fisher. That's what I wanted to tell you."

"What about the bishop?"

"His eternal soul" came the unexpected reply. "But I don't know just what to do 'bout what I'm a-thinkin'."

"Well," Rachel said, "what would *that* be?"

"I've been prayin' for the old bishop."

Rachel wasn't afraid to admit that she was, too. "In fact, I've been wonderin' when a gut time might be to talk to him, just so he doesn't try 'n talk me into accepting Blue Johnny's powwow gift—the transference, you know."

Lavina was still.

Rachel whispered, "You don't think he'd do that—try 'n force me, do you?"

After another long pause, Lavina replied, "I don't 'spect anyone can force a body to receive a gift—holy or unholy."

Rachel thought on that. "I'd hate to see the powwowing thing get stirred up 'round here. After what happened between Blue Johnny and me, well, I'd say a visit to the Old Order bishop would have to be intended by God, pure and simple."

"Don't blame you none for thinkin' thataway." Lavina's voice sounded strained.

Rachel wondered if the woman was nervous 'bout a

visit to the ninety-three-year-old church leader. "You okay?"

"Don't 'spose I'll be if'n I *don't* follow the Lord's biddin' and speak to ol' Seth Fisher . . . afore his next birthday. 'Tis comin' up here real soon."

So *that's* what was bothering Lavina. She was worried the old man might die without hearin' the truth 'bout God's Son and soul salvation, full and free.

"Let's not wait, then, if you feel the Lord nudgin' you," Rachel suggested.

"Don't see how I could do it alone. I'm a shunned woman, ya know. Doubt Seth Fisher would give me the time o' day."

"I'll go with you." The words had flown out before she'd even had a chance to think what she was gettin' herself into.

"Denki, Rachel. Had a feelin' you'd see eye to eye."

Unsure her parents would agree with any of what she and Lavina were cooking up, Rachel leaned against the seat, praying silently. *Dear Lord, help me not get in over my head with all of this. Please, will you lead and guide Lavina and me? Amen.*

❖ ❖ ❖

"I declare, if that shunned woman ain't up to somethin', well, then I ain't Susanna Esh Zook!" She rushed down the stairs, one frustrating thought after another tumbling in her mind.

"Not for you to be worryin' over," Benjamin called

down from the second-floor landing, holding a wrench in his hand.

Susanna knew if she kept it up, sooner or later little Annie might put two and two together and figure her grandparents were fussin' over Rachel and Lavina. "We best talk this over in private," Susanna replied, standing at the bottom of the long stairway. She would give her husband the final say.

"You're right, Susie. We oughtn't cause a scene in front of you-know-who," Ben said, then he went to finish repairing the shower head in one of the guest bathrooms.

Susanna just couldn't get it out of her head that Lavina was influencing Rachel to keep in touch with that fancy woman up there in Reading, slippin' away to death in a nursing home, of all places. Amish folk wouldn't think of abandonin' their ailing and elderly. Plain and simple. They made a home for them right under their own rooftops.

'Course, then again, Adele Herr had no real firsthand knowledge of the Old Ways, and 'twas understandable, seein' as how she'd turned down Gabe's proposal of marriage. Just as well, though. The People would have shunned her right along with the young preacher-man. And would've shunned Gabe all the harder for marryin' outside the church. As it turned out, the troublemaker had got himself killed on his way to speak at a church somewheres in Gordonville. No doubt it was God's way of quieting the voice of a disobedient soul, though she *had* heard various accounts of the "why" behind the accident.

Still, 'twasn't something Susanna cared to discuss, not even with her wise and discerning husband. Both she and Benjamin preferred never to air the superstitious nature surrounding Gabe Esh's untimely death. Jah, best those things be kept buried, and she figured they would be, too, considering old Bishop Fisher was comin' up on ninety-four years. Once he passed, only one other person besides Benjamin and Susanna herself even knew of the strange circumstances surrounding Gabe's death. A good thing, too. 'Twasn't something a snoopy New York reporter could get ahold of and sink his teeth into. As far as she knew, her sister Leah was the only other person with even the slightest knowledge. The secret was safe with the four of them. For sure and for certain.

Sighing, Susanna's thoughts flitted from one problem to another. For all she knew, Rachel and Lavina were prob'ly jabberin' right now during their ride north 'bout all the things Philip Bradley had set in motion when he discovered that no-gut postcard. Things that oughta be kept hush-hush and forgotten. Just the fact that the problem was bein' talked 'bout by Rachel, Lavina, and who knows how many others bothered Susanna no end. She just knew the old bishop was prob'ly havin' himself a fury over some of the rumors going round— gettin' a-stirred up over 'um.

Oh, she could still kick herself for not snatchin' up the postcard right out of the young man's hands! What on earth had kept her from it? Seeing the message, written in Pennsylvania Dutch, of all things, to that wicked Baptist girl who'd torn the community upside down, inside out. Falling in love with the very hope of the Amish church, no less. Well, if it hadn't been for Gabe Esh gettin' his worldly eyes on Adele Herr, who knows just how the powwow doctoring in the area might be flourishing these days? 'Twasn't that they didn't already have several folk healers. It was just that the community had grown, what with couples having upward of eight children or more, in some cases. Jah, they truly needed another *Brauchdokder*—powwow doctor—and with the many giftings her daughter possessed, surely someone other than herself oughta be able to persuade Rachel to accept the revered position. Surely.

❖ ❖ ❖

At Fairview Nursing Home, Lavina sat next to Rachel in the small, yet sunshiny, room marked Rm. 147—the very room Adele Herr had called home for the past two years and some odd months. A single hospital bed flanked one wall. The patient was dressed for the visit, wearing a pale pink bed jacket around her slender shoulders. The color brought out the slightest hint of pink in her cheeks, though Lavina was sure the rosy hue had been dabbed on, prob'ly, the way most fancy folk—women—did. Adele's eyes were just as blue as ever, and her smile was the same as it used to be.

At the far end of the room, plants hung gracefully near a window with wide blinds for its covering, no curtain. A dresser with a gilded antique oval mirror sat just beyond the bed, so that the mirror faced out. And Lavina thought it was a gut idea, too—not havin' to look at yourself if you were so awful thin and ill. Mirrors were far too revealing, 'specially at her and Adele's age. Best just to leave them be, a cold reminder of the youth everyone must lose, sooner or later.

Jah, it was a right gut thing Rachel had brought her here today. Otherwise, she'd have never recognized the meager little woman perched amidst her bed pillows. She figured, though, the reason Adele Herr looked to be so different wasn't necessarily age. No, she just wasn't the selfsame girl who'd come to rent a room at Lavina's farmhouse forty years ago. It was mighty clear to see that the disappointments of life had brought the biggest changes on Adele's face.

Lavina had squeezed the dear woman's hand the minute she set foot in the room, not waiting for Rachel to take the lead. "You have Rachel here to thank for this visit," she insisted. "It was *her* idea to come and pass 'round some Christmas cheer."

Rachel spoke up, blinking as she seemed to look around, though not seeing. "But *Lavina* was eager to bring her tart and tasty apple butter along . . . for you and your friends here." Both Rachel and Lavina had brought baskets filled with mouth-watering homemade sweets.

Adele smiled, seemingly amused. "Well, what does it matter *which* of you decided? The fact that you're both here is a blessing to me. A joyous pre-Christmas blessing. You'll never know how pleased I am to see you again, Lavina. And you, too, Rachel."

"Didja want us to call you Lily or Adele?" asked Rachel out of the blue.

The older woman sighed, smiling. "I understand why you might wonder about that, Rachel, but to tell you the truth, I prefer Adele. The name Lily was a crutch. I don't have to hide behind my middle name anymore. The Lord has freed me from those insecurities. Even the nursing staff has agreed to change my name, so to speak!"

Lavina truly hoped she wasn't staring just now, but she couldn't seem to keep her eyes off the woman in the hospital bed. Was this really Adele Herr—Gabriel Esh's old sweetheart? She studied the features even more closely. Could this be the selfsame young girl who'd come to Bird-in-Hand those many years ago, filling in at the schoolhouse? She'd changed more than Lavina thought such a beauty ever could. 'Course, they were each growing older, and who was *she* to be thinkin' any such haughty thoughts, with plenty-a wrinkles spreading across her own face? Enough to share with Adele *and* Rachel—both!

Combed into a short bob, Adele's former chestnut brown hair was now snowy white, nearly silver-hued. 'Least, certain ways she turned, it looked thataway.

Lavina could hardly sit still, anxious to join in the conversation. But she listened as Adele brought up Philip Bradley, the reporter from New York she'd heard 'bout from both Adele's letters and from Susanna Zook while making apple cider a few weeks back.

"I've been giving some thought to possibly inviting

my new friend Philip for a visit," Adele announced, her eyes shining.

"Nice thing to do," Lavina spoke up.

Rachel said nothing.

"He could come for our Christmas party," Adele continued. "Maybe he would like to write an article on all us old folks."

Lavina noticed the sudden flush on Rachel's face and wondered what *that* was all about.

Adele glanced up at a bulletin board, not far from the side of the bed, and pointed to a slightly yellowed card. "There's the postcard Philip found, and it's changed everything . . . absolutely *everything*." She went on to say, "Philip is such a forthright person. And, you know, he's following the Lord again."

"You mean he wasn't before?" Lavina asked, feeling awkward because Rachel had hardly said a word.

"He wrote that he'd strayed from his first love, his commitment to Christ . . . as a boy." Adele turned and seemed to observe Rachel, and at one point Lavina's eyes met Adele's. The two women shrugged, but Adele went on. "Philip's attending a men's Bible study twice a week, I believe he said. He's full of questions in his letters, and more recently he's started calling long-distance."

Rachel spoke at last. "What sort of questions?"

"Life questions, he says," Adele answered, catching Lavina's eye once again. "He's preparing himself for ministry."

Lavina wasn't exactly sure what that meant. "Gonna be a preacher, then?" she asked.

"Not a preacher, I don't think. But he feels called to something—just *what*, he's determined to find out. And from our exchange of letters, I believe it's safe to say he's open to God's leading."

Lavina found this information to be mighty interesting, but more than that, she wondered what on earth had come over Rachel. Why had she closed herself up like this? Was it something one of them had said out of turn?

She observed the beautiful blind woman, thinking back to when Rachel had first blushed crimson. Then she remembered, and the startling realization caught her truly by surprise.

Hearing Adele speak of Philip in such glowing terms had Rachel nearly beside herself. She felt her face growing warm as Adele commented on the New Yorker's attributes. Jah, she'd also experienced Philip's straightforwardness, among other things. And she was ever so glad to know he'd returned to his faith in the Lord. In fact, she was a bit surprised to hear that he might've neglected his childhood covenant to God. But it was Adele's mention of her possible Christmas invitation that had flustered her so. She knew it was the thought of Philip coming to visit his ailing friend—here in Reading. Why, it was only a hop, skip, and jump down to Lancaster. 'Course, that would be silly to think he'd come see her, too. He had no way of knowing how very often she thought of him, how she remembered his well-chosen words, the way he seemed so taken with Annie . . . and with her, too.

Lavina's words jarred her back to the visit at hand, and she straightened in her chair, taking a deep breath. Oh, she hoped the red had gone from her cheeks, lest either woman discover her most guarded secret.

"I hafta take all the blame for what was written on Gabe's headstone," Lavina was saying. "Poor fella couldn't speak for himself . . . but he must've knowed how much ya loved 'im, Adele."

Rachel thought it right honest of Lavina, admitting her truest feelings to the woman whose heart was awful close to giving out. She, on the other hand, couldn't begin to think of revealing *her* feelings. No, it wouldn't be prudent for her to voice any interest in Philip. The correspondence was ongoing between Adele and him, and she could fully understand why the man had reached out to the kind and gentle woman. Ever so nurturing, Adele Herr was like a wise older relative to Philip. And Adele, in turn, had obviously found a dear friend, as well.

She was truly happy for their friendship—anything to bring a little joy to a woman who'd lost so much early on in life.

Still, Rachel wished she felt more at ease just hearing his name unexpectedly, let alone being told that he'd called Adele Herr and discussed "life questions." Such comments made her truly long to know him better—even to *see* his face. But, of course, regainin' her sight was a matter for the good Lord—and Him alone.

Eight

Friday, December 17

Dear Philip,

How are you? Keeping your head above water with your many assignments, I trust? You have my prayers, as always.

It occurred to me that you might be pleased with an invitation for a visit here. I know you have family in New York, but it never hurts to ask. At any rate, we're having a small informal get-together of sorts here on the night of Christmas. Several musicians are scheduled for the event, among them a string quartet of which I am quite fond. Another is an ensemble of singers. Sounds like fun.

Please don't feel pressured to make the trip. I don't know your plans, of course, and at this late date, I would probably be fooling myself to think that there might be the slightest hope of seeing you during the celebration of our Lord's birth. If, however, you are so inclined, you are certainly welcome!

On another note, I had the nicest visit from Rachel Yoder and Lavina Troyer yesterday morning. They came bearing gifts, just as the Wise Men of old. I don't know when I've enjoyed seeing someone as much as I did Lavina. The woman is every bit as sweet and compassionate as she was back when she "took me in" years ago. She was quite friendly and talkative, in her own way, and I do believe she may have begun to forgive me for being Gabe's first romantic choice. The way she smiled so at me—speaking of such things as her reason for adding my name to Gabe's gravestone—did warm my old heart.

Rachel Yoder, the dear, dear girl, brought a basketful of various home-baked items—sour cream chocolate cookies, sugar cookies, molasses drop cookies, date bars. Is your mouth watering? I do plan to pass the basket around at the Christmas party—yet another enticement for you to join me.

I had no idea that Rachel's blindness was due to trauma, and she mentioned the fact quite openly, I might add. Poor child, my heart goes out to her. But the good news is that she and her cousin in Ohio are "standing on the promises of God" for her healing. So Gabe's grand-niece is believing for her sight to return. Isn't this the most wonderful news?

Please, no matter where you spend it, you must have a very special Christmas. Know that I appreciate your friendship so much, dear friend. May the Lord bless and keep you always.

In Christ . . . I remain,
Adele Herr

Philip didn't bother to read the letter a second time. Reaching for the phone, he sat at the desk in his home office and dialed the number for Fairview Nursing Home.

When one of the nurses put him through, he was met with a cheerful, strong voice. "Merry Christmas, Philip!"

"How'd you know it was me?"

She laughed softly into the phone. "No one else calls."

"Well, it's good to hear you're in such fine spirits. Must be the advent of Christmas."

"That . . . among other things."

"Such as?" He was eager for a good health report.

"To begin with, my doctor is cutting back very slowly on all of my medication. My old ticker is working better than it has in years."

"That's terrific news!"

"Yes, and I'm able to be up and out of bed, walking the halls. I even helped one of the patients address a few Christmas cards yesterday."

He was excited to tell her his plan. "Say, I received your letter . . . just now read it, and I'm taking you up on your invitation. I'm coming to your Christmas party."

"How wonderful, Philip!"

He heard the joyful ring to her voice. "You really *are* feeling better, aren't you?"

"For which I thank the Lord," she replied. "God has touched my life by bringing you into it . . . and Rachel, as well."

Philip thought about her remark and wondered what she'd make of it if he casually mentioned the research he had been conducting on behalf of, but unknown to, Rachel. Forging ahead, he said, "I've gathered some information, and it's interesting that you mentioned it in your letter . . . about Rachel's hysteria. . . ." He paused, inhaling a bit. "Did she bring it up herself when she was there?"

"Well, let's see . . . Yes, Rachel actually spoke freely of the emotional effects she's suffered since the accident. I think she soon may be ready to face her past head on, though I have no idea what that may involve."

"I have an idea," Philip said, not telling her that he'd talked with several therapists on Manhattan's East Side, upon his brother-in-law's recommendation. Philip felt he had a handle on the sort of questions a doctor might ask to permit the pain and the memories to re-surface, the deeply submerged anguish of Rachel's loss. If he could just spend some time with her, he might be able to befriend her.

"I'm glad I wrote you about the Christmas program. Meanwhile, be careful not to work such long hours," she said, beginning to sound a bit tired. "It's not a good thing to burn the candle at both ends."

"It's what I'm used to. Besides, I'm working my way down a long list of assignments. I'll see you soon. Keep smiling."

"You're a wonder," she said.

"Good-bye, Adele."

"God is ever faithful," she said before they hung up.

He recognized it as one of the last lines of Gabe's postcard message to her.

Before heading out to the kitchen to heat up left-overs, Philip opened his file drawer and located a list of characteristics he'd observed in Rachel Yoder. He'd made the list while waiting at the Lancaster Community Hospital last September for word of Rachel's little daughter's wasp-sting incident.

Soft-spoken, mild-mannered, devoted to Annie were

among the first qualities he'd written. Scanning the words, he recalled the beautiful young blind woman. If ever there was something he wanted to give at Christmastime, it was sight to Rachel Yoder!

❖ ❖ ❖

Monday night meetings were a bit unusual, but Rachel wanted to go to the preachin' service that had been called at the Beachy Amish meetinghouse. 'Specially since a visiting minister was passing through. "Lavina's picking me up," she told Mam, adding, "Wouldja be so kind to tuck Annie in for me?"

"Well . . . how late do you 'spect to be?"

"I really don't know, but I wouldn't think too awful late."

Dat spoke up from the kitchen table, where he was having seconds on cake, prob'ly. " 'Course if he's one of them hellfire preachin' fellas," Dat said, "it'll be close to ten, which is mighty late for young women to be out and about."

Ever so protective, Dat was. Yet she loved him for it. "You mustn't be worryin'," she was quick to say. "Lavina's always careful, really she is."

"Does she know enough to avoid the Crossroad?" Mam probed.

"Jah."

"Well, then, I 'spect you're set," Mam said. "Just make sure Lavina watches the speed of the horse. We got us some nasty roads out there tonight."

Rachel nodded, wishing there was some way she could convince Dat and Mam both not to fret over her so awful much. "God's lookin' out for us," she offered, hoping that would suffice. She found her cane and shuffled out of the kitchen.

Ever so eager for more of God's Word, Rachel sat with Lavina near the front of the meetinghouse, on the side with the women. She felt that her spirit might soar, might need to be brought back down to her body, hearing the things the minister was teaching. Spiritual defense—how to put on the armor of God, as found in Ephesians 6, and how to enter into God's protection— something she wished she'd known and understood long before the accident that took Jacob's and young Aaron's lives. Oh, if only her heart had searched for God's provisions back then. So much might've been different had she known to commit herself to the rock of ages, the mighty fortress, and her shelter in time of trouble.

All the way back to Beechdale Road she chattered to Lavina. "I believe the Lord's gonna let me see again," she declared.

"Well, God bless ya, Rachel."

"Oh, He has . . . He already has."

Lavina was quiet again, while Rachel babbled on. She reached her hand out of the buggy, hoping to catch a few flakes. That's when Lavina made the remark that a certain widower "was at service tonight."

"Who wouldja be talkin' about?"

"John Lapp from Paradise Township. Ya heard o' him?"

"No, and I don't much care," she replied, guarding her words.

"Well, just so ya know, he was lookin' you over real careful-like."

"How'd he know who I was?"

"S'pose the word's got out, Rachel."

"What on earth does *that* mean?"

"You put away your mournin' clothes, now didn'tcha?"

"Doesn't mean I'm lookin' to remarry, though. Just ready to move ahead with my life some."

"You're awful young to be deciding such a thing . . . 'bout not remarryin'. Maybe you should be praying 'bout that."

"What would this John Lapp want with a blind woman?" she asked, wondering aloud.

"Now, Rachel, you oughta know better'n to say such a thing. You'd make any man a fine wife."

Rachel felt terribly uneasy. What was all this talk going on behind her back? She didn't want to know, not really. Still it was unnerving, hearing that someone was looking her over in terms of marryin' potential. She wasn't a sixteen-year-old Maedel—maiden—anymore. The whole idea of being eyed that way . . . ach, it just didn't set well. "You don't 'spose he'll come callin', do you?"

Lavina was slower to respond than usual. "I . . . would hafta say that's what he already done . . . tonight in church, so to speak."

She didn't quite know what to say to that. "He came to church to look at a woman? Why, that sounds down-right sacrilegious, if you ask me."

"Maybe so."

"Well, it *is*," Rachel insisted, marveling at her own courage to speak her mind. And feelin' the better for it.

'Twasn't all that late when Rachel came in the front door. Even still, Mam was waiting up. "Glad to see ya home in one piece."

She accepted Mam's hug and gave her a peck on the cheek. "Honestly, I don't know when I've learned so much," she managed to say, trying not to think about the audacity of widower Lapp.

"How was the meetin'?" Mam asked, the weight of the question hanging in the air.

"Can I tell you in the mornin'?" Rachel said, feeling her way to the stairs. "All's I know is, I'm ever so heart-hungry for the things of God."

"Speaking of which, I forgot to give you a tape mailer. It came today."

"From Esther, prob'ly."

"Well, no, I believe it's from some reverend out in Ohio somewheres."

Rachel was overjoyed to hear it! Esther's pastor had sent along yet another sermon. She thought about staying up till midnight to listen to it. Jah, she just might do that. It would certainly be worth the weariness come morning.

Nine

Not only did Rachel listen to the taped sermon, she played it twice before retiring for the night. And the next afternoon, another tape arrived. This one from Esther herself.

Rachel squeezed time out of her busy day—cleaning, baking bread, and washing clothes—in order to hear snatches of it. Yet she was more than eager to do so, for it seemed that Esther *did* know something of the superstitious nature of Gabe's death.

I've just been made privy to some shocking information, her cousin's words came strong and clear. Rachel was relieved that Esther had seen fit to position the highly personal information in the middle of the taped message. This way, if ever Mam was to eavesdrop on it, she would not discover what the two women were passing back and forth.

She continued listening, then was moved to tears as the strange story began to unfold.

> *Yesterday Levi had the chance, finally, to call his grandfather, your Beachy bishop, Isaac Glick. I just had no idea that Isaac would know one thing 'bout the events surrounding Gabriel Esh's death. But let me tell you,*

Isaac shared some terrible frightening things with my husband. I best be careful how I say this, 'cause I sure don't want to garble the truth. From what Isaac knows, Seth Fisher did put a hex on Gabe Esh! Now, I don't exactly know what sort of spell it was. All I know is the very next day, Gabe and his friend were driving in a car somewheres, and Gabe's friend hit a white dove. The friend turned deathly pale . . . terrified, to say the least. He told Gabe that in the religious circles he was akin to, killing a white dove was an omen, a sign that the person or persons would die unexpectedly, and soon.

Gabe didn't know what to make of it, 'cause he, too, had heard of the powerful superstition. In fact, Gabe knew firsthand of people who'd died after an experience like that.

Oh, Rachel, if only your great-uncle had known to turn his back on such things—if only he'd known what we know now, that those who belong to the Lord can take authority over fears and false beliefs. I don't honestly know if Gabe feared the superstition, and his dread resulted in his untimely death. Only God knows for sure. But fear is such an open door, 'cause when we fear we're believin' the devil, whereas faith is believin' in what God says. The book of Job, chapter three, verse twenty-five says, "For the thing which I greatly feared is come upon me, and that which I was afraid of is come unto me." It may be that Gabe didn't understand how fear can open up a believer to front-line attacks from the ol' enemy. And you know, all that Gabe was doin' for the Lord— speaking out so strongly against the powwow practices— well, of course the devil was out to silence him.

Seein' as how Gabe had followed the Lord so closely, though, it's hard to understand how a hex of any kind *could've affected him, really. We know, from some of the teaching we've had, that there are ever so many curses folk unknowingly put on each other. Even by things like jealousy, gossip, and rejection.*

Even so, Levi and I both believe Gabe is in heaven with his Lord because of the stand he made. Honestly, we do.

Rachel brushed tears from her face. Not only was she shocked, but saddened and confused by her cousin's news. And she found herself wondering yet again why such past wicked activity had been hushed up.

Something rose up in her, and she felt so strongly that the darkness had to be exposed so that the Way, the Truth, and the Life could flood hearts that had been hardened by tradition and deceived by the devil. This, more than anything, she desired for her people. The spreading of the Light was what she also desired for the old, now ailing bishop, a former powwow doctor in the community. Jah, Seth Fisher needed to hear that the Light has come. That God's glory had appeared to at least one humble soul amongst the People . . . a distant relative of Gabe, the young man the bishop had despised enough to curse.

Yet Rachel truly felt she must be able to see, have her sight restored by the power of God—and not by powwowing—before she could ever approach the Old Order bishop. Why, surely, once her blindness was a thing of the past, the highly revered church leader would hear what she had to say—even if she *was* a woman. And she feared, in the shape he was in, his time on this earth was fast runnin' out.

She fell to her knees beside her bed, impulsively claiming one healing promise after another found in the Bible. She knew many of the passages by heart, quoting them aloud in her prayer, as she held fast to God's Word. Deep within she felt a sense of urgency, though she did not think she was demanding anything out of the ordinary from the Lord. No, she was merely acting on the Scripture tapes her father had purchased for her months before.

"Dear Lord in heaven, I ask that you heal me," she prayed. "Body, mind, and spirit. I know your Word says, 'Is any sick among you? let him call for the elders of the church; and let them pray over him, anointing him with oil in the name of the Lord.' Well, I ain't an elder, and I haven't had much faith for my healin' in the past—haven't much cared to see, really. So I'm here to present my eyesight to you just now, askin' you to heal me, as you promised. I am willing to go to the elders of our church, to be anointed with oil, if that is your will. In Jesus' name, Amen."

She lifted her head and opened her eyes, fully expecting to see clearly. But the room was a shadowy gray, and she was ever so disappointed, wondering if her ongoing condition had now become a permanent blindness, yet not allowing herself to dread that possibility.

❖ ❖ ❖

After telling Mam the highlights of the church meeting the next morning, Rachel rushed off to her room between chores to pray fervently for her sight. "Dear Lord Jesus, I'm reminding you this day of your many promises to heal. In your Word—in Luke, chapter four—you said that you were sent 'to heal the broken-hearted, to preach deliverance to the captives, and re-coverin' of sight to the blind, to set at liberty them that are bruised.' Well, Lord, I'm all of those things, ain't so? I'm brokenhearted over losin' Jacob and Aaron, my dear husband and little boy. I've been a captive awful long, too, 'cause of fear and bitterness, and I'm blind because I purposely blocked out every memory connected with the accident." She paused, brushing tears away. "I'm bruised, too, Lord, way deep in my spirit, wounded 'cause of my family's past sins. I know this from the Ohio pastor's sermon tapes that Esther has him send. He teaches that ancestral sin brings curses and conse-quences on a family, whether a person believes in you or not."

Just then, it dawned on her why Bishop Fisher's hex might've actually worked on a Christian like Gabe and his friend. She just didn't know for sure, but she had a perty gut idea that Gabe had had no inkling how to bat-tle such things as the sins of his forefathers. One an-cestor, whom Gabe had been named after, was known to be the originator of the powwow doctoring in the whole community.

The more Rachel thought on it, the more she won-dered if that might've been the problem—the lack of spiritual warfare. From what she'd learned, generational sins had to be identified, confessed, and renounced in order for curses to be put to death on the cross of Jesus.

She knew this only because of Esther's pastor, out in Ohio, yet she was ever so thankful to God for bringin' such teaching into her life. If she could just pass it on to her parents, her eleven siblings and their wives and children, and 'specially to Bishop Fisher. She'd hafta keep praying 'bout that, 'cause she needed more courage to speak out to the People. The way Gabe Esh had spoken out so long ago.

❖ ❖ ❖

"Mamma's spendin' lots of time upstairs," Annie informed Susanna.

"Well, now, you know your mam's busy with her personal correspondence, and all."

"Is it Cousin Esther in Ohio . . . that she's making tapes to?" Annie's round face was filled with questions. "Maybe we're movin' out there to live with Levi and Esther and their children."

"What the world, child? Where'd you get a notion like that?"

"Mamma and I talked 'bout it once." The little girl's words came out a bit lispy, due to a missing front tooth.

"I'd say that's just horse feathers."

"What do you mean, Mammi Susanna?"

She knew she'd better come up with something perty gut, or the bright child would catch on. "Well, it's like this. Your mamma feels right stuck here in Bird-in-Hand, prob'ly, what with her best cousin livin' in wide-open spaces out there in Holmesville. We always want what we can't have. That's just human nature, I'd say."

Annie looked at her with those big, innocent, blue eyes of hers. "I wanna live on a farm, too, just like Mamma does."

"Well, now, if that don't beat all." She couldn't say much more. Truth was, there wasn't nothin' better in the whole wide world, far as she was concerned. Nothin' better'n working the soil of God's good earth.

"I think someday we're gonna end up farmers," Annie said out of the blue.

"You really do?"

"Jah, 'cause I have a powerful-strong feeling."

Susanna perked up her ears at that. Could it be her granddaughter had some of the family giftings passed down through the generations? Could it be that Annie was next in line—after Rachel, of course. If this was true, she'd just received some mighty gut news indeedy. And so close to Christmas. Wait'll Benjamin heard 'bout this!

❖ ❖ ❖

Rachel began the next day with earnest prayer, not the silent rote prayers she'd been taught. She prayed with her eyes wide open, yet not seeing, waiting for the Lord to bless her with healing. Desiring her sight more than ever, she pleaded that God might grant her "a clear vision in time for Christmas. And what a *seelich*— blessed gift that would be," she prayed, once again repeating the promises of God, so determined to receive.

111

"I'm willin' to cross the horrible visions—to remember the accident that took Jacob's and Aaron's lives—to get to my sight. Whatever it takes, Lord. I want to see again!"

When her healing didn't come just then, Rachel rose, washed, and dressed for the day. She didn't want to admit it, but she was getting a bit impatient. After all, God didn't seem to be answerin' awful fast, especially now that she was wanting her sight, more than eager to see her little Annie-girl.

Wanting something so much; why, it was gettin' to be right unbearable. After all, when she'd willed herself to block out the images of the accident, refusing to see, her vision had begun to dim within just a short time. She just didn't understand why the Lord would delay His perfect plan for her life now that she wanted to be whole. Why?

It was as she made her and Annie's beds that the sharp shooting pain began. The needlelike sensations felt horrible, seeming to pierce her skull. The turmoil and horrendous ordeal of the past two years came flooding back with the pain. Oh, she never wanted to go through any of that ever again.

Cupping both hands around her head, she gasped, the agony nearly taking her breath away. "No . . . no, not this way, Lord. Please, not this way."

❖ ❖ ❖

When Susanna wandered upstairs to redd up, she

heard what she thought was moaning coming from the far northwest corner bedroom—Rachel's and Annie's room. *"Was is letz?*—What's wrong?" she mumbled, making her way down the hallway.

Standing at the door, she listened. Sure enough, it was Rachel, whimpering. She tapped on the door, anxious for a reply. "Are ya all right, Daughter?"

"Come in, Mam."

She opened the door to find Rachel lying on the bed, fully dressed. "What's-a-matter?"

Rachel's hands were pressed to her temples, and she was writhing in pain. "It's my head . . . I can't stand this pain."

"Well, forevermore," she whispered. "Will an aspirin help, do ya think?"

"No . . . no, not pills."

She sighed. Dare she mention Blue Johnny just now?

"Not powwow doctors either, Mam. Please don't even think of it."

Susanna shook her head in wonderment. There Rachel went again, saying her thoughts aloud, almost before she thought 'em. How she did it, Susanna did not know, but it was a sign of a true gift. That was for sure and for certain. "Do you want me to call a *medical* doctor, then?"

Rachel didn't answer right away but continued rocking back and forth as if she were being tortured. At last, she said, "I wish you would call Esther . . . ask her and Levi to pray."

"Clear out there to Ohio? Well, you must be crazy

to ask such a thing. Do you have any idea how expensive that could be?"

"Cheaper than goin' to a hospital doctor," Rachel said, surprising Susanna at her spunk.

"Well, now, ain't you nervy today . . . pain 'n all?"

"Mamma, please forgive me. I didn't mean it in a bad way."

Susanna thought on that. "However you meant it don't matter none. Truth is, I'm a-thinkin' it's long overdue for you to settle things with Blue Johnny. Once and for all."

"But, Mam—"

"Nothin' doing. You listen to me, Daughter. He's got the power to heal—sight, too. What in all the world do you think you're doin' refusin' him?" Susanna thought she might burst apart if she stayed in the room another second. So she bolted, leaving Rachel weeping great heaving sobs.

Lord'a mercy, was her daughter goin' backward, starting her mournin' time all over again? The thought of such a thing worried her sick. Never again did she want to go through the past two years, 'specially the first fifteen months or so. Rachel's grief had been like no widow's woe she'd ever known.

"I declare, I don't know what to do 'bout her," she muttered to herself as she hurried downstairs, only to bump into Annie, who looked right surprised to see Mammi mumblin' a mouthful of angry words.

"What's wrong?" the child asked.

"Your mamma's sick just now."

"I'll go up and help her."

"No . . . no . . . no, you best stay down here. Help me make a nice big lunch."

Annie's eyes glistened. "But how can I eat if Mamma's sick? I could never do it, Mammi Susanna. I just couldn't."

The way the child was carryin' on, you'da thought Rachel was dyin' or something. Then it struck her, hard as anything ever had. She knew what to do. "Jah, maybe you should go on up and comfort your mamma, Annie. Just lie down next to her and place your hand on her forehead and say these words three times, 'Tame thou flesh and bone, Mamma dear.' Then make three crosses with your thumb on her forehead, and let's see if you can't cure that ol' headache."

Annie got the biggest smile on her face and hurried out of the kitchen. Susanna couldn't help but grin, too.

Ten

❖ ❖ ❖

Rachel, still lying down, was prayin' hard and fast when another knock came at her bedroom door. "Who's there?" she asked, hoping Mam wasn't comin' up to pester her some more.

"It's me, Mamma . . . it's Annie."

"Oh, darling girl, come on in." She made an attempt to control herself and not let on how pain-ridden she really was.

"Mammi Susanna said I should help you." Annie's footsteps were light as she crossed the room to the bedside.

"Well, now, how are *you* gonna help me, little one?"

"Can I lie next to you?"

Rachel slid over, making room. Then, holding her breath, trying not to focus on the excruciating pain, she felt Annie place her warm hand on Rachel's forehead. "Whatcha doin'?"

"Feelin' your head. And . . . I'm makin' the cross on your forehead three times. Now I'm gonna say something over you."

"Like *what* are you thinkin' of saying, Annie?" She could feel the goose pimples popping out on the back of her neck. "Who told you to do this?" Rachel was provoked, 'cause she knew. Without a shadow of doubt, she did.

"Mammi Susanna said I might could cure you" came the tiny voice.

"Well, don't you believe a word of it!" Rachel sat up, wishing for all the world she could see her daughter. "What Mammi told you is very, very wrong."

"Why would she . . . why?" Annie sounded as though she might cry.

"Oh, it's ever so hard to explain," Rachel said. "But makin' chants over folk ain't what God has in mind for healin'. I know it sure as anything."

"But Josh, my little cousin, makes 'um."

Rachel sucked in her breath, then coughed. "What do you mean?"

"He talks like he's gonna be our doctor someday. It's what Aunt Lizzy keeps on tellin' him. I guess Mammi Susanna told her all 'bout curin' folks's sickness, too."

Rachel's head hurt from the penetrating pain. But it pained her more knowin' how the enemy of the soul was workin' overtime in the hearts of her dear relatives. "We hafta be prayin' for our healing, not lettin' Josh or anybody else make chants or spells over us. The Bible teaches against it. Do you understand?"

"Josh says it's 'the People's way.' "

"Well, that doesn't make it right. *God's* way is always best."

Annie seemed to be satisfied enough with Rachel's answer and didn't continue to question. She offered Rachel a kiss on the cheek and left the room.

Rubbing her temples, she breathed a prayer heavenward.

Rachel knew she had to make a choice. One way or the other. She didn't want to go back to the silent dark days of denying herself, tellin' herself lies. She'd been deceived by her own fears, too terrified to remember the truth of whatever it was she'd witnessed at the corner of Highway 340 and North Ronks Road—the Crossroad—where Jacob and Aaron had passed over into eternity.

She just might have to make herself ride horse and buggy down Ronks Road, coming to a complete stop at the deadly intersection. How she would do such a frightening thing, Rachel did not know. But such an experience was somehow wrapped up in her recovery. She felt sure it was.

❖ ❖ ❖

Fully perplexed at Rachel's desperate state, Susanna told Benjamin she was going to call a driver so she could go into the village after lunch. "I need a bit of breathin' room," she admitted, grabbing her coat and boots. "You understand, jah?"

He looked up from his gardening magazine, frown lines evident. The clothes he wore—long-sleeved white shirt and black broadfall trousers—had been pressed nicely. Rachel's doing. "Are you perturbed, Susie?" he asked, closing the magazine.

She clenched her teeth, trying to maintain composure. "More than I care to say."

"Well, then, go ahead. Get it out of your system."

Susanna had no idea where she was actually headed. A cup of black coffee and Leah's listenin' ear might go a long way toward makin' her feel some better. "I won't be gone too awful long," she said softly.

"Over to Leah's?" he asked, getting up and comin' over to give her a hug.

"Prob'ly."

"Gut idea, if ya ask me." He kissed her lips, though they pouted in spite of the loving gesture. "I'll tend to Rachel . . . if she needs some tea or whatnot."

He went to the door with her when the driver arrived. "Now, run along and have yourself a gut time."

Oh, she would try to do that. Jah, she would. Anything would be better than stewin' in the house just now. Both she *and* Rachel needed space from each other.

Susanna figured she'd wait to fill Benjamin in on Annie's statement: "a powerful-strong feeling" that the girl and her mamma were gonna be farmers someday.

Puh! If that childish notion came true, well, she'd be right surprised. After all, 'twasn't enough land to go 'round in families much no more, in Lancaster County anyways. Where on earth were Rachel and Annie gonna find themselves land 'round here?

She attempted to calm herself, staring out the van windows at the white and wintry fields that rolled away from the snow-packed road on either side. Glistening-smooth, the street lay ahead, fraught with plowed snow, making for a straight and narrow path, scarcely wide enough to allow automobiles to pass.

In the distance, rolling hills of frosted ivory scattered across the southern ridge, and for a moment, Susanna had the strange notion that she'd like to go there, far away from home, and find a place of repose. Away from her grown daughter who was behavin' like a spoiled child.

She thought back to the days when Rachel was just a little girl—bashful as the day is long. A sweet and soft-spoken youngster, Rachel seemed eager to obey. Never once exerted her will, not that Susanna recalled. No, Rachel Zook had been the kind of girl most any Amish parents would be wonderful-glad to have as kin, 'cept that she had always been far different from the older five girls born to Benjamin and Susanna. Rebekah, Naomi, Susie, Mary, and Elizabeth possessed a confident and strong disposition, as did Susanna's own sisters and mother, and the generations of women before her. Stubborn women.

Why Rachel had been prone to faintheartedness, coming from a long line of such determined women, had always puzzled Susanna. But here lately, she had come to the conclusion that her youngest daughter was chosen, over all the others, to be the next powwow doctor in the community. Susanna had pondered this many times of late, but more and more she felt strongly that she was right 'bout this. The Almighty One had planted a receptive and humble spirit in Rachel for a right gut reason. She felt confident of God's plan for the blind woman. Wouldn't be long, either, till the rest of the

People came to understand. She could hardly wait for Rachel herself to grasp the importance of the powwow "blessing," once and for all. As for Susanna, she would never rest till that day came.

Bells tinkled in the air as they came up on a horse-drawn sleigh, slowing so as not to spook the horse. A group of women from the Old Order church district were out for some fresh air; either that, or they were on their way to a work frolic somewheres. Not having been invited, she wondered where they might be headed.

When Susanna turned to look more closely, she spied Mary and Lizzy, two of her married daughters, and their teenage girls, Elizabeth Anne, Mary Beth, Katie, Susie Mae, Lydia, and Martha, along for the ride. Why hadn't she been included? But then again, she s'posed it was plain to see. Folks had declined to ask her to doin's, here lately, knowing full well she'd have to turn them down on account of her work at the B&B. First things first, she always liked to say. And she didn't feel too awful bad 'bout bein' passed over, not on a chilly day like this, anyways.

The more she thought 'bout the women, most of them from her own family and headin' off somewhere—lookin' mighty happy, too—she got to thinkin' that maybe Leah was gone to some frolic, away from the house.

Should've phoned out to their woodshed, she thought. Leah's husband or at least one of the older boys would answer out there. That way she could've found out if Leah was at home before ridin' all the way over there for nothin'.

Oh well, she didn't much care. Truth was, she needed the aimless ride in the frosty morning. Helped clear her head some, made her breathing come a bit more easy. And helped her stop dwellin' on the shenanigans her daughter seemed to be pullin' these days.

And my, oh my, those tapes from Ohio—they just kept a-comin', it seemed. Snow, sleet, or shine. Made her wonder, more than ever, what the two women had to say to each other. If she wasn't such a forthright person, well, she might just be tempted to "borrow" one of 'em and listen in for a change. . . .

Turned out Leah *was* home, and Susanna was mighty glad to see her younger sister. "I had to get out of the house for a while," she confessed.

"Rachel?"

"Uh-huh."

"Well, bless your heart, you'll hafta tell me 'bout it."

That was all it took for Susanna to open up and pour out her distress. "She's got a headache . . . carryin' on so, same as she did right after Jacob and Aaron died. Makes me think she's startin' to recall some of the accident."

Leah's face was tipped slightly, looking at her with keen interest. "You know how it is with certain widows and widowers—they just keep a-livin' the loss over and over. Maybe that's what Rachel's doin', too."

"Grief comes in waves. No question 'bout that."

"Jah, but that's not *our* way. The People don't usually carry on so."

The words jabbed at Susanna's heart. She heard the

disdain in Leah's voice. Her sister thought Rachel
wasn't behavin' like one of them. She was acting more
like a modern, "fancy" woman, though she was Amish
through and through.

"I daresay a visit from John Lapp of Paradise might
change all that," Leah said with conviction.

"You don't mean . . ."

"I most certainly do. And I think you oughta out-
and-out invite the smithy to supper some night soon.
From what I hear, he showed up over at the Beachy
meetinghouse last Monday night."

"John Lapp did?"

"Came lookin' for your Rachel."

"Are you sure now?"

"A gut many folk spied him there, saw Lavina and
Rachel sittin' up close to the front, too. I got my facts
straight on this, Susie."

She thought for a moment. "Hmm, now I just wonder what the smithy Lapp might be doin' for Christmas
dinner?"

Leah was noddin' her head to beat the band, brown
eyes a-smilin'. 'Course, Susanna was smart enough not
to think of mentioning any of this to Rachel. No, it was
better kept quiet.

"Speakin' of Christmas, I got a letter from Esther
yesterday, and it looks like they'll be comin' in on Friday
afternoon . . . Christmas Eve."

"First I heard of it," replied Susanna.

"I'm awful glad your Rachel said something."

"Oh, so maybe *that's* what them two's been cookin'
up."

Leah frowned. "What do ya mean?"

"Well, I'd be lyin' to you if I didn't say that there's been a flurry of taped letters goin' back and forth between here and Ohio lately."

"You're thinkin' that Rachel might be needin' a visit with Esther, is that it?"

She nodded. "I'd say them cousins are as close as two women ever could be."

"Well, now"—and here Leah burst out laughing—"look how close their mammas are!"

Susanna had to smile at that. "And here I thought maybe there was something else a-goin' on."

"What . . . with the tapes?"

"Jah" was all she said. Didn't wanna stir up curiosity on Leah's part. Still, she couldn't help but think there was some mighty important reason for Rachel to be the one asking Esther and Levi to come home for Christmas. Had to be.

Part Two

❖ ❖ ❖

If a man therefore purge himself . . .
he shall be a vessel unto honour,
sanctified, and meet for the master's use,
and prepared unto every good work.

—2 Timothy 2:21

Eleven

❖ ❖ ❖

The sound of busy feet, booted and crunching against polluted snow—shoppers running helter-skelter up and down Broadway and surrounding boulevards—filtered into Philip's head. He purposely kept his own pace, walking nearer the shops than the curb, noting that not a single person caught in the mad dash of holiday buying seemed remotely interested in peering into the exquisite windows along the avenue. Even the locksmith and pharmacy, ordinary merchandisers, were brimming with beleaguered buyers. The Broadway Nut Shop and Starbucks Coffee were crammed with people waiting in line for gift certificates or a quick snack to boost their spirits.

Christmas in New York City was precisely the place to be for many. Not for Philip. Not anymore. He could hardly wait to set out for less peopled climes. Namely, the village of Bird-in-Hand, population: 300.

He planned to leave Manhattan in two days by car, long before rush hour, on Christmas Eve. He had discovered, upon calling his travel agent, that there were any number of inn accommodations available in the Reading area this time of year. He would take his time driving to Pennsylvania, delirious with the idea of abandoning the bustling city for a few days. Typically, things were slow at the magazine between Christmas and New Year's, so the only hurdle had been in getting Kari to understand why he wouldn't be able to spend the holidays with her and her parents. His mother was visibly unnerved by the news, but he had promised her and Dad—Kari too—that he'd make up for being gone by hosting an exciting New Year's Eve party "at my place . . . or we'll go to Times Square and watch the ball drop, if you want to," he'd offered.

But Kari and her parents preferred to attend church for an old-fashioned "Watch Night" service. "There's a European choir," Kari said, her eyes dancing. "I know you'll love it, Uncle Phil. We'll have prayer and communion at midnight."

He actually liked Kari's idea better. So along with the rest of the family, he had agreed to "pray in" the New Year.

Janice and Ken had seemed rather surprised that he wanted to spend Christmas with Adele. But he assured them—all of them—that this was important and reminded them that he'd never missed celebrating the season with them, "not in twenty-seven years."

Time for a new approach to the holy days, he told himself as he slipped into a small corner bookstore, an out-of-the-way spot where he could drink some cappuccino and purchase a gift or two for his niece, a bookworm extraordinaire. He was also on the search for a picture book for Annie Yoder, whom he wanted to see again, almost as much as her mother, Rachel.

❖ ❖ ❖

"I saw Mary and Lizzy and their girls heading over toward Hess Road, in a sleigh, no less," Susanna said while helping Leah wipe down cupboards and later, mopboards. "Thought maybe you'd be goin' out to the same frolic."

"Jah, I heard of it but didn't much feel like gettin' out today, not with the roads so awful."

"What's doin'?" Susanna was just too curious to let it drop.

"Bishop Seth's great-granddaughter's havin' a baby come late March, so some of the younger women were gettin' together to make a batch of crib quilts."

"Oh."

"Hope the old bishop lives long enough to see his first great-great-grandson."

"So . . . it's a boy for sure, then?"

"Well, the powwow doctor tested her with a penny tied to the end of a string, ya know."

"If that's the case, Bishop Seth can count on it, 'cause the powwow doctors ain't never wrong. They can even tell how many babies—twins, triplets, ya know— and the sex of each in correct order."

Leah frowned, her eyes wide. "Ever wonder why that is?"

"What?"

"The accuracy of them powwow doctors . . . what makes them right so often?"

Susanna shrugged. "Just the way it's always been."

131

"But *how* do they know so much? Must be some reason, I'm a-thinkin'.'"

Susanna didn't make an effort to explain. She didn't know for sure, really. Just that the "knowing" powers were passed from one person to another through the generations, same as other gifts of enchantment.

They continued with their cleaning chore, and Susanna came mighty close to bringin' up her concerns over Esther, who just seemed bent on a-fillin' Rachel's head with things she oughta forget. But she kept her peace and let the matter drop.

❖ ❖ ❖

"Hope you get to feelin' much better, and right soon," Lavina told Rachel, offering her the cup of chamomile tea and honey she'd made in the Zook kitchen. "Between you and me, I think the Lord's speakin' to me . . . 'bout visiting the Old Order bishop in a couple-a days."

Rachel plumped a pillow behind her as she sat up in bed. "Is that why you came? To talk to me 'bout goin' along?"

"Honest, Rachel, I felt a nudge—strong as anything this mornin' while I was prayin'. Thing is, 'twouldn't be right—two unmarried women goin' to speak to the bishop."

"I was thinkin' the same thing." Rachel raised the teacup to her lips, her hands trembling.

"Who wouldja ask to go with us—what man?" She

stood at the side of Rachel's bed, looking down at the poor girl, pale as the moon.

"Levi Glick would be the best choice, I'd hafta say, but I haven't heard for sure if they're comin' for Christmas or not."

Lavina studied awhile. "Oughta be prayin' . . . for the Lord's leading, ya know."

"If Dat was in the know 'bout spiritual things, I'd ask him."

"Well's . . . why not? Your father could hear the witness same time as the bishop does." Lavina hadn't thought of that before, but it was an idea worth thinkin' through.

"When wouldja wanna go?" Rachel took another sip of the tea, eyes squinted shut as if in terrible pain.

"Soon as you're able."

"Then I don't know if I can, really. The pain in my head's gonna hafta taper off a whole lot before I can think of goin' anywhere."

Lavina sighed, sitting on the edge of the bed. "Have ya tried a home remedy?"

"I rubbed oil of rosemary at my temples, but the pain seems to be comin' from deep inside my head . . . not like just any headache."

"You be fearful 'bout something, Rachel?" She suspected as much.

"Well . . . maybe I am." Rachel went on to tell her how she'd been praying, beseeching the Lord for her healing.

"Tryin' too hard, maybe."

Rachel cocked her head thoughtfully. "How could *that* be?"

"Rest in the Lord. Wait patiently for Him." It was the best advice Lavina could give.

"So I shouldn't keep remindin' God of His promises to heal?"

"Far as I understand, you don't hafta to remind your heavenly Father 'bout things He's said He'd do. The same way you don't hafta remind your dat when he says he'll take you somewheres. Just rest, Rachel. Your healin' will come in due time."

If she hadn't been in such pain, Rachel would've pressed the older woman. Lavina was sounding ever so much like a wise old sage of a lady, and far as she knew, there was only one woman like that 'round Lancaster County. She'd heard tell of Ella Mae Zook—one of her father's second or third cousins once removed—who lived down in Hickory Hollow a piece. Folk in that church district often called Ella Mae the Wise Woman 'cause she seemed to have answers to life's grittiest questions.

Your healin' will come in due time. . . .

Whoever heard? And how could Lavina know that for sure? Rachel thought long and hard 'bout it even after the kind and gentle woman took the empty teacup, with a promise to refill it, leaving Rachel alone in her room once again. But the more she thought, the more she just figured you had to be a bit slow in some areas to be as quick as Lavina Troyer was in others. Now, didn't that beat all?

Still, she didn't know how she could keep from re-
citing the biblical promises, those wonderful-gut Scriptures her cousin had sent her. How could she *not* pray
the way Esther's pastor had taught on the sermon tapes
Rachel loved to hear?

Ach, she was ever so puzzled now. Didn't quite know
what to do, really.

❖ ❖ ❖

Philip spied a vacant, overstuffed chair in the corner
of the diminutive bookstore. He set down an armload
of children's books on the table in front of him—children's poetry, a humorous takeoff on Noah and the Ark,
a story about two Amish children who make Christmas
preparations, several editions of Nancy Drew mysteries,
and a collection of C. S. Lewis's *Chronicles of Narnia*.
He also wanted to purchase something for Adele Herr.
So many choices, so little time . . .

Glancing at his watch, he began to peruse the picture books and the other books he wanted to buy for
Kari. He made his selections rather quickly, deciding on
the set of the Lewis books for Kari and the book with
the Amish setting for Annie Yoder, though he couldn't
be certain of the accuracy of dialogue and information,
or how Rachel's little girl might perceive the characters.
Regardless, he would take the risk. The illustrations,
after all, were quite eye-catching, and from what he remembered of Lancaster County, the artistic renderings
seemed authentic enough.

He located a beautifully illustrated gift book, featuring American rural scenes, as well as a blank book for journaling—both for Adele.

On his way out of the store, purchases in hand, he spotted a book on the bargain table with a most intriguing title, *Gifts of Darkness*. Compelled to pick it up, he noticed that the author had been a Pennsylvania Amish preacher at one time. He was intrigued and decided, upon reading a portion of the first chapter, that he must have it for his growing collection of Plain books.

Not until he arrived home from work later in the evening did he discover the actual theme of the book. One of the chapters was entitled "White Witchcraft," and once again Philip was reminded that there were certain dark and secret rituals occurring under the guise of faith or "sympathy" healing in many Plain communities. Other than Adele Herr's story of Gabe Esh, he had not heard of occult practices associated with the Anabaptist people, so he read from cover to cover, not stopping until he had completed the entire book.

Most surprising was the seemingly honest approach the former Amish minister had taken in writing the book, revealing the grip of Satan in his own life, how he had been forced as a youth to "receive giftings passed down from an older female relative," as well as his path to spiritual freedom. The author recounted the steps the Holy Spirit had led him to take in order to be released from the enemy's stronghold.

After reading certain chapters a second time, Philip began to rethink the timing and his purchase of the book. No longer a believer in happenstance, he had recently entrusted his very life and future to the Lord. He began to pray on behalf of people everywhere who might indeed be under the "deceitful spell of the devil," as the Amish writer had stated. Philip had no one in mind, though he wondered later, while reheating leftovers in the microwave, if what he knew of Gabe Esh's story might have subconsciously triggered his encounter with the pocket-size book.

After a light supper, he began to pack for his trip. He was eager to share his find with Adele; even wondered if Rachel Yoder had ever encountered such practices in her present-day Amish community these many years since Gabe's death. Most remarkable were the steps to deliverance from generational curses and what the author called "familiar spirits" in families, and how to become free of bondage through the power of Jesus' name.

He was anxious to head for Pennsylvania, now more so than ever, praying that what he had just read might be something he could share with a needy heart. He recalled the unique sermon at the Mennonite church, back in September, where his historical society contact Stephen Flory and wife attended. It had been the first message on spiritual warfare he'd ever heard—how to make a rock-solid covenant to truth. "The very arrows intended for God's people shall enter into the evildoers' own hearts, 'and their bows shall be broken,' " the pastor had preached with reference to Psalm 37 from his unadorned pulpit in the meetinghouse.

At the time, Philip hadn't known what to make of such a sermon. Now, since renewing his faith and study-

ing the Bible daily, his "eyes of faith" had been opened
to redemptive truths. He could see the Lord's hand in
his life so clearly these past few months and could
hardly wait to share this teaching.

Closing his suitcase, he knelt beside his bed, the way
he had often prayed as a boy. "Dear Lord, it has occurred
to me that you have placed in my heart an urgency to
minister. I cast myself on your mercy, thanking you for
bringing me back to the Fold. It is my desire to commit
my life, one hundred percent, to your work and to your
kingdom.

"As for Rachel Yoder, if it is your will, allow me to
present to her the information on conversion disorder.
I entrust her sight to you, as well as her future. In Jesus'
name I pray. Amen."

❖ ❖ ❖

Rachel didn't wait till Annie was asleep to kneel at
her bedside. She prayed with her daughter, her arm
around her dear one. "Lord Jesus, I have never asked
you for my healing in front of my little girl. But Annie
knows now how much I want to see again . . . how badly
I want to be whole, too—healed from the memory of
what happened the day of the accident. She and I come
before you just now, prayin' that you'll hear and answer
our prayer."

Annie continued, quite unexpectedly. "I don't
know how you're gonna do it, Lord, but Mamma really
wants to see what I look like now. So could you do that

for her? And could you do somethin' else, too, Lord? Could you please take away her awful headache? Amen."

Rachel nodded in agreement. Jah, it would be ever so wonderful to be free of the throbbing pain, especially that intense and thorny penetrating sensation that filled her entire day. The acute, raw pain that accompanied the return of terrifying visions.

Long after Annie was tucked in, the memories continued to present themselves. A horse rearing up on its hind legs . . . her dear husband struggling to control the mare. Screams of children . . . a car horn wailing . . . the hideous, grating sound of the crash.

She did not reject the visions as she had in the past, but made a futile attempt to shield herself from the persistent pain that seemed to accompany them. She was willing to walk through the nightmare, through the memory. Jesus had promised to be with her—even through the valley of the shadow of death.

Wrapping her arms about herself, Rachel rose and reached out to feel the wall, locating the windows across the room. "Oh, Lord Jesus, I want to remember what happened that day," she whispered. "Because I want to be healed . . . no matter what."

But she could speak no more, for the tears threatened to fall. Determinedly, Rachel waited with open eyes, hoping to regain her sight, to witness the moon's rise over the neighbor's barn, to see her beautiful child who lay sleeping.

Sometime later, Rachel groped her way back to bed and crawled in, curling up under the layers of quilts. She placed both hands next to her face, as if in prayer, her knees nearly touching her chin. Then she wept softly.

Much later, Rachel thought she heard voices, possibly Mam and Dat arguing. She wished to fall asleep without pain, either emotional or physical, yet she experienced great stress at the thought of her parents' fussing.

Getting up, she made her way down the long hallway, her hand on the wall as she counted her steps to the top of the staircase. Then, turning away from the stairs, she followed the voices and stopped well within earshot of their bedroom.

"I daresay our Rachel was the one who invited Esther and Levi home for Christmas. She wants to talk 'em into takin' her and Annie back to Ohio with them, prob'ly," Mam was saying.

"Well, now, how could that be?" Dat replied.

"You just see if I ain't right."

Dat was quiet now, and Rachel wondered if he had been talkin' in his sleep. After all, it was much too late for her father to be carryin' on any sort of intelligent conversation. Mam oughta know that!

"There's more," Susanna continued.

Rachel thought she heard something of a grunt, but she couldn't be sure. Still, Mam persisted.

"Annie's talkin' like she and Rachel must've discussed farmin' someday, so I'll betcha I'm right 'bout this."

Dat was beginning to snore. So much for a two-sided conversation. Poor Mam. She never knew when to quit!

"And . . . you listen here to me! Our granddaughter's showin' some interesting signs, I tell you, Benjamin. She might just be the next powwow doctor 'round these parts. If'n I can ever sneak her out of the house to see Blue Johnny. Or maybe Bishop Seth's the one to see before he passes on. . . ."

Rachel cringed, turning on her heels. She hurried down the hall as quickly as possible, though she didn't want to go fallin' headlong down the stairs. *That* would never do!

Back in her room, she knelt at her bedside again. "Oh, Lord Jesus, I need your help tonight! I don't even know how to pray 'bout much of what's on my heart just now, but I believe you know and you care. And protect Annie from what Mam might be planning to do. Mam needs you ever so much, Lord. She really does. . . ."

Susanna waited long into the night, past her usual bedtime, to slip into Rachel's bedroom and snatch up one of the tape recordings from Esther Glick. She'd promised herself months ago she'd never do such a thing, listening in on her daughter's and her niece's personal "letters" to each other. Still, she figured the Lord God heavenly Father would understand and forgive her just this once. After all, it was high time she had an inklin' why on earth Rachel would ask Esther and Levi to return to Bird-in-Hand for Christmas.

Twelve

❖ ❖ ❖

Lavina sat on her big feather bed—her grandmother's ancient bed—with artwork strewn around her. *Gabe's* . . . when he was a young boy, back when he had shown occasional signs of actually caring about his friend, who just so happened to be a girl one year older and a mite skinnier.

Studying each picture closely—one, a pencil sketch of a two-story bank barn and silo in early summer; another, a rusty water pump with a lone daisy growin' to one side, nearest the handle. The third was her favorite—a watercolor picture of his father's meadow in full spring, with purple and pink wild flowers and sunny-yellow dandelions, too, all colorful and eye-pleasin'. She'd decided she wanted to take them—or at least color copies of them—along to show Adele next time she and Rachel paid a visit.

Next time? Well, she was hopin' she could get Rachel to go again real soon. In time for the nursing home's Christmas program, maybe. After all, sounded to her like Adele was going to invite Philip Bradley— the man whose name had caused Rachel to blush red as a ripe tomato. Jah, he was prob'ly coming down from New York for the special program. Sure as anything, made sense to get Rachel back there, too. That is, if she could bring up the idea without Rachel 'specting something was up.

For sure, she didn't much wanna to be playin' matchmaker. She'd come mighty close to urgin' young Adele to return to Bird-in-Hand one summer, forty-some years ago, just weeks before Gabe was killed in a car accident. Still, she knew without question that the English schoolteacher had dearly loved Gabe, without a smidgen of help or matchmakin' from an old maid, let alone a woman with only half her wits.

Carefully she gathered up Gabe's drawings, setting aside her three favorites. She wouldn't risk losing them; couldn't part with 'um, either. She would drive horse and buggy over to her married brother's place—he had a copy machine in back of his woodworking shop. Color copies would make a right nice Christmas gift for her friend. And 'twould be a gut excuse to return to the Reading nursing home . . . with Rachel Yoder.

She couldn't help but snicker as she headed to the hall closet to put on her warmest coat, artwork in hand.

❖ ❖ ❖

The next day, Lavina made a point of goin' to see Rachel. Mainly it was to show little Annie the perty drawings Gabe had made so long ago. There was another purpose in her visit, though. She wanted to chat with Ben Zook 'bout accompanying her to see Bishop Seth Fisher, who folks were sayin' here lately was real bad sick with flu and other complications.

"High time he hears from *me* 'bout my shunning," she said as she sat in the Zooks' parlor, with both Susanna and Ben sharing a couch across from her. " 'Least 'fore he dies, I believe I oughta go."

Ben put down his paper, looking over his glasses at her. "Well, now, I wouldn't be opposed to such a thing. That is, if you're goin' there to repent." He paused, his frown growing deeper by the second.

Susanna spoke up. "That *is* what you had in mind, ain't?"

Lavina felt flustered all of a sudden. She'd come to ask a favor, and Benjamin and his wife were puttin' her on the spot. "There's somethin' else I best be doing, too." She didn't go on to say that Rachel had agreed to go with her—to witness to the old bishop—but now that seemed out of the question, what with Rachel sufferin' so with crippling headaches.

Ben's face seemed even more ruddy than she'd remembered, but she figured it was due to the fact that he was vexed. She could be wrong, but she thought the color creepin' up in his neck and face prob'ly was just that.

His fingers worked up and down his tan suspenders, makin' her even more nervous. "Well, Cousin, what is it?" he pressed for her answer. "What's it ya wanna do?"

Avoiding his serious gaze, Lavina was wishin' she'd left well enough alone. Still, she believed God wanted her to speak to Bishop Seth. "Has the Lord God heavenly Father ever put somethin' strong in your heart, so powerful-strong you knew you best do something 'bout it?" Lavina managed to say as she sat there on Susanna's brown tufted settee.

Ben's face broke into a most pleasant smile, and for a moment she was relieved. "Why, sure He has, and I can tell you 'bout one of them times, too. It was back when Seth Fisher was one of our preachers and had just been chosen by lot to be our bishop." He stopped, inhaling slow and easy, as though he was enjoying the recollection. "I was no more than ten years old, seems to me."

Lavina wondered how old the *bishop* had been at the time, but she didn't have to wait more than a second to find out.

Ben continued. "Seth Fisher was close to forty years old, and one of our ordained preachers, when I felt led of God to help out the church's new leader . . . or soon to be."

Susanna's eyes were fixed on her man, prob'ly having heard this tale many-a-time. She nodded her head, listenin' like Lavina had never witnessed before, 'specially since Susanna Zook was known to be frisky at times, and quite a talker, on top o' that.

"Jah, I was just a boy when I assisted the man of God by hangin' a small bag of ingredients 'round a sick horse's neck. I watched Seth Fisher cure my uncle's best drivin' horse thataway."

Lavina wasn't too surprised to hear this. Plenty of youngsters had been eager to help the bishop—or anyone who had "magical powers"—down through the years.

"You can imagine my surprise when I thought he

wasn't lookin', and I peeked into that there little burlap bag." Ben's smile was contagious, and Susanna was grinning, too. "I found nothin' but a handful of sawdust mixed with oats, of all things!"

"Still, the horse was cured," Susanna pointed out.

Lavina didn't think Ben's boyhood tale had much to do with being led of God, but she sure wasn't going to argue. Just listened, waiting for the man to agree or disagree on going with her to talk to the respected bishop. One of the two.

It was after Annie came into the parlor, telling Susanna that her mamma wanted to "talk to Lavina," that she remembered the drawings. "I've got something right nice to show you," Lavina said, getting up and heading for the stairs.

"What is it?" Annie asked.

"Perty drawings, that's what. I'll be right down, dearie."

Annie nodded and pranced out of the room. And Lavina hurried upstairs to see about Rachel, poor thing.

"You still sufferin', child?" Lavina asked, going quickly to the side of Rachel's bed.

Rachel kept her hands on a wet cloth that was wrapped 'round her forehead. "No need to worry over me, 'cause what I have to tell you is ever so important. My cousin Esther said some mighty interesting things on her latest tape."

"I'm all ears," Lavina said, perching on the edge of the bed.

Rachel's face was drawn, her eyes downcast. "I think you should know what Esther said 'bout the hex put on

Gabe Esh." And she went on to tell her what was told to Esther's husband about Bishop Seth's "death charm." "Must've sprung out of Seth's anger against Gabe for not comin' under his authority. Gabe was a right stubborn fella—stubborn for God, you know."

Ach, she was shamed to hear such horrid things 'bout the man who'd led the People all these years. Lavina clamped her hand over her mouth when Rachel mentioned the hex and the encounter with the white dove.

"But remember, Lavina, the enemy will use anything—even superstitions—and you know how we Plain folk are 'bout that," Rachel added. "Esther says it's ignorance and irrational fear that make superstition work."

Lavina couldn't agree more. "Jah, but it's time we take back our families, our community, for God!"

Nodding, Rachel whispered, "I'll be prayin' for you when you go to the bishop, and I'm ever so sorry I can't go with you . . . on account of this horrible headache."

"I think your father's comin' with me. And I'm hopin' and prayin' he'll stay and listen . . . when I talk to Bishop Seth 'bout the hex . . . and the dove."

Rachel frowned. "What'll you say if the bishop asks you to repent for goin' to the Beachy church?"

Truth was, she couldn't show remorse. "The Lord will hafta give me the words to say. That's all I know."

Seemed to be what Rachel needed to hear, 'cause her face brightened, and for a moment, Lavina wondered if the pain in the poor girl's head just might be lettin' up some. "You just stay here and pray, and I'll go and do the speakin' for the Lord," she said before getting up and kissing Rachel's cheek.

"You can count on me," Rachel replied, still rubbing her forehead.

Lavina headed back downstairs to show Annie the perty artwork by the little's girl very own great-great-uncle Gabe.

❖ ❖ ❖

The phone rang almost as soon as Lavina and Dat left by way of the front door. Rachel had heard the doors close behind them, and when the phone rang, she was glad Mam had stayed home. That way she wouldn't have to bother getting up to answer it.

Soon, though, it was Mam calling up the steps to her. "Rachel, are you up to talkin' to Mr. Witwer?"

She was sure their Mennonite driver must have some information 'bout "Auntie" Nancy Beiler. Maybe located her, though she wished the call had come on another day. When she felt better.

"Jah, I'll take it up here," she succeeded in saying loud enough to be heard. Hobbling down the hall, she sat on the small chair next to the phone table.

Turned out, Calvin Witwer *had* found where Nancy Beiler was living. "She's stayin' with her married sister, over near Gap."

"Really, so far away?" Rachel replied.

"I just now talked to her, and she says she wants you to give her a call sometime, when it's convenient."

She memorized the woman's number, still holding one side of her head with one hand, the phone cradled in the other. "I'll be glad to. Thank you ever so much, Mr. Witwer."

Hanging up the phone, it was all she could do to make it back to bed. Yet she'd promised to pray for Lavina, so she lay there on her back, her head stinging with every pulse of her heart, trying to make sense of her prayer. "Dear Lord, please help my father's cousin as she goes and talks to the old bishop 'bout you. Help her remember the deliverance prayer she learned from Esther's tapes."

She sighed, hesitant to ask the Lord for her healing again. "Help Seth Fisher show grace and mercy to Lavina . . . help her not to feel rejected if the shun is put on her for gut. Oh, Lord, just help her. And help me, too." That was all she said 'bout herself. She wanted to "rest in the Lord" as Lavina had instructed so wisely yesterday. With everything in her, she was trying her best to do just that.

So she would set her mind to resting. Then in a few minutes, she would get down on her knees and pray again, remembering her dear friend and relative, Lavina, whom God had called to testify for Him.

Thirteen

❖ ❖ ❖

The elderly bishop lay lifeless—gray 'round the gills—his bed marked only by the colorful blues and yellows of the quilts and the modest walnut headboard and footboard. His plain white nightshirt was visible, though only the neckline, as he was covered securely with a mound of blankets and quilts. His gray hair was damp with perspiration at the crown, and strands clung to his wrinkled brow. His beard, grizzled and untrimmed, was *schlappich*—disheveled. Overall, he looked downright wrung out.

The room was typically Plain with rag rugs scattered here and there—one rug on either side of the low double bed and a long narrow one directly in front of the dresser. A lone rocking chair sat near the corner windows across the wide hardwood plank flooring. Lavina noticed that the bishop's wife had draped her bureau mirror with jewelry—mostly glittery necklaces and bracelets. Truth was, many Amishwomen decorated their bedroom mirrors with colorful jewelry and shiny trinkets, since they weren't allowed to wear such things.

"I've sent for Blue Johnny and his black box," Rosemary Fisher said, her wrinkled face solemn and drawn as she stood near her husband's bedside.

151

Lavina hoped Rachel was callin' her name out to the Lord just now. Oh, she needed divine wisdom! She could scarcely hear the bishop breathing, but then she set her gaze on his chest and saw that it was rising and falling ever so slowlike.

She found herself concentrating on the beloved bishop, the tall, dignified-lookin' man who'd overseen her baptism into the Amish church back when she was only eighteen years old. Now he lay still as death, looking like a bag o' bones beneath the many bedclothes. "Is he conscious?" she whispered.

Rosemary shook her head. "He's been sleeping 'round the clock, so it's all right if you wake him." Then, she asked, eyeing Benjamin Zook, "Are ya here to confess for sinning . . . against the *Ordnung?*"

The sick man perked up a bit, his eyes fluttering open. Just in that instant, Lavina remembered how those serious dark eyes could pierce a body through, although just now there seemed to be a flicker of relief in his countenance. Mighty confusin' to Lavina, to say the least. She recalled, too, his stern preachin' voice, the way he used it to exhort the People.

"Lavina Troyer's here," Ben said softly, stepping back to allow her to move closer.

Rosemary also moved toward her, stooped over and leaning on a cane. "So you're here 'bout confessing, then?" She seemed anxious for an answer, her gaze intent on Lavina.

"I've come in the name of the Lord." Lavina was somewhat surprised at her own sudden boldness.

"That don't answer my question." The bishop's

wife, feeble as she was herself, was unyielding, and Lavina couldn't blame her for wanting to protect her husband, as ill as he seemed to be.

"Jah, I'm here to 'fess up, all right. I own up to bein' right headstrong 'bout attending preachin's over at the Beachy meetinghouse. Guess I ain't been forthright with the bishop 'bout that, and I'm sorry. Should've spoken up weeks ago 'bout the way the Lord's touched my life over there . . . how He's taught me things I never knowed were in the Bible. Jah, I'm just sorry I didn't speak up sooner."

Rosemary took a step or two back, frowning and looking ever so befuddled.

"What's that, Rosie?" the bishop was saying, struggling to raise his head off the pillow. "What's the woman want?"

"Lavina Troyer says she's sorry," Rosemary told him. "She wants to tell you that—"

"I'm here to give you a message from the Lord who loves you, Bishop Seth," Lavina interrupted. All she could think to say was the Scripture passage in Luke she'd memorized just this week. She began slowly, deliberately, sayin' the words as clearly as she could. " 'In the synagogue there was a man, which had a spirit of an unclean devil, and cried out with a loud voice, saying, Let us alone; what have we to do with thee, thou Jesus of Nazareth? Art thou come to destroy us? I know thee who thou art; the Holy One of God.' "

The bishop's eyes blinked several times, and a scowl settled on his brow. "What . . . what do you want with *me?*"

It was the pitch of his voice that made Lavina wonder. Didn't sound like Seth Fisher's voice at all. Sounded eerielike. Dark and distant, too.

She sensed an unusual heaviness in the air. Yet in spite of the troublesome oppression, she felt something else just as strong, if not stronger. She recognized the presence of God in the room. The very closeness of His Spirit.

" 'Hold thy peace,' " she spoke the Scripture, " 'and come out of him.' "

Without warning, the bishop began to shake and twist on his bed, winding the ends of his sheet into what looked like a coiled rope, holding on to it as if convulsing. His face broke out in heavy perspiration, and his eyes kept rollin' back in his head. Then he began to cough and sneeze repeatedly.

"What's happenin' here?" Ben Zook gasped, his face turning ashen.

"The power of God's on him . . . and evil spirits can't stay where God is," Lavina answered, praying silently all the while.

"Well, whatever it is, I best be gettin' Blue Johnny, but quick," Rosemary said, leaning hard on her cane.

"Won't be needin' him," Lavina was quick to say. Again, she was unsure where the words were coming from, so fearless were they. "Just wait a bit . . . and pray for God's peace to pour over him."

The bishop's wife scratched her salt-and-pepper head through her formal veiling.

Ben was shaking his head in amazement, staring at both Rosemary and Lavina. "This ain't 'bout the powwow gift, is it? This writhing and whatnot?"

Lavina explained as best she could. "If you're thinkin' I've got the conjurin' gift, no . . . no. But if you're a-thinkin' the magical powers—and the curses—are comin' out of the bishop just now, jah, I'm trustin' and believin' the Lord Almighty for that."

Ben's face turned from white to bright red, and he spun on his heels and fled the room. Rosemary stayed put, though, wiping her husband's brow with a cloth, trying to soothe him. "I'd heard tell of things like this," she muttered. "Just never seen it with my own eyes."

"Let's pray," Lavina said, not wanting to get caught up in idle talk. "God's been wantin' to deliver our bishop ever since Gabe Esh died of the hex."

Rosemary's mouth dropped open. "Whatever are you talking 'bout? How do *you* know 'bout. . . ?" She clapped her hand over her own mouth.

"The hex . . . the white dove . . . and the all-consumin' fear that surely must've killed Gabe and his friend that night on their way to Gordonville—that's what the Lord wants out in the open. Once and for all."

"But that happened a long, long time ago."

"Jah, but the Lord sent me to pray for Bishop Seth 'bout all that. I can't think of disobeyin' the Lord God, now can I?" Lavina could see the sick man was beginning to relax, sighing, and taking long, deep breaths. His eyes were still fluttering, but his expression seemed to be changing—softening—right before their eyes.

"I wanna pray for you, Bishop Seth," she said, leaning closer. "The Lord wants to save your soul 'fore He takes you home to heaven."

"Now, you wait just a minute," Rosemary spoke up, eyes casting fiery darts her way. "My husband don't need no soul-savin'. He's the bishop, for pity's sake!"

At that, Seth Fisher motioned with his finger to his wife weakly, but motioning all the same. "Closer," he muttered.

Rosemary, quite shaken, bent down while the bishop whispered something in her ear. "Well, I'll be!" She straightened to her full height.

But the bishop gestured to her again. "Come closer, Rosie."

Turning pale herself, the bishop's wife leaned down again to hear what her husband had to say.

Lavina was beginning to wonder if the Lord would allow her to finish the work He'd started here and was greatly relieved when Rosemary stood to her full height once again. Facing Lavina, her eyes glistened as she spoke. "My husband insists on hearin' what you've got to say."

"He does?"

"Jah, but best make it snappy."

Seth Fisher's voice was raspy and weak. "I had a vision earlier this morning . . . hours before you came. Never has such a dream haunted me like this one, and I didn't know what to make of it. But now I understand that it was God preparin' me, for I saw an angel of the Lord come to me, tellin' me that what I've been doin'— hexing and powwowing—is wrong, dead wrong." His voice, though thin, was every bit normal-sounding now.

"Don't wear yourself out, Seth," his wife spoke up, stroking his shoulder with her free hand.

But he persisted. "The vision was as real as you are standin' right here, I tell you." He looked right at Lavina. "God knew you would be comin' today to wake me up out of my sin-sickness . . . to cast the evil out of my soul."

The gray pallor was slowly disappearing. Even as the women stood over his bed, the color began to return to his face. A moment passed, and the room was still as night.

Lavina felt it was time for her to speak again. "Bishop Fisher, God wants to forgive you for the death-hex you put on Gabriel Esh," she said gently. "And for the way you've kept the People in the grip of the enemy all these many years."

The bishop's eyes grew moist, and a tear slid down his crinkled cheek. His deep brown eyes shone with compassion, like beacons in the darkness, yet he remained silent, not speaking for a gut long time.

At last, the words poured forth. "I've been waitin' for this day. Who would've thought the Lord God would send a simple-minded woman to me." He sighed, eyes closing. "But it don't matter, not no more. I'm ready to receive forgiveness."

"I can help you say a prayer," Lavina said, glad that she'd learned how to in the past weeks since attending Rachel's church. "Is that all right?"

There was no hesitation. Bishop Seth nodded his head, the muscles in his jaw relaxing as Lavina looked on him in mercy and kindness, this man who'd shunned her unfairly.

"Lord Jesus, I come to you," she said.

He repeated her words, slowly, purposefully.

"I believe you are the Son of God . . . the only way to the heavenly Father." She paused for him to recite the simple, yet all-important words.

"You died on a cruel cross for my sins, took my place there, and rose up from the dead." While the bishop repeated after her, she inhaled slowly. "It's high time I give up the fight against you, Lord. I won't resist you no more. I repent of all my sins. Take me, Lord, I'm your child . . . your servant from this day forth."

Rosemary was sniffling now, and Lavina wasn't sure, but she thought the woman might be whisperin' the words right along with her husband.

"I'm askin' for your forgiveness, Lord . . . 'specially those sins of my forefathers, who passed down curses and their consequences on me and my children. Make us free from the sinful patterns of our ancestors, in Jesus' name."

The bishop recited every word without questioning her. Lavina continued her prayer. "I turn my back on the devil and cancel the claims wickedness once had on me. And I ask to be forgiven for Gabe Esh's death, for the evil that I harbored in my heart."

Not only did the bishop say the prayer after her, he cut in and finished it himself. "And, Lord God in heaven, I do ask to be forgiven for the *many* hexes and charms I called forth." He stopped to cough several times. "I pray you'll see fit to forgive me for denyin' the People your truth . . . all these years. And for not livin' up to my own name, Seth, which I understand means 'anointed one.' Jah, I want *your* anointing on me . . .

now as I live out my final days."

Lavina held her breath, believin' that the Lord might keep him alive a bit longer because of the witness his life could be. . . .

"Please, Lord, heap blessin' on our bishop where once there was cursin'," Lavina ended the prayer. "In Jesus' name. Amen."

"Amen," Rosemary repeated, then reached over and gripped Lavina's hand. "Oh, dear girl, thank ya for comin' . . . today of all days."

"Thank the *Lord.*" She didn't want to go on and on, not really, tellin' the bishop's wife 'bout the divine help she'd been given. She'd just have to let the Lord do His work in Rosemary's life.

The bishop breathed a long ragged breath and looked straight up at Lavina. "I saw the mercy of God's Son, Jesus, in your eyes today, Lavina Troyer. Bless you for coming . . . thou wise and righteous woman."

Lavina felt mighty happy and could hardly wait to share the miraculous account with Rachel. My, my . . . who would've thought?

Soon after, she left for home with Benjamin Zook, who was visibly shaken over the visit to the ailing bishop. He tried to put the blame on her for upsetting the poor man, but she turned a deaf ear to him. No, she wouldn't begin to argue the truth or describe what she'd seen with her own eyes as the bishop was released from the evil spirits that had controlled him for so long. And she didn't wanna spoil things by recountin' the blessed moment just now.

Lavina heard from the bishop's wife, later in the afternoon, that Blue Johnny had shown up at last, though his services "weren't needed . . . or wanted, neither one," Rosemary said when she phoned from an English neighbor's house. "Denki for whatcha did, Lavina. I can't say thank you enough for the miracle that happened between my husband and God today."

"What 'bout you, Rosemary?" Lavina was bold enough to ask. "Did you pray the prayer, too?"

There was a slight pause, then the bishop's wife admitted she had. "I've always followed my husband in whatever he chose to do, ya know, as married couples oughta."

"But you believed it for *yourself*, ain't so?"

"Oh, my . . . more than words can say!"

So Lavina hung up the phone and set about cleaning house and bakin' molasses bread, thanking the Lord for helpin' her lead two dear souls to Himself.

And she knew, without a shadow of doubt, the angels were rejoicin'—twofold—as they wrote down the bishop's and Rosemary's names in the Lamb's Book of Life!

Fourteen

❖ ❖ ❖

𝒜 festive tree, decorated with slip-glazed ginger-bread figures, stars, hearts, angels, tiny mangers, and white twinkling lights, literally brushed the ceiling with its tip-top sprig.

Philip watched his niece busy herself with the glee-ful task of distributing gifts to her parents, grandparents, and Uncle Philip himself. He had felt somewhat obliged to attend the pre-Christmas Eve gathering when his sister called with her "great idea to get the family together before you leave" and sounding nearly breathless with her pleading that he "must come." There was the promise of prime rib and, naturally, the family gift exchange.

And he had come, not so much reluctantly as cha-grined that his impromptu travel plans had inspired Janice to throw a last-minute party.

He sat in the corner, nearest the tree, in the lone hand-painted Hitchcock chair, one of the many prized antiques his sister had collected over the years. Gazing about him, he took in the bank of windows to his right, where, in the near distance, a spectacular night view of midtown New York's skyscrapers shimmered against the black sky. Across the room, Janice had decorated a mock mantel, encasing a wide bookcase. On it was a splendid array of evergreen garlands, white candles of varied sizes, ivory roses, and pine cones lightly sprayed with fake snow. Scattered about the room, white poinsettias and fragrant paperwhite narcissus added to the simple, yet elegant, holiday decor. The coffee table, partially covered with a lace doily, was the showcase for dessert—a bundt cake with icing drizzled down the sides and powdery doughnuts to boot. "Homemade," Janice had insisted upon first carrying the silver tray into the room, followed by "oohs and aahs" from Philip's mother, especially. Ken, too, seemed impressed, as did Kari, whose wide eyes told the truth.

The word *homemade* caught Philip off guard, though he should have been prepared, but he wasn't. His thoughts went twirling away to Lancaster County, although Kari's interruption brought him back quickly.

"For you, Uncle Phil." She stood before him, holding a large, rectangular present.

"Thank you." He accepted the gift, then began his usual dramatic shaking of the box, leaning his ear down to determine if there were sounds emerging. "Hmm, *what* could be inside?"

"Not yet." Kari gave him a playful poke.

Philip's mother, sitting prim and proper in her white woolen suit and aqua blue brooch, smiled demurely, eyes shining. Dad, looking fit in his perennial red sweater vest, grinned when Kari handed him the family Bible.

"Time for the Christmas story, Grandpa," she said, recommending Luke's account.

He began to thumb through the pages. "Luke's my favorite, too."

Philip and Janice's father was a small wiry man, yet a "softie," as Kari liked to refer to her grandpa, Howard Bradley, a retired Long Island businessman. But when he read the Bible, the family paid close attention because he read with authority, as well as a semblance of tenderness.

The evening went smoothly as family get-togethers go, and when the slightest fussing about "too much money being spent on your parents this year" commenced from none other than Philip's mother, he rose and excused himself to get some more eggnog in the kitchen.

Janice joined him in a flash. "She makes the same comment every year," she whispered.

Philip poured his eggnog. "It's not important."

She nodded, shrugging. "So . . . when do you leave?"

"In the morning, as soon as I can get out of town."

Janice stepped back to survey her brother, hands on hips. "You're not yourself tonight, and I think you know what I'm talking about."

"Wouldn't have a clue." He made a serious attempt to mask his expression.

She eyed him curiously. "I read your Amish feature last week . . . nice work."

"Thanks."

"C'mon, Phil, there's more to that article than meets the eye. I *know* you."

"You're dreaming." He forced a droll grin and

pushed past her, back to the living room and the merry-making.

❖ ❖ ❖

"Never been s' happy in all my life," Lavina exclaimed the next morning, bright and early, when she stopped by to visit Rachel. "After I got home from the bishop's yesterday, I hafta admit I felt like kickin' up my heels and dancin' a jig. 'Course, we don't believe in such things, but I felt like it, all the same."

Rachel had to smile at her friend's remark, ever so glad to hear the news of Bishop Seth's glorious conversion. She sat in a chair near the bed, still wearing her bathrobe and slippers. "I believe I prayed so hard for you while you were at the bishop's house that my head actually quit paining me," she said. "It's a miracle."

"That's wonderful-gut news."

"Jah, and just in time to help Mam get ready for Christmas dinner tomorrow, for which I thank the Lord. Mam says Esther and Levi and the children are comin' in from Ohio for a few days. It'll be a fun time for all of us—Annie, too, 'cause all she's talked 'bout here lately are her young cousins from Ohio, and when is she ever gonna get to see them again."

"They'll stay at Leah's?"

"My aunt and uncle wouldn't have it any other way," Rachel replied, excited to see her cousin and family again.

"So . . . sounds like Susanna's having Christmas dinner here this year."

"Jah, but we're all goin' over to Aunt Leah's and Uncle Amos's tonight after supper for hot cocoa and cookies. We'll sit 'round the kitchen, talking 'bout the olden days with all the relatives, prob'ly. One of our Christmas Eve rituals." Rachel enjoyed hearing the old stories, one after another, at such gatherings. Things like hearing how Great-Aunt So-and-So had fun helping her mamma sort potatoes back when, or the first flood of the twentieth century and how they managed to bale water out of the cold cellar, or the time Uncle Samuel heard about "Amish dirt"—as a young boy— and how dumbfounded he was to learn that such dirt held more than six times the water an average no-till field did, due to crop rotation and manure application.

'Course, then again, discussing such farm-related things might not be the best topic for discussion at Christmas. But if she knew Levi and Esther, there'd be plenty talk of farming and reminiscing over their child-hood days in Lancaster County.

Remembering—one of the best things 'bout the Christmas season. And she had her own private memories to cherish, though they had nothin' at all to do with Christmas or any other holiday, for that matter. No, her memories of Philip Bradley had not a single connection to the Amish life and heritage.

❖ ❖ ❖

"You did *what?*" Ben said, hurrying to close the bedroom door behind Susanna.

"You heard me right."

He shook his head, coming 'round the side of his plump wife. "Well, what's our Rachel gonna think of such a thing?"

"Ach, she'll be just fine with it." Susanna's eyes flashed with her connivings. "Besides, it's high time she meets someone."

"Well, now, I don't know 'bout that," he insisted, going to the window and looking out. "When's the smithy due over here, anyways?"

"Straight up noon, Christmas Day."

"And you called him?" he said, turning to look at his wife, still skeptical 'bout what she'd gone and done. Without asking his advice, of all things!

"*I* didn't call him."

"But you had a hand in invitin' him?"

Susanna pursed her lips, trying to smother a smile, it seemed. "John Lapp has received an invitation to dinner here." That was all she was gonna say 'bout the stunt she'd pulled. He knew it was, 'cause she flounced off to their private bathroom and locked the door with a resounding thud.

Knowin' there wasn't much he could do now, Ben left Susie to have her little snit if she wanted to. He headed on downstairs to sit and read *The Budget* by the fire. Soon it would be time to leave for Susanna's sister's place. He just hoped Leah's daughter and son-in-law, back home from the Midwest, would mind their manners and watch what they said 'bout their religious be-

liefs and whatnot. Why, he'd seen enough strange spiritual goings-on since yesterday at the bishop's house.
And that thing Lavina did, quoting the "deliverance"
Scripture over the bishop, or whatever it was she'd
called it, well . . . he wished he'd never agreed to take
her over there, causin' such a ruckus she had. Should've
asked her what the world she was thinkin', annoying
the poor ailin' man thataway.

Far as he was concerned, it was a gut idea to keep
things solemn just a bit, seein' as how the People might
hafta be laying their bishop in his grave soon, sick as he
was.

Copper came bounding into the room just then,
wagging his tail like nobody's business. "Well, hullo
there, pooch," he said, bending down to pet him. "I
'spect you're lookin' for a nice Christmas treat, and I
know of just the thing."

He rose with a grunt and marched out to the
kitchen, where he knew Susanna kept tiny bone-shaped
doggie biscuits. "There, now, that oughta make ya
happy," he said, offering Copper a whole handful, not
caring what his wife might say 'bout so many.

❖ ❖ ❖

Philip unpacked his clothes and hung up the shirts
and trousers quickly, hoping to discourage wrinkles. He
didn't mind touch-up ironing, but only if necessary, and
there were more important things on his mind today.
Once he was settled in his room at the inn, he planned

to make a surprise afternoon visit to Adele Herr. She wouldn't be expecting him until tomorrow evening, but a lady like Adele shouldn't be alone on Christmas Eve without the love of family or close friends. He would see to it that she laughed and enjoyed herself *both* days. After that, he wasn't sure of his game plan. He would trust the Lord to guide his every step. Whether or not his steps led him back to Bird-in-Hand remained to be seen.

The walkway leading to Fairview Nursing Home was trimmed with white lights, and along the porch, boughs of evergreen and an occasional lantern dressed up the outside, offering the warm home-away-from-home atomsphere. An enormous holly wreath, composed of white flowers, fake blueberries, and clusters of cinnamon sticks, provided the initial welcome as Philip pushed open the door.

Inside the foyer area, garlands of evergreen, bedecked with red velvet bows, hung over deep casement windows. A large multiroomed birdhouse made a showcase for colorful glass Christmas balls and was perched on a lamp table near a splendid tree adorned with strands of golden beads and red, white, and gold ornaments.

He heard laughter and muffled talking, and because the receptionist was nowhere in sight, he wandered down the hallway toward the sounds.

Philip spotted Adele first. The dear lady was seated in a chaise lounge, an afghan thrown over her legs. A harpist—a young girl not much more than twelve or so—had just begun "O Holy Night." Standing in the back of the sunny room, Philip folded his arms, listening in rapt attention to the angelic rendition, already glad he'd made the decision to come for the holiday.

When the carol was finished, he applauded with the rest of the patients, and, quite unexpectedly, Adele turned and glanced back at him, almost as if she'd sensed that he was there.

Quickly, he made his way to her. "Merry Christmas, Adele." He stooped down to greet her.

Her smile warmed his heart. "Oh, it's so good to see you again, Philip."

"You're looking well," he replied, accepting a chair from one of the nurses with a nod and a thank-you.

"I'm getting better, and the doctors are amazed." She folded her hands on her lap, grinning up at him.

He was about to make a comment, but a young boy was standing before them, ready to recite a poem. Philip felt as if he were playing hooky from his upcoming assignments, scheduled conference calls, and the like, but sitting here next to his surrogate relative, he felt rejuvenated by the message of the young man's poem and the musical performances that followed.

"What a lovely program," Adele said when it was over.

He agreed. "And to think you have something just as wonderful to look forward to tomorrow evening."

Her eyes brightened. "All I need is right here," she said, reaching for his hand and squeezing it.

Nodding, he continued to sit with her, welcoming her company. For two hours they engaged in animated conversation, talking about whatever Adele wanted to discuss, until supper was brought to her on a tray and he said his good-byes.

"I'll come again tomorrow," he told her, promising to bring "a surprise from the Big Apple."

"Well, what could *that* be?"

"That's *my* line," he said, describing the shenanigans he always pulled for his niece's sake.

"Then you must've celebrated Christmas already with your family."

He admitted that he had. "But the most special part of my Christmas this year is being here with you." Indeed, he'd wondered if this might not be the woman's last celebration of Christ's birth on earth, but as he gazed on her dear face, noting her bright eyes and rosy cheeks, he had a feeling that Adele might fool everyone and live a while longer. And he was elated at the prospect.

❖ ❖ ❖

Susanna and Benjamin greeted their relatives as they made their way up the snow-swept walk. "*En frehlicher Grischtdaag!*—A Merry Christmas!"

"*S'naemlich zu dich!*—The same to you!" Amos and Leah called out in unison, meeting them with warm hugs and smiles at the kitchen door.

Amos took their wraps and disappeared into the front room with an armload of coats and scarves.

Leah leaned on Susanna's arm, chattering a mile a

minute. "Come, have some sand tarts, sugar cookies . . . whatever you like."

Susanna made herself right at home, taste-testing her sister's cherry pudding first thing after they said their "hullos" all 'round, 'specially greeting Esther and Levi and their youngsters.

Leah and her daughter-in-law Lyddie Stoltzfus, along with an elderly aunt—Auntie Ann—on Leah's husband's side, had put a nice spread on the kitchen table, even used all the table leaves to extend it gut and long. 'Course, they wouldn't be sittin' down, but still there was plenty of room for an array of pastries, cookies, and cups of hot cocoa with marshmallows peeking over the tops.

Leah and Amos's married sons and their wives and children had come, and, of course, Sadie Mae and Molly were on hand, whispering and grinning from ear to ear, along with ninety-year-old Auntie Ann. In the middle of the kitchen stood Esther, Levi, and their brood, like they were on display after bein' gone all this time. Esther was just a-huggin' and a-kissin' Rachel and Annie, babbling to beat the band, standing right under a string stretched clear across the width of the kitchen. Little red and green paper bells hung from the string, and Susanna s'posed that Leah's grandchildren had made the decoration or brought it home from school. One or the other.

She decided it best to let them talk as much as they wanted. Get it out of their systems. 'Course, then again, she must be very wise and not let on that she'd listened to one of Esther's tapes late last night. Wouldn't let on one bit. Far as she was concerned, that business 'bout family patterns and sins of ancestors and whatnot was downright ridiculous—for the birds, really. Esther and Levi had gone and gotten themselves caught up in some mighty strange teachings. And she'd already planned to put her foot down if there was the least little bit of talk 'bout Esther and Levi cartin' Rachel and Annie off to Ohio!

Still, while making over her sister's wonderful-gut recipe, she couldn't help but overhear a little of what Esther and Rachel were sayin' to each other. Made her think back to that tape, and a little shiver came over her, recalling some of the Scripture verses. They were passages she'd honestly never heard of ever in her whole life. 'Course, if they were really and truly recorded in God's Word, well, then, she s'posed she oughta be lookin' them up and findin' out for herself. And once Christmas dinner was behind her tomorrow, that's just what she intended to do.

When all was said and done, it was the applesauce nut cookies that won her vote, if there was to be one. And she told Leah so. "I daresay you've outdone yourself, Sister."

Leah grinned, showing her gums, and reached out and hugged Susanna. "Well, if you must say so, then I'll hafta be sayin' Denki for it."

The People weren't big on giving compliments, usually didn't do it at all. Truth be told, Susanna felt mighty odd with all the attention being showered on Esther and Levi. My goodness, they were standin' there in the middle of everything awful long, though Leah and Amos didn't seem to mind a'tall. Prob'ly assumed the evening's visit was for this very purpose, to get reacquainted with their Ohio relatives.

At long last Susanna made a point of catchin' Molly's eye, and going across the kitchen, she stood with the seventeen-year-old girl, Leah's youngest, not too far from where Esther and Rachel were still gabbing up a storm. She whispered that she appreciated the "help" Molly and a certain boy cousin had given while over in Paradise Township not so many days ago. "It was right kind of you."

"Oh, it was nothin' really," Molly said, smiling. "I just hope everything works out tomorrow . . . for Rachel, ya know."

Well, Susanna hoped it more than anyone, but she couldn't be sure how her daughter would take to the outspoken smithy Lapp. 'Least not the way she seemed to be comin' into her own more and more these days. Susanna truly hoped she hadn't stuck her neck out too far, invitin' a near-total stranger for Christmas dinner.

Fifteen

❖ ❖ ❖

Lavina really wanted to take the copies of Gabe's artwork to Adele for a Christmas surprise. She'd even asked Rachel if she wanted to go up to Reading, but Rachel hadn't seemed much interested. 'Least she hadn't responded the way Lavina thought she might, seein' as how she was sure the young woman was sweet on one Philip Bradley. 'Course, it was best to let things happen as they might, in God's way and His time, too . . . if'n the friendship was meant to be at all. Besides, who was to say that Philip would come all the way down from New York City, anyways.

"Mam says we're havin' company from Paradise," Rachel told her, looking worried. "You don't 'spose it's—" She stopped right then, her face drooping.

Lavina gasped upon hearing it. "Don't think it could be the smithy Lapp, do ya? Not unless . . ."

"What?"

"Whoever'd do such a thing? Not your mamma!"

Rachel shook her head in dismay. "You must not know my mother very well, if you're askin' that. She's a conniver, she is. And I surely ain't the first person to tell ya so!"

Lavina thought on that and had to agree that

Rachel was right 'bout at least one thing. Jah, Susanna was a schemer, all right. As for invitin' a stranger into the Zook house to share Christmas dinner, well, Lavina didn't have an opinion on that, really. Lots of Amish families had outside guests comin' in on Christmas Day, 'specially. Guess Rachel would just hafta wait and see what happened.

❖ ❖ ❖

Rachel was awful glad to have Esther over for the noon meal. Levi and the children played checkers on the floor in the commons area with Annie—where B&B guests usually spent their time. Not *this* Christmas. It was the first year since they'd had overnight boarders that not a single lodger would be sharing the day or the feast. Rachel wasn't as happy 'bout *that* as she was to have more time with Esther.

The older women, all six of them, helped Mam put the finishing touches on the roasted turkey, stuffed with corn bread, and laid it out in the dining room on the longest platter Mam owned with all the trimmings: mashed potatoes and gravy, buttered homemade noodles, cut sweet corn, lima beans, cabbage slaw, sweet and sour pickles, two kinds of olives, and plenty of celery and carrot sticks. To top off the meal, there'd be enough pumpkin pie for seconds, ice cream, and a variety of cookies. Not to mention the many small dishes of candy and nuts scattered here and there.

Mam had made certain that the younger children—

ten of them, including Annie and Joshua, Lizzy's little one—had places in the kitchen. "That way we won't worry who spills what," she'd said as Rachel and Esther worked to set the tables in both the kitchen and the dining room. There would be an overflow area, where folding tables would be used, but every detail of the dinner had been carefully planned, as Mam was known to do.

Only one aspect of the meal was left to be discovered, and Rachel encountered that rather abruptly when the doorbell rang. Just as they were preparing to sit down, she heard Dat's voice as he answered the door, welcoming someone inside.

"It's John Lapp . . . the blacksmith widower," someone whispered, though Rachel couldn't tell who, not for sure.

All she knew was that her stomach was churning and her face felt warm. What had Mam gone and done now?

She made herself scarce, hiding out in the kitchen as Dat went 'round introducing the smithy from Paradise like he was the most important guest under their roof, now that he was here, anyways. She didn't quite know how to act, seein' as how this man had been invited for *her* sake—unbeknownst to her and without her consent.

Was Mam so eager to have her courtin' again that she'd do such a thing? Why, it was beyond her how Mam could've gone and spoiled Christmas dinner for her like this. Now that she thought of it, she almost wished she'd agreed to go to Reading and visit Adele Herr with

Lavina, after all. Maybe it wasn't too late for an afternoon visit. . . .

❖ ❖ ❖

Philip arrived at the nursing home, bearing gifts. "It's looking like Christmas around here," he said, placing two colorful packages on the dresser near the foot of the hospital bed.

"Oh, Philip, what have you done?" Adele was sitting in a chair across from the bed, gazing at the gifts. "Those aren't for me, are they?"

"You and only you." He pulled up a chair and sat facing her, amused at her naiveté and childlike comment.

"What a blessing you are to me."

He thanked her, once again, for the spiritual encouragement she had offered during their months of correspondence. "I've learned so much from you, Adele, and in such a short time." He reached for his New Testament, pulling it out of his sports coat pocket. "I have a Scripture to share with you before you open your gifts."

Adele's eyes closed briefly; then opening them, she dabbed at her face with a tissue, apologizing. "Oh, look at me go on this way. For goodness' sake, it's Christmas morning, and my favorite person is sitting right here."

He reached for her hand. "It's all right, Adele."

She sighed heavily. "My eyes should be void of tears after all these years."

He shook his head, wishing to cheer her. "But they're joyful tears."

"Yes, I believe they are." She was smiling now, motioning for him to read from his Testament. "Don't mind me. I want to hear the verses you've chosen for Jesus' birthday celebration."

Locating the very passage his father had read two nights before, Philip shared the story of the first Christmas from Luke's gospel with the woman who had adopted him as her own, at least in her heart.

After they prayed together, he showed her the book he'd found in the small-scale New York bookstore. "It has an unusual title and topic, don't you agree?"

"Yes . . . yes it does," she said, turning to the back of the book. When she'd finished scanning the copy, she looked up. "*Very* interesting."

"If you'd like to read it, you may. I'd like to have your opinion, as well."

"Oh, I'll read it, all right, but this looks like a book that should be circulated among Plain folk."

He didn't know if she was thinking of any particular community, but one thing led to another, and soon they began to talk about Philip's investigation into conversion disorder.

It was Adele who first brought up the topic. "I've been thinking a lot about your hysteria research . . . with Rachel Yoder in mind."

"There's certainly a lot of information on the subject, and I've brought it with me. I just don't know exactly how to go about getting it to her."

"Keep in mind, Lavina Troyer's a good friend of

Rachel," Adele remarked. "She might be able to help."

"I'd thought of Lavina," Philip admitted. "But I don't know her, only know *of* her."

"Well, seems to me, Lavina's a person who can be trusted. And I should know, because I lived in her house a good many years ago."

"True, Lavina might be the best choice. I'd wondered about mailing a packet of information to her, and would even be willing to write a brief letter to explain what I hoped she could do . . . for Rachel's sake."

"So you would ask her to read the contents to Rachel—is that what you're thinking?"

"Would Rachel think it presumptuous of me, sending it through Lavina?"

Adele glanced at the ceiling, then shook her head slowly. "I just don't know how Lavina would manage all those technical terms. But it *would* be a shame if all your work came to naught."

Philip wouldn't come right out and say he'd much prefer to deliver the data in person and discuss some of the ideas with Rachel directly. But how that might come about, he didn't know.

When Adele's turkey dinner arrived on a tray, Philip excused himself to go eat at the inn's dining room, where he was staying. "I'll return in time for the Christmas program this evening," he promised.

"Good idea, Philip, especially since the nurses will insist I have a nap after this sizable meal." She glanced at the generous portion before her and shrugged. "Have you ever seen so much food?"

He didn't have to think too hard to recall the six-course candlelight suppers he'd experienced at the Orchard Guest House B&B last fall. "Eat what you can, but don't overdo it," he suggested. She extended her arm, and he was glad to go to her for a hug. "Will you be all right until I return?"

"Never better. Now, you go enjoy yourself . . . wherever you're bound."

The glint in her eye made him wonder. Did she suspect that he might be headed to Bird-in-Hand for a short visit with Rachel? Did Adele know him *that* well?

❖ ❖ ❖

They were sitting around the fire, tellin' one story after another—the children in the sunroom 'round the corner, playing games and sneakin' cookies—when Benjamin came up with a humdinger of a tale. 'Course, Susanna knew it was every bit true, but it was just so surprisin' to her that her husband would wanna reveal something so personal.

"Back in the days when corn huskin' bees were still goin' on 'round these parts, Susie and I showed up at one of them work frolics—not together, really. We was just gettin' acquainted at the time."

Susanna could feel the heat risin' in her face, and she wondered if it was such a gut idea for Benjamin to be tellin' this one in front of John Lapp, who most definitely had his eye on their Rachel. Why, from the time the womenfolk finished cleaning up the kitchen and joined the menfolk, who'd come into the front room to relax a bit, the smithy Lapp sat across from her daughter, just a-starin'. Truth was, his big brown eyes hardly strayed once since they all finished eatin' and come in here. 'Twasn't that John wasn't a right gut-lookin' fella, even though he was older than Rachel by three or four years, no doubt. He was clearly attracted to her daughter, and Susanna was ever so relieved 'bout that. Appeared as if her plotting might just pay off.

She watched the smithy, careful not to be caught staring. He was a tall, solid man. His dark hair was thinning just a bit on top, but his beard was thick and full, which implied that he'd been married and lost his spouse to death. 'Course, if folks hadn't known of his widower status, they'd be thinkin' he was married, due to the untrimmed beard and, of course, no mustache. The beard was their way of lettin' folks know who was hitched up and who wasn't.

She was gawkin' now, noticing his long fingers and callused hands. John Lapp was a hardworkin' blacksmith and the father of children—how many she didn't rightly know. 'Least if Rachel paired up with him and they eventually wed, little Annie would have herself some stepbrothers and sisters, and prob'ly more, too, before long, knowin' how Rachel loved children. Sad thing, though, she'd be losin' her girl to another township if that happened. It was the one thorn in her flesh as she thought 'bout all this.

Benjamin continued his story. "Susie and I'd gone to this here Singin' over near Smoketown, and the older folk had departed for home along 'bout ten o'clock, so we knew it was time for a little pairing off and square dancin' amongst the young people. 'Course I knew that the folk games we often played to the tune of 'Turkey in the Straw' and 'Skip to My Lou'—on a fiddle, guitar, and a mouth organ or two—wasn't really considered dancin' by the Old Order." Ben stopped here and, right in the middle of the tellin', turned and asked John Lapp, "How 'bout your church district over in Paradise?"

"Jah, same as here," John said, nodding his head. "Most of the bishops are sticklers when it comes to any sort of dancin', you know, for the young folk. Same thing with music at them Singin's." He spoke with authority, like he was mighty confident 'bout his answer.

Susanna liked that, but she wondered 'bout his blunt approach. Almost sounded as though he had something to prove. She wasn't sure how that would set with Rachel, her bein' as timid as she was. Most the time, anyways. 'Cept here lately . . .

"Be that as it may," Ben went on, "Susie and I each took a corn shock—same as the other couples there— tryin' to see who could finish shocking their corn first. And wouldn'tcha know, it was *my* girl who found the red ear of corn, put there by the hostess, and she had no choice but to receive a kiss from her partner, which, of course, was me." Ben was glowing. " 'Course, you all know who I ended up courtin' and marryin' soon after that."

The group burst out clapping. Even Rachel joined in, though she kept her face down, prob'ly because she didn't know precisely where John Lapp might be seated.

Susanna was startin' to blame herself for the whole setup. She'd clearly made her daughter miserable on

Christmas Day. The smithy was no dummy, neither. Her own husband pullin' something like this? Why, she could hardly contain herself.

Straightening herself a bit and taking a few deep breaths, Susanna hoped her husband would start thinkin' of poor Rachel, how she might be feeling along 'bout now. As for John Lapp, she could tell he was a mite embarrassed, too, by the looks of them bright red ears peekin' out from under his brown hair.

Esther, bless her heart, saved the day for both Rachel and the smithy, changing the course of the afternoon. In a clear and strong voice, she led out in a well-known carol, followed by two more. And if anyone had asked Susanna privately, she would've agreed that singing "Joy to the World" and the other songs was a right gut move on her Ohio niece's part.

Jah, 'twas.

❖ ❖ ❖

After carols were sung and several of Leah's and Susanna's married sons and their families headed back home for milkin' chores, Levi began sharing certain things from his heart. Listening more closely now, Rachel was ever so interested in hearing what Esther's husband had to say. He was explainin' some of the life-changing teachings he and Esther had discovered at their Ohio church, and began to read from the Old Testament book of Deuteronomy. " 'Let not your hearts faint, fear not, and do not tremble, neither be ye terrified because of them; for the Lord your God is He that goeth with you, to fight for you against your enemies, to save you.' "

Levi went on to explain that "fear is the opposite of faith," and that "we" must turn away from it in the name of Jesus. "It's time we do spiritual battle against the enemy. But we mustn't shrink back in fear. We must keep our eyes set on the Lord—gaze on Him—as He leads us on to victory."

He was startin' to sound ever so much like a preacher, Rachel thought, and she wondered how her own parents would receive his forceful words . . . on Christmas Day, of all things.

And what of John Lapp? Was he hearin' some of God's Word for the first time, maybe? Honestly, she didn't want to give a second thought to the Paradise widower, not the way her heart beat for Philip Bradley since first meeting him. And, goodness' sake, the way John had dominated the conversation at the dinner table, well, she was right surprised at a stranger coming in and taking over like that, almost as if he was showin' off for the whole lot of them!

Just as she was wonderin' what she'd say if the smithy asked her to go with him somewhere, sometime, the doorbell rang.

"Well, now, who's this?" Dat said and went to the door.

Immediately Rachel recognized the man's voice. Philip had come back. Just like he said he would!

She sat still as anything, trying not to get her hopes up that he'd come to see *her*. No, she oughtn't to be so quick to think such a wonderful-gut thing. Still, her heart pounded with delight.

"Merry Christmas, Mr. Zook," Philip said, standing on the doorstep, his present for Annie tucked under one arm.

Ben eyed the gift. "I'm surprised to see you here . . . again."

"I was in Reading, visiting a friend, and wanted to drop by and wish you folks a Merry Christmas."

"Well, the same to you," Ben said, but he didn't budge an inch or indicate that Philip was welcome inside.

Philip tried but failed to call upon his journalistic skills, those used in interviews and research. "Are, uh, Rachel . . . and Annie at home?" A ludicrous question. Of course, they were home. It was Christmas afternoon! He struggled with what to say, having experienced the same cotton-mouthed situation months ago, when he'd come here the first time.

Ben glanced over his shoulder. "Jah, Rachel's home, but she's entertainin' company just now, and Annie's busy with some of her cousins." The man turned back to face him, eyes narrowed and brow furrowed, nearly hissing through his front teeth. "It's Christmas Day, for goodness' sake."

While Ben admonished him, Philip was able to see past him into the living room, where he spotted Rachel. She was sitting next to a woman about her age, someone who might be a cousin, perhaps, since they looked very much alike, only this woman had darker hair and eyes.

But it was the man, a bearded Amishman in his thirties or so, who caught Philip's attention. He sat directly across from Rachel, gazing at her intently, as if awe-struck. And understandably so. Rachel's face was aglow with color, and there was something more to it, although he couldn't pinpoint what. Nevertheless, it was obvious the blind woman was the object of *someone's* affection. Even a momentary observation was enough to see that.

"I . . . I guess I made a mistake in coming," he managed to say. "Merry Christmas, Mr. Zook." Philip turned to go, present still in hand, undecided as to whether to leave it or take it back to his car. So disconcerted was he that he had not a thought of what he might've said to Rachel—or little Annie—if he *had* been given the opportunity. And there was the pertinent information on conversion disorder in his briefcase, representing hours of work. . . .

Opening the back door to his car, Philip placed the lone Christmas present inside on the seat. Just as he was standing up to close the door again, he heard someone call out his name. Looking toward the house, he saw that it was Rachel's adorable daughter. "Well, hello there, Annie," he replied.

"You mustn't be goin' just yet, Mister Philip." She was running out the door and down the driveway.

He went around the side of the car to greet her, though he was cautious, touching only her head. "I should've called first, I suppose."

Annie's eyes widened and her mouth dropped open. "Why wouldja wanna do that on Christmas? Nobody calls first before they come. It's just fine to drop by. All the People do that 'round here."

"All the *People*," he echoed, standing up and noticing that both Ben and Susanna were standing in the doorway. "But, you see, I'm not one of the People, Annie."

The child seemed surprised at his remark and shook her head, her little white prayer bonnet slipping back slightly. "I think Mamma'd be ever so glad to see you," she whispered, leaning closer.

"Your mother has company today."

She wrinkled up her nose. "John Lapp, that's all 'tis."

"Oh, *Mister* Lapp, eh?"

"He's lookin' to marry Mamma, but I won't let him."

Chuckling, Philip backed away, thinking he ought to exit the premises before Benjamin came out and bodily shooed him off. "You're a lively one, Annie," he said, wishing there was a way to give her the present he'd purchased for her.

"Wait, you mayn't leave just yet," Annie said.

"Annie!" Susanna was calling from the front door. "Come inside, child. It's much too cold!"

Philip motioned for her to heed her grandmother's warning. The next sound he heard was Rachel's gentle voice. "Annie, dear, you best be comin' inside."

Reaching for the car door, he caught himself just before thoughtlessly waving to the lovely blind woman in the long blue dress and full-length white apron. "Merry Christmas, Rachel!" he called instead, relieved that her parents had moved back into the house.

"Same to you, Philip." She smiled at him from across the front yard. "Can you come in for a bit?"

Could he? That was the reason he'd come—but how was this precarious situation going to work itself out? He thought of the Amish suitor John Lapp and Rachel's crestfallen parents.

Annie reached for his hand and began to pull on him, attempting to bring him back up the driveway. "You hafta come in and sit a spell," the girl said. "You *hafta* . . . it's Christmas!"

"I do?" he teased, thankful for Annie's tenacity. He would get the opportunity to visit with Rachel, after all.

"We got cookies and candy and—"

"Candy? What kind?"

"Come see." And she continued to tug on his hand.

In Philip's entire life, only one other female had ever tried such a tactic with him—his niece, who was equally as spunky as Rachel's young daughter.

Philip's coming was the perfect remedy for gettin' John Lapp out of the house and on his way. 'Course, it was downright awkward, what with both men there in the same room. And no man, 'cept for her dear Jacob, had ever been interested in her back when she was courting age and able to see just fine. The present situation was ever so peculiar, and Rachel was more than relieved when the smithy bade his farewell, not only to her, but to everyone else in the room. Then, before actually leaving, he asked if he might call on her again. "Would that be all right?" he asked, so close that she honestly felt his breath on her face.

Stepping back, she gave him her answer softly, so as not to call attention. "I . . . I'll be thinkin' on it."

"Gut then, I give you a few days."

She didn't say "Thank you" or "Have a nice Christmas" or any such polite thing as he prepared to leave. Truth was, she could hardly wait for him to exit the house. And once he was gone, she wondered what on earth she would do now with Philip Bradley here again, the very man she'd found herself thinking of so often since the day he'd left. If she could've seen the expression on Mam's face, she may have been sheepish, but she was spared that. And Dat did his best to cover his tracks, and he made small talk with Philip, having been a bit aloof at the door. But it was truly Esther and Levi who were most kind.

About the same time as John Lapp left, Aunt Leah and Uncle Amos said they'd best slip out and get on home. And so did each of their married children and spouses and Molly and Sadie Mae, of course, which left only Esther, Levi, and their four children and Annie in the house with Philip and the elder Zooks.

The job of introducing Philip to Esther and Levi fell to Rachel. But Philip had a remarkable way of setting her at ease, once again, and did an excellent job of fillin' Esther and Levi in on his whereabouts, where he'd grown up, why he'd first come to Bird-in-Hand—to do research for a magazine article—and how it was that he'd come to write for a New York magazine called *Family Life*. Things like that.

She wasn't sure how it happened that they got to talking 'bout a book Philip had purchased in New York.

Sounded like something she wished her own father might be willin' to read. All about the life of an Amish preacher who'd found himself caught up in age-old practices of powwowing and other occult activities. Philip didn't mention the title of the book, but he was asking if any of them had heard of it or knew the author, and he gave the name.

"Does sound familiar to me," Levi said.

"And it's high time we had someone Plain speaking out 'bout such things in our communities," Esther put in.

Dat was quiet; Mam, too, though she didn't stay put long, excusin' herself to go out and "check on the children," which she gave as her reason for leavin' the room.

"There *was* someone like that—someone who wasn't afraid to speak out against the witchcraft in high places," Philip said. "He lived here in the area a long time ago."

Rachel was worried over what Dat would think. What was Philip going to say 'bout Gabe Esh?

Fear is the opposite of faith. . . .

Just then, Dat cut in. "And that there fella got himself excommunicated and shunned for it, too. We have our ways, and that's that." Then he got up and marched out of the room, making the floor shake as he rumbled past her.

Fear not, and do not tremble. . . .

"I guess I shouldn't have brought *that* up," Philip was saying in an apologetic tone.

"No . . . no, don't be feelin' doubtful," Levi encouraged. "I believe that's one of the reasons these things keep bein' covered up and never discussed. I believe it's the reason we find so many of the People in bondage to darkness . . . to the evil one."

"Why don't I mail the book to you when a friend of mine finishes reading it," Philip offered.

"Jah, do that."

They talked awhile longer, mostly 'bout what they could do to band together in prayer for the community, though Rachel just listened, finding it interesting how very well Philip seemed to fit in with her cousins. In many ways, he was a man her family would approve of. Except for one glaring problem. He wasn't Plain. 'Course, then again, she was gettin' way ahead of herself. It wasn't as if they were courtin' or any such a thing.

All too soon, Philip mentioned that he needed to get back to Reading. "I came to visit Adele Herr for Christmas," he explained.

"Lavina and I were just up to see Adele a week ago Thursday," she offered. "Adele told us 'bout the Christmas program comin' up."

"That's where I'm heading now."

"Will ya tell her Merry Christmas for me?"

He was silent, but only for a second or two. "You could tell her yourself, if you wanted to," Philip said, surprising her completely.

"What . . . what do you mean?"

"Come with me to the program." He didn't wait for her answer, then added, "Adele would be delighted, I'm sure."

Is Philip speaking for himself, too? Rachel wondered, hesitating, not sure how to answer, really. After all, Esther and Levi wouldn't be staying 'round Lancaster for too much longer, and she really wanted to have some personal sharing time with her beloved cousin.

"Sounds like a gut idea to me," Esther chimed in.

"Jah, go ahead and have yourself a nice time," Levi added.

They must approve of Philip, she decided, finding the situation to be rather comical. A fancy New Yorker invitin' an Amish widow—a blind one at that—to a Christmas program at a nursing home, of all things! "Well, if Mam won't mind lookin' after Annie, I 'spose I could go."

"Ach, don't worry over Annie. I'll see to it she gets fed supper and has a gut time with her cousins," Esther offered. "And tomorrow, we'll do some catchin' up, just you and me."

Rachel paused, thinking that it was high time she told Esther what she'd been planning to do. "Uh, tomorrow, I'm lookin' to go to the Crossroad. Sometime after church." She hadn't got up the nerve to tell anyone before now, but she'd thought it through, all the same.

"How will ya get there?" Esther asked, sounding flabbergasted.

"You and Levi will take me, won'tcha?" she said, her voice growing softer, and a lump filling her throat. "I've been waitin' an awful long time."

"What's this all 'bout?" Levi sounded concerned.

"I wanna see again, that's what. I feel I hafta go to

the scene of the accident. After all this time, I'm ready to face up to whatever happened there—every last bit." She didn't go on to say that she'd suffered severe headaches due to some of her memory returning. But she was past that and wanted to force herself to remember *everything*.

"Well, now, have ya prayed 'bout this?" Levi asked, sounding more like a father than her cousin's husband.

"Oh, I've prayed like nobody knows. And I believe the Lord's in it—me goin' to that intersection, in a horse and buggy . . . on Second Christmas." She wasn't exactly sure if Philip knew what "Second Christmas" was, but if he'd done a thorough job of researching Plain Christmas customs, he'd surely know that it was merely another day set aside for visitin' and relaxation in Lancaster County. 'Course, when it fell on a Sunday, like this year, the Old Order Amishfolk would have house church. Beachy Amish had church *every* Sunday in celebration of the Resurrection, like most Bible-based churches.

Just then Philip spoke up. "If you wouldn't think it too bold of me, Rachel, I'd be more than happy to accompany you and your cousins to the Crossroad."

Esther seemed to take the decision right away from her. "Jah, I think Philip *should* ride along."

Oddly enough, Rachel didn't resent her cousin for speakin' up that way. Not one iota.

❖ ❖ ❖

Susanna had promised herself she would go and look

up certain Scripture verses in the old German Bible once the busy day was behind her. But with Rachel off into the night with that Mister Bradley, she was lookin' after Annie. Esther hadn't stayed, but had given in when Susanna insisted she and Levi go on back to Leah's to bed down the children at their *own* mammi's house.

"Ach, are ya sure?" Esther had asked, indicating she wanted to help with Annie as she'd promised Rachel.

"No . . . no, you go on. There's no need for you to stay up all hours. Besides, who knows when Rachel will be back."

So Esther, Levi, and the children had got their coats on and scurried off, almost as if they'd been pushed out against their will.

Later, Susanna was fit to be tied when Annie started askin' her things like "Why's Mister Philip so awful nice to Mamma?" Those sorts of questions flyin' out of Annie's mouth served to rankle her all the more. And she could scarcely get the little one bathed and into bed fast enough.

"He brought a Christmas present along," Annie said as Susanna pulled up the quilts on the small bed. "I saw it."

"Well, now, I think you must be dreamin'."

"No . . . no, I *saw* some perty paper and a big green and red bow and—"

"Time for prayers now." She cut off the girl's chatter.

Annie blinked her big eyes. "Why don'tcha like Mister Philip?"

Susanna sucked in her breath. "I think you have no idea 'bout that man."

"Well, I think he's just 'bout the nicest I've ever met, Mammi Susanna."

"Your dawdi Ben's a *nice* man." She was desperate to turn the conversation 'round before lights out.

"But Mister Philip is, too."

"Guess I don't know him as well as you seem to."

Annie giggled. "Oh, I know him, all right." And she went on and on 'bout how the tall, smooth-faced Englischer had saved her life from the wasp sting she'd got down by Mill Creek, out behind the house. "He smiles real nice, and Mamma says he's followin' the Lord God heavenly Father. That makes him a gut man, don'tcha think?"

"*I* think you've talked quite enough for one night," she said, getting up and heading for the door.

"I'm sorry, Mammi. Honest, I am. I talk too much sometimes . . . even on Christmas, I 'spose."

"Ach, Annie, just say your silent prayers" was all she could think to sputter before flicking off the light.

Annie said her prayers all right, but they weren't her ordinary prayers. No, she said "prayers from her heart," just the way Mamma had been praying lately.

"Dear Lord Jesus," Annie began. "Please watch over Mamma tonight. Mister Philip, too. And thank you ever so much for bringin' him back for a visit. I'm thinkin' it's the best gift I could've ever had, come Christmas Day."

Part Three

❖ ❖ ❖

For, behold, the darkness shall cover the earth,
and gross darkness the people:
but the Lord shall arise upon thee,
and His glory shall be seen upon thee.

—Isaiah 60:2

Sixteen

◆ ◆ ◆

*R*achel decided it was real thoughtful of Esther to pack a meal for both her and Philip. She was also completely dumbfounded when Levi had suggested that Philip check in at the Zooks' B&B for the night. "It'll save him from havin' to drive all the way back to Reading tonight." Not only was it surprising, but Philip had actually agreed to the idea, making financial arrangements on the spot with Mam—who was tolerant of the idea—before they ever left the house.

Mam, she was sure, had had a change of heart toward Philip. Possibly toward other things, as she had not lashed out at Esther and Levi when they were talking 'bout their church in Ohio and some of the teachings. She actually wondered if Mam wasn't mellowing somewhat. And if so, it had been a long time comin'!

So once again, Philip would stay temporarily in the southeast guest room—one of their very best. Rachel could hardly believe this was happening! 'Course, she knew better than to get her hopes up that anything would come of this visit. No, she would be foolish to assume such a thing. Philip was a busy man, and though she had no idea what a magazine writer did besides write stories to earn a living, well, she was perty sure he kept a fast pace in New York City.

They rode along in Philip's car, Rachel enjoying the easygoing conversation with this modern fella in the driver's seat. She still got little shivers when he said her name, though she found herself making an effort to shield her heart. She must make herself not care so much!

Together, they ate their sandwiches, then sang along with familiar Christmas carols on the radio. Later Philip said, "I bought a book for Annie . . . a Christmas present. I thought it would be all right."

"Jah, 'tis. And Annie does like her books."

"This one has full-color illustrations . . . set in Amish country," he explained. "It very well could be Lancaster County, though it doesn't say for sure."

"You're very kind," Rachel said, meaning it. Oh, how she meant it, but she guarded her response so as not to let on just how much.

They traveled awhile in complete silence, except for the soft radio music, until Philip spoke. "I don't know how to bring this up . . . wouldn't want you to misunderstand, but I've been doing some research. On your . . . type of blindness." He said it with empathy, almost apologetically.

Rachel felt a sudden rush of warmth to her face and neck. "Then you must be recallin' what my mother said that day on the phone—'bout her own daughter bein' 'mental.' "

"I think I understand why she may have said that."

"Jah, I've forgiven her. Mam means well." She was eager to know what he'd discovered. "What did you find out . . . from your research, I mean?"

"Many interesting things." He paused for a moment, then continued. "Have you ever thought of talking to a professional, Rachel? For some initial counseling, perhaps?"

She didn't know how befitting it would be to tell him that she'd memorized many Scriptures dealing with divine healing but hadn't thought of counseling much at all. She wasn't sure if she should open herself up to this kind and ever so thoughtful Englischer. "I do happen to have the name of a therapist," she said softly. "From a doctor at Community Hospital."

"Then you've talked with someone?"

"Not a therapist . . . not yet."

Philip didn't speak again for a moment. Then, "What made you decide to go to the Crossroad?"

"I guess I've just been puttin' it off long enough now, that's all."

"But the day after Christmas . . . is there some special reason?"

"Has nothin' to do with it, really."

"This is a big step for you, Rachel."

She thought she might cry, hearing him speak so tenderly, as though he truly cared.

"All I know is I'm standin' on the Word of God. It may sound a bit odd to you, but I believe the Lord's been leadin' me to the Crossroad for a gut long time. My whole life changed there in a split second of time." She felt a bit more comfortable now, sharing with him the accident story, at least the things she'd begun to remember just in the past week. How Jacob had been driving the enclosed market wagon, their precious little children—Aaron and Annie—sitting behind them, playing and cuttin' up a bit. "Honestly, I must've told Aaron to hush several times, at least," she confessed. "But now, knowin' what I know, that it was to be the very last day of his dear life, well, I'd give anything if I could take back those words."

"Your little boy knew you loved him. I'm sure he did."

"Oh jah, he most certainly knew," she said, the strangest feeling comin' over her now. "I can't change a thing by talking 'bout it, but I just know it's better for me not to hold all those memories inside any longer."

"Do you remember what happened?"

"Most everything, jah, except after the car hit the wagon. I don't remember much at all after that." And she'd told no one 'cept Lavina the extent of the horrendous pain she'd endured this week—days of ceaseless headaches, stabbing pain through her skull. With the memories and the acceptance of them, though, the headaches had gone away completely. At last.

Now she was anticipating the next step on the road to healing. Her sight must surely return. Oh, she was ever so hopeful!

"I had wanted to be able to share some of the information I gathered . . . with the possibility that it might help you see again, Rachel." Philip trod gently, trusting she would understand that his research was meant to be helpful, not pushy. "I prayed that the Lord would guide me to know what to do." He went on to tell her he'd thought of contacting Lavina, sending the materials to her.

"Well, it's a gut thing *you* came, 'cause Lavina's reading skills are a bit limited, I must say."

He smiled at her insight. "You're right. I'm glad we could visit." He sighed, thinking how relaxing it was to be in her company again. Rachel Yoder was a pure breath of fresh air. She had it all over the erudite women he worked with, and though they were articulate, witty, and climbing the success ladder, they lacked Rachel's simple and refreshing common sense, her ability to perceive the world in an uncomplicated way. No wonder he'd thought of her off and on all these weeks.

He wondered what Adele would say about his bringing Rachel along to visit her on Christmas night. She was a wise one, his seasoned friend. No doubt she would suspect there was something happening between him and this beautiful Plain woman. But more important than initiating a romantic situation—out of the question entirely—his true goal was to help Rachel accomplish her own objective: regaining her sight. But he wouldn't interfere in her life while doing so. It was a fine line he must walk in his pursuit of Rachel's wholeness and ultimate healing.

So he would. But in the interim, he would continue to pray for God's leading.

Rachel waited in the car while Philip checked out of his room at the Reading inn. She found herself becoming giddy at the thought that they were to share the evening with Adele, enjoying a Christmas program, of all things. She'd always enjoyed music played on instruments but hadn't been much exposed to it in church or 'round the community. Amishfolk relied more on human voices for their music of worship. But to think that she would be hearin' a quartet of stringed instruments with Philip at her side, well, that thought made her as joyful as she'd been in two long years. Jah, she was perty sure this night would be most exciting.

❖ ❖ ❖

Opening the German family Bible, Susanna read the words she'd first heard on Esther's tape: *Our fathers have sinned, and are not; and we have borne their iniquities.*

Our fathers have sinned. . . .

She paused, thinking 'bout such a Scripture. How could it be that the sins of the fathers were passed down through the family? Through the bloodline?

We have borne their iniquities. . . .

She closed the Bible, wondering. Yet here it was, stated ever so clearly in God's Word. Right there in Lamentations—the Old Testament, of all things. She knew their preachers much preferred to admonish them from the Old Testament. Still, in all her days, she'd never heard a single sermon on any of the verses Esther had talked about on her tape to Rachel. Not one time. And why was that?

'Course, she'd be asking Benjamin 'bout this just as soon as possible. Right now the house was quiet and peaceful, what with Annie asleep and all of Leah's

grand-youngsters finally gone, too. Ben would be snorin'
up a storm here before long. The thought never crossed
her mind to talk to Leah 'bout any of this. No, Leah was
actin' awful strange these days. My goodness, for her sister to question the validity of the powwow doctors.
Why, it was beyond her what would make Leah say such
a thing. She knew better. 'Least, she oughta by now.
Leah had lived a gut long time here in Bird-in-Hand,
for goodness' sake—same as Susanna. Folks living
'round here had sense to believe in what they'd been
taught. Down through the years, comin' straight from
their fathers' lips and their grandfathers before them.

The sins of the fathers . . .

The words stuck in her head as she outened the lantern and slipped into bed. Her silent rote prayers
seemed awful heavy this night, like stones weighting
her down. And she didn't understand why, really, but
she began to weep into her feather pillow, wishing she
didn't feel this way—not on the night of the celebration
of Jesus' birth.

❖ ❖ ❖

"I do believe the Lord has His guiding hand on that
young Englischer, Philip Bradley," Levi said as he and
Esther prepared to retire for the night.

"Jah, I feel the same way," Esther replied. "That's
the reason I encouraged Rachel to go along with him to
Reading."

"I thought so." He paused, weighing his words. "I'm

thinkin' it's a gut idea that Philip goes with us over to the Crossroad tomorrow . . . the four of us together."

"Why's that?"

"Let's just be prayerful as we take the horse and buggy down North Ronks Road. The Lord's impressed on me that this trip is necessary for more than Rachel's memory."

"Oh?"

"I believe Philip, too, has a need to make such a journey." He watched as Esther stood at the dresser, brushing her long flowing hair, without the prayer veiling. His wife's hair, thick and dark, was her glory, meant to be shared only with him.

Esther put down the brush and crossed the room to turn down the bed quilts. "I believe something else, too," she said softly.

"What's that, dear?"

"Rachel's falling in love again."

Levi didn't quite know what to make of that. Could be Esther was so in tune to her cousin, so close to her, that she could rightly make such a statement. As for himself, he could only pray that God would guide and direct his wife's blind and widowed cousin. Surely the Lord had a plan for Rachel Yoder's life, as well.

❖ ❖ ❖

Rosemary Fisher sent for her grown children and grandchildren. The great-grandchildren, too. Clear as anything, the bishop was dying, and on Christmas of all things. It was like a blessed sign, and she sat near the bed, whispering a prayer as Seth's eyes fluttered.

"There's something I hafta say, Rosie" came her husband's words. With great effort, he began to reveal the truth behind the many hexes he'd put on folk during his lifetime. But it was Gabe Esh's death that troubled him most.

"Gabriel was one of *us*. . . ." Her dear, dear Seth struggled to breathe. "Mighty cruel . . . I was."

"The Lord God's forgiven you." She touched his brow, beaded with perspiration. "No need to struggle anymore."

He shook his head, making a futile effort to sit up. "I was bent on seeing Gabe dead . . . full up with loathing, I was. Wanted revenge . . . he turned his back on me." Weeping, he continued. "Don'tcha see, Rosie? Gabe never would've died that day, but I . . . I called up the spirits of darkness . . . enchantments against an innocent man."

His tears fell freely as he told, for the first time, how he'd seen a dusky vision of Gabe and a Mennonite friend, riding in a car toward Gordonville. How the accident took place just before the preaching service. "Just as I conjured it up to be."

"Ach, dear, must ya go on so?"

His voice was but a whisper now. " 'Twasn't God showin' me them things that night. No, I sold out to the devil."

She listened, gripped by his sorrowful confession.

"And all because of a grudge," he murmured, his eyes pleading pools, searching hers. "Will *you* forgive me, Rosie, for my wicked ways?"

Brushing tears from her eyes, she nodded. " 'Course I forgive you, and . . . so will the People."

He gripped her hand. "Tell them for me, will ya?"

Kissing his cheek, she felt his hand go limp in hers. "Jah, they'll hear the truth. I promise ya that."

Then, closing his eyes for the last time, her Seth— the People's bishop—passed through Glory's gate with a smile on his lips.

Seventeen

❖ ❖ ❖

*A*dele Herr seemed pleasantly surprised to see Rachel again, and Rachel, too, was delighted to spend time with the woman who might've become her great-aunt had Gabe Esh lived . . . and had Adele agreed to marry the young Amishman.

The nursing home Christmas program was unusually enjoyable, and as she sat with Philip and Adele, Rachel found herself wishing the evening might stay young, that it might not end. She was having such a wonderful-gut time here with her friends, even though neither was Plain. Yet it didn't seem to matter. She felt right at home with Philip and Adele because they belonged to the Lord.

After the program of instrumental carols came refreshments. Philip offered to get her some punch and cake, but she had not become accustomed to being waited on, in spite of her disability. So she went with him to the table, accepting his arm to guide her.

Walking slowly together, she recalled his cologne, that subtle scent that had first caught her senses off guard the day they'd strolled together in the cemetery, searching for Gabe Esh's gravestone. She felt now, as she had then, that Philip's coming had given her great courage. The pluck she'd always sought for—her whole life—and had never quite found. It wasn't something as frivolous as the smell of nice cologne on a considerate man—oh no, it was far more than that!

"Would you care for white or chocolate cake?" Philip asked.

She had to smile. He would have no way of knowing that she could *smell* the different choices from where she stood. "Chocolate, please," she said, allowing him to serve her, at least for the moment.

"Mints?"

"Thank you."

They made their way back to Adele, through the crowded room, together. Rachel carried her cake plate in one hand, the other tucked under Philip's strong arm. She'd had oh so many lovely dreams of walking with Philip this way, yet she'd never allowed herself to think twice 'bout ever spending more time with him.

Philip got her situated in a comfortable chair, then excused himself, leaving her alone with Adele, preparing to fill the older woman's order for white cake. "No punch, please," Adele insisted.

He chuckled at the comment. "Surely you'd like something to drink."

"Oh, I'll have my hot tea if there is any—"

"I'll locate some if I have to brew it myself." And Philip was off.

One bite of the chocolate cake, and Rachel recognized it as store-bought. What a difference between her own German sweet chocolate cake and the artificial taste of this dessert. 'Course, it should not be so surprising, as she sensed that not a stitch of butter had been put in the mixture. In all likelihood, *this* cake was straight out of a box. Still, she wouldn't think of saying so out loud. She could only imagine Mam's sentiments after biting into such a flat and disappointing pastry. She listened to the chatter of the patients in attendance, glad that Adele had, indeed, shared the homemade cookies both Rachel and Lavina had lovingly baked and brought days before.

Adele was content to sit quietly, and Rachel assumed that the older woman was tired from the long day, prob'ly. So she allowed her thoughts to drift back to the days when she was first learnin' to bake alongside her mamma. Amish mothers were bound and determined to pass on domestic skills to their young daughters just as soon as a little girl could hold a measuring spoon right steady. Being close to four years old, often she had to be called in from outside, where she loved to feed the ducks down by the pond. Oh, the happy, noisy creatures were always eager for day-old bread crumbs. They would come right up close to where she and Dawdi David crouched in the tall grass.

"Look-ee there at how hungry they are," her grandfather would say nearly in a whisper.

"What do they eat when we ain't here?" she had asked, peering down at the smallest ducklings.

"Ah, the Lord God heavenly Father watches out for 'um. You don't hafta worry 'bout that."

"But what do they *eat*?" she'd insisted.

"Bugs."

"Where from?"

"Floatin' on the surface of the water." And he'd point, sayin', "You'll see 'um if ya look hard enough."

Rachel scanned the pond, tryin' ever so hard to see the dead flies, mosquitoes, and whatnot. Ach, she hated the thought of the perty little downy ducks havin' to eat such awful-tastin' things as bugs. And she knew just how nasty they were, too, 'cause one of her big brothers had tricked her into eating an ant once. He'd rolled it in sugar, sprinkled cinnamon in his hand, and told her it was candy. But once the sweetness melted away in her mouth, she knew it wasn't no candy.

When she tried to *bapple*—tattle—on her brother, Mamma just shooed her off, back outside to Dawdi, who was always waitin' patiently for her to come and tell her troubles.

Dawdi David Zook was the quietest man she'd ever known, and she figured that's why she liked to feed the ducks with him. He was so silent the ducks came right up close, as if they weren't afraid of either of them— Dawdi or Rachel—neither one.

Till the summer she was ten, Dawdi lived in the *Dawdi Haus*, built on to the main house, after Rachel's grandmother passed on to Glory. And every single day, if it wasn't rainin', he'd gladly hike down to the pond with Rachel. Fact is, they went every day till the day he died.

Every so often he'd come out with what young Rachel decided then and there were wonderful-gut, important words 'bout life. She figured he wouldn't be 'round forever, and he prepared her for his passing by talkin' ever so softly—and joyfully—'bout heaven, "where Jesus is." He once told her that he "sneak-read" his Bible—from cover to cover in less than a year. "But that's my secret," he'd said with a serious look on his old, wrinkled-up face.

She had wondered then why such a thing had to be kept quiet, but she grew up to find out later. The Old Order preachers used select Scripture passages repeatedly, Sunday after Sunday. "Old favorites," Dawdi would say sometimes as he sat in the high grass, a stone's throw from the pond. Seems they didn't want the People reading the whole Bible on their own and tryin' to interpret the passages the way the Mennonites liked to do.

"Jah" was all Rachel would say whenever Dawdi whispered things like that, just enjoying her oldest living relative and the sounds of nature all 'round them.

So the outdoors was the place to be for her when she was but a young girl. Still was, 'cept now she wasn't free to run through the meadowland or the woods as she had when she was sighted. But, Lord willin', that was all 'bout to change. Come tomorrow.

When Philip returned with cake and tea for Adele, he asked Rachel if she'd enjoyed the music.

"It was wonderful-gut, jah."

"The string quartet reminded me of the kind of music there will surely be in heaven," Adele remarked.

"I wouldn't be surprised," Philip said. "But please don't plan on going anytime soon, all right?"

"You don't have to worry about that," Adele said, making a high-pitched clucking sound.

"You're feeling much better, ain't?" Rachel said, knowing it sure as anything.

"Why, yes, I believe I am, dear."

Rachel couldn't be sure, of course, but she thought Philip's eyes were on her just now. She wondered if he would talk more to her 'bout her sight problems on the drive home. Or would they talk of other things, maybe?

As much as she enjoyed visiting here with Adele Herr, she was actually anticipating the drive home, having Philip's attention all to herself. And even though she'd always been taught *not* to crave such attention, she did not think it displeasing to God—the way she felt just now.

Philip was reluctant to leave Rachel in the waiting area, but he wanted to assist the nurse in taking Adele back to her room. And he wished to have a few minutes alone with his dear friend.

"I believe you're fond of Rachel Yoder," Adele said when she was settled into her chair. "I see it in your eyes."

He didn't quite know how to respond. The truth was, Philip didn't know how he felt about Rachel, how he *should* feel. "I think you must be seeing things," he said at last, laughing off her comment.

"Well, I see what I see."

"If I can help Rachel regain her sight, that would be my greatest joy." He didn't reveal to Adele that he had invited himself to ride along in a horse and buggy to the Crossroad tomorrow afternoon. Adele might read too much into it. He was content to say nothing about his plans for the Lord's Day. Second Christmas, as Rachel had called it.

"You can say what you like, Philip, but I wonder if the same thing is happening between you and Rachel as happened with Gabe and me." She paused a moment, then continued. "I don't mean to sound bold, but do pray about Rachel. See what God has in store. Don't make my mistake and miss out on the love of a lifetime."

Adele's words took him by surprise. How she would have perceived any sort of emotional attachment between him and Rachel was puzzling, at best. But then, his own sister had questioned him on various occasions in her curious, off-the-cuff style.

So what *was* it that people sensed in him? His joyful countenance? His increased energy? A spring in his step? All of the above?

Philip had thought he was in love before, years ago, but things were completely different with him at that time. Surely, his feelings for Rachel Yoder were purely friendship, admiration. Nothing more. Certainly nothing on which to build a home.

"I believe you must be mistaken about Rachel," he told Adele.

She smiled a knowing smile, which Philip dismissed, and he began to wind down his visit. "I enjoyed your company very much, Adele. Thanks so much for inviting me."

"You mustn't wait until next Christmas to come again." Her azure eyes were bright with expectation.

"Oh, you'll see me long before that," he promised,

taking her hand in both of his. "Shall we pray together?"

She agreed, and he bowed his head, asking the Lord to continue to give her health and strength and many blessings.

Before he could end the prayer, Adele whispered, "And, Lord Jesus, please lead and guide Philip's life and ministry. In Jesus' name. Amen."

She picked up the book *Gifts of Darkness*. "I do intend to read this, beginning tomorrow."

"Good. I'll give you a call in a couple of days."

Nodding, she smiled again. "We'll discuss the book then."

It was difficult to say his final good-bye, even though Philip fully intended to see her again. Soon. There was just something so comfortable about Adele. She seemed to know and understand him better than most of his own relatives.

"Merry Christmas, Philip," she called softly as he stood to go. "Remember, seek God's will above all else."

God's will above all else . . . Her words followed him as he walked the long hallway, and as he looked ahead to the waiting area, his heart quickened at the sight of Rachel.

Eighteen

Susanna's sleep was fitful. She tossed so much she
worried she might wake up Benjamin, and that would
never do. Slipping out of bed and heading downstairs,
she went to sit in the parlor for a bit. She hadn't turned
on the hall light, though she knew she oughta, 'specially
since Ben was forever warnin' her not to "creep 'round
the house at night in the dark." Well, they'd grown up
thataway—with little or dim light, at best—so she figured she was used to it. Had only experienced the luxury
of electricity for a little more than two years now, 'cause
Bishop Seth had permitted it—due to the B&B. She
and Ben had agreed it was best to continue with oil
lamps in their own private quarters, obeying the bishop
on the issue.

'Course, they'd just gotten word that Seth Fisher
was dead now—and would be buried soon. She wondered who'd be drawin' the lot to fill his position in the
church district. Any number of preachers 'round the
area would do. But she hoped it might be God's will for
Preacher King to be their new bishop, the man who'd
helped them oust Gabe Esh ever so secretly forty long
years ago. She couldn't help but think the People would
be needin' a grieving period. Seemed only *kluuch*—pru-

dent—that they not replace the bishop too soon, but she, bein' a woman, had no say 'bout such matters whatever.

All the talk in the community just now was that Bishop Seth had gotten salvation two days before Christmas, thanks to Lavina spreadin' the word 'bout it. Only thing was, the People—for the most part— didn't believe it, 'cause it sounded downright fishy. 'Specially comin' from a simple-minded woman. A shunned one at that.

When she'd asked Benjamin 'bout the day he took Lavina over to the Fishers', Ben had clammed right up, lookin' a mite peaked, too. She'd wondered why and pushed for an answer.

"Ach, don't be so nosy, Susie," he'd chided her.

"I don't mean to be," she'd said softly.

"Well, ya are, and that's all there is to it!"

In spite of Ben's blunt retort, Susanna still s'posed there oughta be someone who knew what had happened while Lavina talked to the bishop on his sickbed. After all, where was Rosemary during all the supposed soul-savin' goings-on? Well, she'd just hafta go over and pay her respects to the bishop's wife before too long. Tomorrow after preachin' service, maybe.

Climbing back up the steps to their bedroom, she thought again of the Scriptures she'd read before retiring. They just kept a-goin' 'round and 'round in her head, and before she slipped under the covers again, she opened the old German Bible to the now-familiar passages. Just then, as she was reading, she thought of Rachel, wondering if she might not be talkin' to Philip

Bradley 'bout all the Bible lessons she'd learned from Esther.

Susanna didn't quite know why the thought popped in her head just now, but she had a strange feelin' Philip was gonna be hearing 'bout them verses one way or the other. Why, the way Levi Glick had launched off on his view of Scripture and such things this afternoon—right there in the living room—she had a powerful feeling Rachel would also be sharin' some of the same things.

Here lately, it seemed her daughter couldn't stop talking 'bout the Lord, repentance, and whatnot all. Susanna had truly wanted to put a stop to it in the worst way, but something kept her from confronting Esther like she'd wanted to. Something *else* was keeping her from worrying so awful much 'bout Rachel tonight, too. Truth be told, she didn't know why she hadn't thrown at least a slight fit when Philip wanted to rent a room for the night. Why on earth had she agreed to take his reservation and his money?

What *had* come over her?

❖ ❖ ❖

Before heading south toward the highway, Philip suggested they stop for coffee. "It's still early," he said, opening the car door for Rachel. "Are you hungry?"

"Let's see what's on the menu," she said, taking his arm.

He noticed for the first time that Rachel had come without her walking cane. Had she merely forgotten?

Deciding not to inquire, he led her carefully into the restaurant, pointing out each step along the way.

Inside, they followed the receptionist to a table near the back of the restaurant. The woman looked them over rather indiscreetly. Philip supposed they did make an odd-looking couple—Rachel in her cape dress and apron, and he in his dress slacks and sports jacket. But then, how would anyone know for sure that they weren't simply brother and sister? The "brother" having left the Fold of the People—or never joined—and the "sister" . . . well, it was quite obvious where her church loyalties stood.

They sat facing each other in a padded tan booth. Philip leaned back, inhaling slowly as he studied the woman across the table. "I think it's time we had a real supper," he offered.

"I'm not *that* hungry," she replied, smiling.

"I suppose not, after cake and punch."

"And Esther's turkey sandwiches earlier," she reminded him.

"You'll have to tell Esther thank you."

She smiled unexpectedly. "You can tell her if you like. Remember, we'll all be goin' to the Crossroad tomorrow."

Philip wouldn't risk saying that he'd nearly forgotten the plans to ride in a horse and buggy, accompanying Rachel and her Ohio cousins to the busy intersection.

"Are you sure you're ready to go to the Crossroad, Rachel? I mean, do you feel comfortable with the thought?"

She blinked her eyes several times before she answered, almost as if trying to see him. "I believe I'm ready for whatever the Lord wants me to experience," she said softly.

Rachel's face was lovely and smooth; even without makeup she was truly beautiful. Eyebrows perfectly arched, cheekbones well formed, and lips . . . He stopped his analysis there. "I'll pray that the Crossroad will bring you the healing you long for."

"That's just what I've been asking the Lord to do. I believe He will heal me . . . tomorrow!" she whispered emphatically.

Such faith he had never witnessed. Rachel literally glowed with anticipation, and he felt, for a moment, that he, too, was catching her vision of hope. "More than anything, I wish that for you."

"Denki," she said, nodding her head sweetly.

And it was then he noticed again the gentle curl of her hair, where a strand or two had sprung free at her neck.

He almost told her how pretty she looked in the vibrant blue dress and white apron—Sunday attire, he supposed—instead of the gray and black mourning clothes he'd become accustomed to seeing her wear. But he caught himself, coming to his senses just as the waitress arrived at their table, bringing two water glasses and a fistful of clean utensils. "I'm very sorry, Miss," he said, begging for more time. "The lady and I haven't even looked at the menu yet."

The waitress glanced at them, offering the same shrewd smile that Adele had given him earlier. "I'll come back in a few minutes."

"I appreciate it," he said, realizing his mouth had suddenly become dry. He reached for his glass of water just as Rachel put her hand out, seeking her own glass. Without thinking how Rachel might react, he touched her hand lightly, guiding it.

"Oh!" Her face flushed instantly.

He wished to slow his heart, wished he could think more clearly. Could it be that Adele's assessment was correct? Was he actually fond of the blind widow before him? "Annie, uh . . . how's your little girl?" he blurted the ridiculous transition.

"Ach, a happy one, she is" came the sweet, yet baffled reply.

Each time Rachel answered, he attempted to think what her vernacular style reminded him of—aside from the initial conversations of the past fall—since first he'd met the reticent young Amishwoman. It was unlike any dialect he'd ever encountered anywhere. Except, perhaps, the "village talk" he'd come across during his school vacations spent in an isolated sector of southern Vermont. There he had listened in on a few old codgers, tottering friends of his grandpap. Folk who sat in ancient rocking chairs, watching the sun go down from their paint-peeled porches, sipping iced tea. Every summer night without fail. "Tip-top entertainment, yes, indeedy," one old gentleman had lisped through missing teeth, in regard to the sunset. Philip had never forgotten.

"Will Annie attend school next year?" he asked, shaking off thoughts of New England.

Rachel nodded. "She missed going this year by a few months, but I think she'll be ready come next fall."

"What a wonderful little girl."

"Jah, and she likes you, *Mister* Philip."

They laughed together, which broke the ice even more. And that was an excellent thing, he decided, because the way things had been going for the past few minutes, he was beginning to wonder if stopping off here for a bite was a mistake. Perhaps, talking while driving toward Lancaster might've been a better choice for them. But the truth was, he felt drawn to Rachel and wanted to get to know her better.

Shifting to his journalistic mode, he asked if she'd mind answering a question or two about the Plain life. "I know from the things Adele Herr shared about Gabe, there were one-room schoolhouses for the Amish children back in the sixties. Is that still the case?"

"Jah, they go through eighth grade."

"Then what, after that?"

She cocked her head as if recalling a distant memory. "Most of the boys work alongside their fathers, same as the girls do. We go back home to our mammas, learnin' how to can and quilt and keep house—that is, if we didn't already know how by that time."

"And if you did already know those things, what then?"

"There's ever so much to know 'bout woman's duties."

"Then are you saying that women and men have specific chores? That men, for instance, wouldn't clean or cook?"

Rachel actually giggled. "Not to laugh at you, but no, they wouldn't think of doin' our work. The men know what's expected of them; so do the women."

"And just what *is* expected of an Amishman?" He was aware of his own voice, that he was speaking much softer now, and he leaned forward, his elbows on the table, peering into Rachel's lovely face.

"Outside work," she replied. "A young boy is trained to work with his father and older brothers in the barn, the tobacco shed, the fields. That way, when the time comes for him to finish up with book-learnin', he can help farm the land or help his pop in the wood-workin' business or blacksmithing."

When she mentioned blacksmithing, he noticed she raised her eyebrows awkwardly, then shook her head as if she wished she hadn't alluded to that particular job. "What is it, Rachel?"

"Oh my." She looked positively flustered. "I don't know what came over me just now—bringin' up the job of a smithy and all."

"Because of John Lapp's visit?"

She put her hand to her throat. "Himmel! I'd never want to go anywhere with that man!" she confessed, spilling the words out like he'd never known her to do. "He is overbearing and outspoken. And Mam should've never invited him for Christmas dinner, for goodness' sake!"

"Your mother did?"

She folded her hands on the table in front of her. "It's our way. We often ask folk in at Christmas. But ever since I quit wearin' my mourning clothes, Mam has made it her duty to try 'n match me up with someone."

"Why is that so annoying?"

"I'm a grown woman. I can go 'bout my life without help from Mam."

"This must bother you a great deal." He could see from the frown on her face that it did.

"Jah, ever so much." Rachel sighed, then continued. "It's not such a carefree thing to be a young widow in the Amish community. People talk; they hope to put widowers together with younger women who've lost their husbands. All for bearin' more babies—future church members—especially the Old Order folk feel that way."

"So . . . the more children born, the better?"

"That's right."

The waitress was heading their way again, and they still had not looked over the menu. "What's your special tonight?" he asked the woman in the pale green waitress outfit.

"It's our Christmas special—chicken and dumplings" was the quick reply. "Would you care for that?"

"Does that sound good to you?" he asked Rachel.

She nodded her head bashfully, her eyes cast down, and Philip ordered the same. "With black coffee, please."

"I'll stick with water to drink," Rachel said.

Quickly, they resumed their conversation, and Philip was amazed that they'd fallen into the same comfortable dialogue they had experienced last fall on their drive home from the Reading cemetery. How was it that a young Amishwoman and a modern journalist could have this kind of rapport? How? He didn't understand in the least, but he knew it was a reality. Their spirits had found communion. Yes, he preferred that far better than the secular terminology of "soul-mates." More suitable for two people who loved the Lord and wanted, above all things, to serve and honor Him.

"Tell me 'bout the information you brought for me," Rachel said out of the blue. "On my blindness."

He was quite surprised, but pleased, that she had inquired about it and began to recount the information to the best of his ability. More than ever, he believed Rachel was ready to receive the help she surely needed.

During the drive back to Bird-in-Hand, Rachel explained for Philip what "ach" meant. He said he'd heard the word used often while in the Lancaster area and was curious.

"It just means 'oh!'—that's all."

"Oh."

"No . . . *ach*." He laughed at that, and she honestly didn't know what came over her to joke with him that way. 'Course she would never say she felt homelike with him. Prob'ly didn't need to, now that she thought 'bout it.

They fell to talkin' of less serious things. He wanted to know if she ever visited with Emma at the antique store in Bird-in-Hand village.

"Every so often Mam goes there to look at Emma's new items, but it's been a while now since I've gone. Why do you ask?"

"I've been thinking that I might order a desk, something similar to the one in the guest room where I'll be staying again."

"It's a nice piece," she said, though she'd never laid eyes on it, only dusted its pigeonholes. "Mam's mighty glad to have it."

"I can see why."

"Jah, it's a gut place to hide a postcard, right?" Again, they laughed together, and his chuckle was ever so joyful.

Their talk soon turned to Esther and Levi. "Wonderful people," Philip remarked. "Any chance they might return to the Lancaster area?"

"Funny you ask, 'cause I've been wishin' they'd come back. But I think it's out of the question. They've got the land they've always wanted in Holmes County," she explained. "And they waited an awful long time for it." She went on to say that one of her heart's desires was to farm again. "It goes without sayin' that we Amish have a cravin' for the soil." Unexpectedly, she thought of a comment her Jacob had often made—that he was born with dirt under his fingernails.

Philip said, "My grandpap on my father's side owned a large amount of acreage in southern Vermont, near the Battenkill River—the most beautiful place on earth, I thought as a boy. Grandpap built a summer cottage there, surrounded by trees and vegetable gardens. Whenever I go there, even now, it's a little foretaste of heaven. So I think I know what you mean."

Rachel had to smile at his comment. Something else they had in common, it seemed. "I don't know why, but I believe someday Annie and I will work the land again.

But only the dear Lord knows how that's gonna come about."

"Trusting God for His plan isn't easy, is it?"

A little surprised at his question, she answered softly, "Lavina says to 'wait patiently for Him,' and, believe me, I'm learnin' to do just that. Every day of my life since I lost half of my family at the Crossroad."

"I can't imagine what you've gone through."

"You mustn't feel sorry for me," she was quick to say. "I don't seek pity."

"You've been courageous, Rachel."

His voice was tender just now, and she wished for all the world she could have one glimpse of his face. Surely he was a handsome man. Annie had said as much. Told her repeatedly, in fact.

"I've been meaning to ask you something," she said, eager to change the subject, get the focus off herself. "And if ya think I'm pryin', just say so, but I'm interested in hearing 'bout your preparations for the ministry. Adele mentioned to Lavina and me that you felt the Lord callin' you."

"I believe He is, but that's where trust comes in." Philip sighed, taking his time. "I'm praying daily for guidance."

"Does that mean you're not so happy with your writing job? At the magazine?"

"That may be too long a story for this particular night. Perhaps, though, we could have dinner together again before I leave?"

He was asking her to go with him somewhere, yet again! Oh, she wanted to say "Jah" without a bit of hesitation but knew it was best not to. "I don't know. I believe I oughta concentrate on first things first—the Crossroad . . . tomorrow."

Philip was quiet for the longest time, and she worried that she'd offended him. When he spoke, his words were gentle, yet somewhat disquieting.

"Your vision is more important than anything, Rachel. I wouldn't think of distracting you from that."

"No . . . no, I understand. Honest, I do."

"After the Crossroad, we can decide about having dinner or not."

She felt helpless to give a worthwhile answer, so she kept her peace. Best not to lead him on, anyways. What made her think that a man like Philip would ever be content for long with a friend with such obvious . . . limitations?

❖ ❖ ❖

Long past ten o'clock, Susanna awoke from a hair-raisin' dream. She sat straight up in bed, wiping the perspiration from her brow, attempting to catch her breath, which had been perty near snuffed out in the middle of all the nightmarish confusion. She'd dreamt the most peculiar thing, and its murky undercurrent was still pulling at her, even in her wakefulness. Blue Johnny and the newly deceased bishop, Seth Fisher, had been talkin' to her. The bishop was sending a warning from the grave, and Blue Johnny was trying to block it, rebuffing every word Seth Fisher was shouting out. There was screamin' and rantin'—all comin' from an angry Blue Johnny—worse than any nightmare she could've ever imagined.

She'd heard folks say that there was sometimes a meaning in a dream like this, but she daresn't think such a thing. No, 'cause she had a powerful-strong feelin' she knew just what the meaning was. Jah, she did. The bishop *had* found salvation, full and free—'least in the dream, he had—just like Lavina was spreading 'round amongst the People, but Blue Johnny was madder'n a hornet 'bout it. That's why he'd kept a-hollerin' to drown out the things the bishop was tryin' to say.

For the third time this night, Susanna crept out from under the bed quilts. This time she fell to her knees, clasping her hands in fervent prayer. "Lord God Almighty," she began, "if any of what I've read in the Bible tonight concerns me and the sins of my fathers, if any of it oughta be confessed and renounced, as my daughter keeps sayin', well, then, O Most High, I ask you to show me what to do. Amen."

She s'posed it was all right to talk that way to the Lord God heavenly Father, 'specially if no one was 'round, listenin' in on important things a body had to say.

❖ ❖ ❖

Rachel felt sure she could trust her feelings for Philip, that she knew who he was deep inside, even after only a few visits with him. She also thought she understood what made him tick, so to speak, and that he was trustworthy as the day was long. Why else would she have allowed herself to be alone with an outsider on two separate occasions? Yet she could not grasp a sound reason why they had been brought together. Did God intend them to be more than accidental friends?

Rachel knew she'd best cast the matter into God's hands. Let Him work things out. So she lay awake, long after talking to the Lord 'bout Philip Bradley and all that had taken place this Christmas Day. She thought 'bout John Lapp wantin' a bride younger than himself to bear him more children. And she sighed into the night, wonderin' what it would be like to be married again to someone of God's choosing. To someone as dear to her as the handsome blond husband she'd married at eighteen.

It was nigh unto impossible to think of the cocksure smithy that way. And as much as she liked Philip, she was ever so hesitant to consider an Englischer when it came to marriage. Yet beneath his "fancy" layers— speech patterns, intellect, and his perception of the world—she thought she saw glimmers of yearning. A longing for a more simple life. She saw it in the questions he asked, the way he drew her out. Besides all that, his patience seemed to have no end. And he had the ability to reassure her. She truly liked him for everything that set him apart from John Lapp. He was the sort of man her family would have smiled on had he been born into the Amish community—the thoughtful farm boy down Beechdale Road or Maple Avenue, harvestin' corn and baling hay along with his pop and brothers.

Oh, she knew his spirit, knew it through and through. Jah, with Philip she could see ahead to the future, her confidence being handed over to her, the doors of timidity cracking open and swinging wide at long last. Sun-filled days, a spread of land burstin' with crops, ponds a-plenty, and woodlands to run through at dawn. The Lord's name to be praised together with a man set on servin' Him, too. These were the things she wanted most out of life. Nay, *needed*.

But would Philip have understood these late-night thoughts of hers had she been able to put them into words? *Prob'ly not.* Still, she knew, deep within her spirit, Philip Bradley was a God-fearing man, full of faith. And he was ever so kind and playful with Annie. A right gut father he'd make! But would she be willing to go "fancy" for him?

Before she drifted off to sleep, she thought again 'bout what Philip had shared with her—therapeutic ideas, grief groups, and whatnot. All the information he had so kindly brought for her to consider. Yet she felt the Lord was prompting her to have the church elders pray over her, first and foremost. Emotional healing had been hanging in the balance far too long; her ability to see was bound up in it. She was ever so sure of that. It was time she mustered up the courage to follow through with biblical teaching, found in the book of James.

Come tomorrow, after the preachin' service, she would ask to be anointed with oil in the name of the Lord Jesus.

Nineteen

The tiny gap, where Annie's front baby tooth had once been, caught Philip's attention as he helped the young girl and her mother into his car the next morning. He had offered to drive them to church during the course of breakfast, much to the unspoken astonishment of Rachel's parents. It seemed they, too, had church plans. But Susanna was quick to make the distinction between what she viewed as the wayward Beachy Amish and the Old Order. "We haven't forsaken the assembly and tradition of our forefathers," she'd said, eyes flashing. "We attend *house* church."

"Whose turn is it to have Preachin', then?" Rachel asked, diverting the subject almost effortlessly. Or so it seemed.

"Thomas and Mary Beiler," Susanna replied, then turning to Philip, she kindly explained. "That's my oldest living sister and her husband."

"And Thomas ain't no doubter neither," Benjamin piped up, bringing the conflict back into play. He was dressed for the day, wearing a pressed white shirt, tan suspenders, black broadfall trousers, and vest—"for gut" clothes—or so he'd said when first Philip was seated at the dining room table.

"Thomas is an upstanding Amishman," Susanna added, and it almost seemed as though they were united in an attempt to make a point. For Rachel's sake?

Rachel, who was sipping her coffee, did not so much as crack a smile. Philip assumed she was contemplating her visit to the Crossroad, this long-awaited day of days. Observing her more closely, he saw that she was pensive, even prayerful. He reached for his juice glass, recalling how, last evening, his hand had innocently guided hers to the water glass. Their first dinner alone. No matter what happened, he would fondly remember that Christmas night.

❖ ❖ ❖

Singing from the hymnbook at the Beachy Amish Church was somewhat similar to his own church, with the exception of the fact that each hymn was sung without musical accompaniment. Even so, Philip, who shared the hymnal with Levi Glick, found the harmonious, full sound of human voices entirely refreshing. He was glad, too, that Levi and his wife had chosen this house of worship today. A visitor in "secular" attire, he might have felt even more conspicuous sitting with the Plain men in their conservative dark coats and trousers had it not been for Levi, who welcomed him with a warm smile and friendly manners, putting Philip completely at ease.

In the middle of "O, For a Thousand Tongues," he happened to glimpse Rachel and Annie, sitting toward

234

the front with an older woman, whom he assumed was
Lavina Troyer, as well as Esther Glick and her two little
girls. All the women and young children sat on the left
side of the church aisle, the women in modest cape
dresses—blues, purples, and greens—and white prayer
veilings, as was their custom.

Verse five of the hymn was especially meaningful as
he blended his voice joyfully with Levi's and the men
around him.

> Hear Him, ye deaf; His praise, ye dumb,
> Your loosened tongues employ;
> Ye blind, behold your Savior, come;
> And leap, ye lame, for joy.

Philip contemplated Rachel's intended trip to the
Crossroad, as she called it. During his short stay in Bird-
in-Hand, he had become familiar with the junction of
North Ronks Road and Route 340. In fact, on several
occasions he had passed through on the main highway,
noticing a line-up of horses and buggies at the red light.
He'd thought it a wise and sensible move, installing a
traffic light at that particular intersection. But to think
that Rachel and her young family had experienced a
fatal accident there was more than he cared to ponder.
No wonder Rachel and Annie had been traumatized
these many months. No wonder it had taken so long for
the young widow to bring herself to this day. What
courage—with God's help—she would have to muster
to revisit the scene of the accident, sight or no, that had
so altered her life! He would offer whatever support he
could, though his guess was that Levi and Esther would

be the key proponents. Yet he was going along. Had actually volunteered. And Rachel seemed altogether pleased.

During the last hymn, Rachel felt her faith rise up powerful-strong. *Ye blind, behold your Savior, come . . .*

She could scarcely wait for the church elders to pray for her. This was her day of deliverance. She believed it with all her might!

The pastor took his place behind a simple wooden pulpit immediately following the passing of the offering plate. There was no special Christmas music, no wreaths or decorations. Plain and off-white, the walls were devoid of crosses or pictures of Christ. A single small chandelier hung in the center of the aisle, offering sufficient light. The windows were clear, no stained glass here.

A gentle rustle of pages turning came as soon as the minister announced his sermon text. Philip, too, located the Scripture passage, a bit surprised that its focus was divine healing. He wondered if perhaps Rachel had had recent pastoral counsel, inspiring such a sermon topic the day after Christmas. Or was it that the pastor knew of Rachel's plan to visit the Crossroad this day?

He found himself paying close attention, yet, at the same time, wanting to be in an attitude of prayer. Philip concentrated on God's great mercy in sending Jesus as divine provision for the healing of mankind—accomplished by the beating Christ suffered prior to His death on the cross. Praying silently, he believed that this would indeed be Rachel's day of restoration.

Along with Rachel, several other church members
met the elders and pastor in the altar area after the service. Philip stood in the back of the sanctuary with Levi
and his four children, waiting without speaking for both
Rachel and Esther to join them.

The elders anointed Rachel with oil, and Philip
bowed his head, as well. *Lord Jesus, please give your child
the desire of her heart . . . today, if it be your will,* he
prayed silently.

After the elders' prayers, Rachel fully expected to be
able to see, but when her sight did not return immediately, she felt she wanted to go straight to the Crossroad, postponing the noon meal "for just a short time,"
she told Esther and Levi in the church parking lot.
"Would it be all right if we go now?"

Graciously, Lavina Troyer offered to stay at the
church with the children, including Annie. Levi agreed
to drive his in-laws' horse and buggy over to North
Ronks Road and down to the Crossroad. As planned,
Esther and Philip went along. Rachel's cousin guided
her carefully across the driveway and into the enclosed
carriage.

It was Levi who suggested that she sit in the second
seat with Philip, behind him and Esther. She was taken
aback by his insistence, yet she didn't question, doing
as he requested. Surely, Levi wasn't in favor of encouraging her friendship with an outsider. Surely, he had her
best interest at heart—sitting in the second seat was a

way to cushion her a bit from the stark realities, maybe. From the return of memories that surely lay ahead.

By agreeing to go on this ride, Philip realized he was putting himself at risk, as documented in recent newspapers. Due to increased population and drivers impatient with slow-moving carriages on busy thoroughfares, more and more wrecks were occurring in Lancaster County. So here he sat, in a dilapidated old buggy, next to an attractive young woman, who was determined to see her way past the pain. Beyond the agony of the Crossroad.

Levi, their experienced driver—all the way from Ohio for Christmas—tapped the reins gently, and the horse pulled the carriage forward, out of the church parking lot and onto a two-lane road. If someone had told Philip—his sister, for instance—that he would spend the day after Christmas in such a peculiar manner, he would not have believed it. Yet he had volunteered only yesterday to go along on this, Rachel's journey to healing. The fact that he was here, hoping for the very best—praying too—meant that he must care more than he had let on to anyone. Most of all, himself.

❖ ❖ ❖

Susanna waited till Rosie Fisher was alone to approach her 'bout what was on her mind. She offered her sympathy, then said, "Nobody seems to know, for sure and for certain, 'cept maybe Lavina, so I'll just up and ask ya. What happened the other day . . . at your place?"

"Well, *I* know 'cause I was there, but I don't rightly understand what happened, not really," Rosemary told her after Preachin' service at the Beilers'. "All's I know is Seth whispered to me that he wanted to hear what Lavina Troyer had to say. He didn't want me or anyone else to keep her from speakin' whatever was on her heart. And he said something else to me, too."

"What's that?" Susanna was all ears.

"Seth said the Lord God had prepared his heart for her visit."

"Well, I'll be," Susanna said, heading with Rosemary to the kitchen to help set up for the common meal. "If I hadn't heard it from you, I'd hafta say I wouldn't believe it a'tall."

The elderly woman nodded, her eyes shining. "I wisht you could've been there to see it for yourself. My husband's face was just a-glowin'."

"Where was Benjamin during all this?" She had to ask. Had to know what on earth went on that her husband hadn't witnessed any of what Rosemary was a-sayin'. Or wanted to forget, maybe.

"I daresay, if Ben didn't up and leave the room like a scared 'possum."

"Why, do ya think?"

"Well, a kind of glory come in and filled up the place."

Susanna didn't know what to make of this. "A *glory*, you say?"

"Jah, come right in and sent the evil a-spinnin' out."

"Evil?"

"Twistin' and a-turnin' right out of Seth. I saw it with my own eyes. He coughed and sneezed nigh unto thirty times."

"But what *evil?*" Susanna insisted.

"Them curses . . . all the years of hexin' and enchantments, that's what. My Seth got clear free of the powwowin', too, surprisin' as that might seem."

Susanna gasped. "What did you say?"

"The 'knowin' gifts' got prayed right out of him by your husband's shunned cousin. It was mighty surprisin'."

Susanna thought on that. Lavina castin' out wickedness? Why did Bishop Seth need such a deliverance as that? What was *wrong* with powwowing? The more she mulled over what Rosemary had just said, the more one certain Scripture came to mind. *Our fathers have sinned, and are not; and we have borne their iniquities.*

Was that verse the explanation for the bishop's need? Could it be? Well, now that she thought on it, she wished she *had* been on hand—at Seth Fisher's bedside—that day. She would've been downright interested to see what shunned Lavina had witnessed with her simple eyes and childlike understandin'.

She decided she'd be listenin' to Esther's tape yet again.

❖ ❖ ❖

Snow-laden wheat fields met them on either side of

the narrow road. In some places, large patches of frosted grass showed through, reminding Philip that one day, months from now, the pastureland would spring to life once again. The density of the snow and ice weighed down certain enormous tree branches as the horse pulled the buggy and its passengers down North Ronks Road. Philip began to wonder if Rachel were able to see the snowscape encompassing them, if she might not have associated the ice and heavy snow with her own personal state. That she, too, had been burdened with a ponderous mass.

Because Rachel was so silent, sitting next to him, he chose to accommodate her obvious need for quietude. Doing so, he created a mental picture—the best-case scenario for Rachel—that her sight would indeed be restored. Her life would return to normal, and the mission he'd hoped to accomplish would be fulfilled. He would go back to New York, proceed with his pursuit of Bible study and fellowship with the Christian businessmen of his community, and continue asking God for direction. He could throw himself back into his writing, even accept an occasional free-lance assignment.

Rachel, on the other hand, was sure to have many more opportunities to remarry. She wouldn't have to settle for the outspoken smithy from Paradise Township, after all. Even better, Annie would have a sighted mother once again!

God's will above all else . . .

❖ ❖ ❖

"Why'd Mamma and her cousins and Mister Philip hafta go off without us?" Annie asked Lavina as they stood in the vestibule of the Beachy Church.

"Well, now, girlie, I think your mamma already explained that," she told the little girl with bright eyes.

"But how's goin' to the Crossroad gonna help Mamma see again?"

"Jah, I wanna know, too," asked young Ada, Annie's second cousin.

She wondered what more she oughta tell the children. Seemed Rachel had done a right gut job of sayin' what should be said. She sighed, wonderin' what she'd got herself into, offerin' to stay with the five little ones. "Sometimes a body's just gotta go back and see what's in the past . . . for their own selves," she said simply.

"But if Mamma can't see," Annie said, "how's she gonna do that?"

"Jah, Rachel's blind," James added. "Been that way for over two years now." And Mary and Elijah were shaking their wee heads in unison.

"I'd hafta say if God wanted Rachel to go in a buggy to the Crossroad, well, then, who are we to question that?"

That quieted them down, and Lavina went in search of a Sunday school lesson to read to her young charges. She'd have to sit them on the floor and pretend to be their teacher, something she'd always admired 'bout her old friend, Adele Herr. That's just what she'd do till Rachel and the others returned, and Rachel's sight was back to normal. Leastways, she'd be hopin' and prayin' for the dear girl. . . .

❖ ❖ ❖

The morning had been breezy and cold when Philip first had awakened, the wind coming out of the north with a few flurries. But now a stillness fell over the region, gray and gentle, as if they in the buggy were nestled in the eye of a storm, protected from future fury; far enough removed, almost to be convinced that the storm did not exist at all.

His thoughts turned to Adele and her discerning reply to one of his recent letters, written before leaving New York. He had unburdened his soul, sharing his personal and professional concerns for the future.

I'm delighted to know that you are relying on God's help with your "fork in the road," she had said in her letter.

He didn't exactly know why her reply had continued to make such an impact on him. Was it because he had come to believe, as did Adele, that she had made an irrevocable life error? That she had missed God's will for her life forty long years ago? He cringed anew each time he recalled Adele's account of her refusal. Gabe's earnest love had gone unheeded; she'd broken the young Amishman's heart, rejecting his marriage proposal.

The four of them rode in unbroken stillness. He presumed Levi and Esther had immersed themselves in intercessory prayer on behalf of Rachel's healing. He, in turn, asked the Lord for divine help during and after the possibly traumatic journey they were embarking on, searching his own heart as he did.

As he opened his eyes, the wind began to blow again, pushing back the clouds. All at once the landscape and the road ahead were bathed in radiant light. Liquid gold spilled across the snow-packed road ahead, flowing across field and stream, casting a bold sheen over every farmhouse and barn as far as the eye could see. But most interesting was the effect the sudden burst of sunlight had on Rachel.

"The sun's just come out, ain't?" she whispered, leaning close to him.

Turning, he was amazed at what he saw. Her lovely face was wet with tears. "Yes, Rachel, the sun *is* shining," he said, trying to compose himself.

The noonday sun was ablaze in the sky, and he took for granted that he should have felt subconscious warmth. But beneath the layers of his fur-lined topcoat, Philip shivered.

Twenty

❖ ❖ ❖

*R*achel kept her eyes closed, seized by the radiance around her, thinking that it might vanish. *Heart, you must not fear!* she commanded her timid spirit, recalling the verses in the Old Testament. *For the Lord your God is He that goeth with you. . . .*

Taking several slow, deep breaths, she asked the Lord to give her an abundance of courage for what she might remember, and that she would not be afraid to see again. *Please, dear Lord Jesus, help me get through to the other side*, she prayed silently. *To the other side of the Crossroad.*

Unexpectedly, a thought came to her—the term given the dangerous intersection had another meaning. 'Least for her, it did. The Crossroad could also mean the *road* to the Cross. Why she'd never thought of it, she didn't honestly know. The path to the Cross was ever so excruciating for the dear Savior. A grievance no one should ever have to endure, yet He chose to walk the way of it. Surely then, He would understand and see her through this day. Jesus himself would carry her to the brink of her memories, through the horrific visions she'd repressed and rejected. She pictured in her mind the Lord gathering her up, blind and tormented, into His own strong arms.

Brushing tears away, she fixed her heart on the painful journey the Lord had called her to. And she allowed herself to think back to the very day of the accident.

Two long years ago . . .

❖ ❖ ❖

The day had been exceptionally hot for mid-June. But there was a breeze, which helped circulate precious little air through the enclosed market wagon. Jacob hurried the horse toward North Ronks Road. She was a bit on edge 'bout taking the shortcut to market, but Jacob reassured her that it was the best way "to make gut time." They'd gotten a late start, and she blamed herself for sleeping past the alarm, causin' this rushing 'round in the first place.

Leaning her head on Jacob's strong shoulder, she closed her eyes, enjoying the sounds of birds, crickets, and the cadence of the horse's hooves on the road. There was the humming sound of a windmill, too, and an occasional passing horse and carriage. In back, Aaron and Annie played happily.

In her hand, she clutched a letter, one she'd written the night before. It was to Esther, her close cousin, transplanted to Ohio from Bird-in-Hand, Pennsylvania.

❖ ❖ ❖

"We're comin' up on the intersection," Esther said

from the front seat. "Thought you should know."

"How much farther?" Rachel asked, her heart in her throat.

Levi answered. "A quarter mile or so."

She tried to settle back, cautiously thinking through—step by step—the events leading up to the accident, aware of Philip's presence. Yet she felt as if she might be floating through space and time, knowing full well she was conscious.

❖ ❖ ❖

"Look at Dat's handmade toy trains and helicopters!" young Aaron was saying as they rumbled toward the Crossroad.

Jacob joked with his son, and right then the wind plucked the letter out of her hand. Sent it flying through the window. She told Jacob she'd get it "right quick," which she did. Jumped out while the traffic light was still red and chased the letter across the field.

When she retrieved it, she turned in horror to see the mare rearin' up, carrying on like their driving horse had never, ever done before. Jacob was struggling, trying to control the spooked creature. Oh, it was the most frightening thing she'd ever witnessed, and she felt her very breath go out of her lungs. And then the horse charged forward into a stream of traffic.

Just now, reliving the dreadful events, she fought her way through it, clawing her way out of what seemed like a long black tunnel. She agonized anew over not being able to locate her little children, their bodies surely wracked by pain, in shock. Searching, tripping over debris in the road, she kept callin' out their names, stumbling over Jacob's handmade toys and the mutilated pieces of what had once been their market wagon.

A flash of light! Suddenly, Rachel remembered something submerged so deep in the recesses of her soul—ever so precious a memory—one she'd lost, repressed with all the others.

She was kneeling on the hot blacktop, on the road, cradling Jacob in her arms. He was breathing, and she was oh so glad for that. He began to stir, looking up, his eyes fluttering open as he struggled against full sunlight.

"Rachel . . . I see the Lord Jesus . . . His arms are open wide . . . for *me*." Pausing, he breathed a ragged sigh, then coughed, wincing with the effort. "Heaven's here, radiant and bright . . . ach, it's so beautiful."

His eyes closed slowly, and she could feel the life draining from him. "Oh, Jacob," she whimpered, "I love you so. Please live. Stay with us. Please, don't give up."

Yet, in the stillness, as her husband lay dying, Rachel felt utter peace. Like a divine balm of Gilead, drenching her, warming and soothing her very soul. She longed to linger in its indescribable glow, letting the amazing feeling flow over her. Jacob, her beloved, was going home to heaven right here in her arms.

The sweet reality filled her spirit, soul, and body. In that moment, she felt sure that nothing could ever move her again in such a profound way. She wanted to stay here for always, holding her husband just a handclasp from eternity. So close to that glorious hereafter, promised to all those who belong to the Lord. Heaven's door was near, at least for that one instant, and the glimpse of it was precious beyond words.

Her peace was short-lived as a crush of sounds flew at her—footsteps, whispers—and hot, dense air flurried 'bout her as Jacob fell limp against her.

"Step back," someone commanded, and she felt an opening in the wall of commotion.

❖ ❖ ❖

"Rachel . . . it's over," Philip said, reaching for her hand. "You've passed the Crossroad . . . to the other side." He could not go on, so filled with emotion was he. He continued to cradle her fragile hand in both of his, gently stroking, offering whatever comfort he could.

Esther turned around in the front seat, her hand reaching out for Rachel's free one. "It's all behind you now, dear Cousin. The Lord is with you."

"Where are we?" Rachel murmured, tears spilling down her cheeks.

"Just south of the Crossroad, on Ronks Road," Esther explained. "Levi pulled off the road when you started to cry. We'll stay put here till you're ready to go again."

"You just say the word," Levi spoke up.

"I feel I hafta tell all of you what happened just now," Rachel began.

And the memories poured forth from her as if pent

up for a lifetime. But it was the account she gave of her husband's heavenly homegoing that touched Philip most.

Rachel made several futile attempts to control herself, to make the tears stop. It didn't help that in spite of her faith-filled prayers, the return of her memory, and the striving she had felt in her spirit, she was still blind. Oh, there were the murky and occasional bursts of light at the end of the darkness, but as for seeing clearly, well, she simply couldn't. And she was ever so glad that neither Philip nor her cousins were asking her 'bout that.

Truth be told, she had come out on the other side in one piece, and yet there was only the gloom of reality. Jacob and Aaron were still in their graves, buried in the Amish cemetery on the hill. She was still a widow with only one of her children left living. No hope for a love like she'd had with dear Jacob Yoder.

No hope . . .

She began to sob in deepest despair, her body trembling with the truth she'd had to face. She covered her eyes with both hands, letting go of both Esther's and Philip's handclasp. Then she felt Philip draw her near as the horse and carriage continued down the road— away from the Crossroad. She gave way to his gentle touch, scarcely aware that her head had come to rest on his shoulder or that he whispered soothing words. In her grief, she also mourned the fact that Philip would be leaving soon, returning to his own world, where she did not belong.

"Your vision is more important than anything," Philip

had said last evening. More important . . .

The memory of those words drowned out his compassion now. The carriage clattered onto Lynwood Road, heading toward the direction of the church. The long way back . . .

❖ ❖ ❖

Lavina had read through all the Sunday school lessons and was makin' an effort to sing "Jesus Loves Me" on key when Annie asked where her mamma was. "I'm gettin' awful hungry," she said.

"Me too," young Ada added.

"My tummy's gonna cave in," Mary said, getting poked by her brother.

Lavina figured it shouldn't be too much longer now. "Let's count to one hundred in Dutch, and maybe they'll be back."

Elijah tried his best, but the four-year-old was havin' a hard time, mixing up the numbers. It reminded her of how troublesome counting had been for her back when she was a schoolgirl. "You'll hafta count along with your big brother," she suggested, knowin' how awful bad he felt.

He nodded and the other children were eager to help him. But it was Annie who seemed most distracted. She was clearly worried 'bout her mamma.

And now, as she thought on it, Lavina was, too.

Twenty-One

I can't tell you how glad I am to have that ride over," Rachel told Esther in the privacy of her bedroom. "It was ever so frightenin', but I know now that I blocked out the most beautiful memory of all, right along with the horrifying ones."

"Jacob's homegoing?" asked Esther.

She nodded. "I just don't know how I could've rejected such an experience."

"Well, your heart was breakin', that could be why. Go easy on yourself, dear one."

"S'pose I oughta."

"Maybe the Lord saved this special memory for just today . . . when you most needed to remember," Esther said softly. "Ain't it true that God gave you Jacob for a short time, only to take him out of this present life to be with Him? I've thought so often since the accident that surely there was a lesson in it . . . for all of us, maybe."

"And I think I know now what that lesson might be."

Esther was silent, and Rachel reached for her cousin's hand as the women sat on the bed. "The lesson I believe the Lord would have me learn is not to take life's blessings for granted. The morning we drove to market for the last time, Jacob even said that we always miss what we don't have. I had to learn the hard way, I guess. Every single day's a gift from God."

"The Lord's grace is abundant . . . new every morning," Esther replied.

"And even though my sight hasn't yet returned, I still have hope that it will . . . in God's perfect time." Rachel truly wanted to believe it, fightin' hard against the hopeless feelings inside.

They sat quietly in the stillness of the bedroom, where both Rachel's large bed and Annie's little one had been neatly made with homemade quilts and Rachel's crocheted afghans.

"Wouldja like to talk about Philip?" Esther surprised her by saying. "A special young man, he is. Levi's very impressed with him . . . thinks he must surely have a call of God on his life."

Rachel thought on that. "But why should we talk 'bout him?"

" 'Cause God's call is on *your* life, too, Rachel."

"I . . . I just don't know what you're tryin' to say, bringin' Philip Bradley up this way." Honestly, her mouth turned dry as cotton.

"Don't be shy 'bout prayin' for Philip, that's all. Could be that God has a plan for your lives . . . together."

She wondered if her feelings for Philip had begun to show. If that was why Esther had brought up the subject. She daresn't ask. Not even Esther must discover *this* secret.

❖ ❖ ❖

Philip was enthusiastic to spend time with Levi. The house seemed nearly uninhabited at the present time, even though he knew the Glick children and Annie were off playing in the sunroom. He knew, too, that Rachel and Esther had disappeared upstairs. A good thing, presumably, what with Rachel's emotional state by trip's end.

They'd had a sumptuous dinner of baked turkey and ham, mashed potatoes and gravy, along with a number of side vegetable dishes, "wonderful-gut leftovers from Christmas dinner," Esther had said. It was amazing how she'd single-handedly whipped together such a meal while Rachel was resting.

The fact that Ben and Susanna were away from the house—having a meal with other Old Order church members—meant that Levi and Philip could talk more freely. And with the food cleared away and the kitchen cleaned up, he and Levi had the front room to themselves.

"I'd hoped to help Rachel regain her sight by coming," he ventured, specifying the information he'd discussed with Rachel. "Clearly, her sight hasn't returned, and I wonder if she might benefit from a Christian counselor, or even a secular therapist who has experience with such cases."

"Maybe." Levi smiled sympathetically.

"Do you know of anyone locally?"

"Well, I know that Rachel talked with her pastor's wife on several occasions."

"Is there a grief group she might join, as well?"

Levi frowned. "I don't know if she needs a group like that, really. Seems to me she's moved past her heartache over Jacob and Aaron."

Philip didn't press for an explanation but trusted the man's opinion. It was hard not to. Integrity emanated from Levi. "I hope I didn't stick my neck out with Rachel, sharing some of the materials I gleaned. I even went so far as to tell her about discussions I had with several New York psychotherapists."

"Well, how'd she take it?"

"Fine . . . just fine. But I hope she understands that I came to help . . . not to cause her confusion."

Levi eyed him curiously. "*Just* to help, is that it?"

He shrugged, uncertain of what to say.

"I think there may be more to it, Philip."

How Levi Glick, whom he had met only yesterday, seemed to know and understand Philip's personal struggle, he did not know.

❖ ❖ ❖

The Lord's Day was turnin' off right nice as Susanna and Benjamin rode home from Preachin' service. Now it was much lighter, what with the sun shinin' bright and hard against a backdrop of snow and ice, nearly blinding. The road ran downhill past farmland, now dormant for the winter, and gently sloping yards of one Amish neighbor after another.

Susanna wondered how things had gone for Rachel,

going in a buggy to the Crossroad, of all things. First time in well over two years. Well, her girl was in right gut company, so to speak. 'Least there was plenty of them, seein' as how Philip Bradley had gone, too, along with Esther and Levi.

She thought it best not to bring up the matter to Ben just yet. He'd been right quiet the past few days. Still, she'd been itchin' to talk to him 'bout Rosemary's account of the "deliverance" that had supposedly occurred at Seth Fisher's.

Susanna knew she oughta pick her conflicts carefully, this one weighin' mighty heavy on her mind. So she tilled the soil for discussion, hoping Ben wouldn't put up too much of a fuss. "Rosemary told me 'bout the bishop's change of heart before he died," she opened the subject. "Thought maybe you and I oughta be talkin' 'bout it, too."

"That's all well and gut, but I have nothin' to add."

"But you saw what she saw, didn'tcha?"

" 'Twasn't a perty sight, Susie, I'm tellin' you."

"Well, the bishop told Rosemary that the Lord had been preparin' him for Lavina's visit. Now . . . what do ya think of that?"

Ben's eyebrows arched high and long over his eyes. "You don't mean it."

"That's what she said."

"Well, I'll be . . ."

Not permitting a delay in their conversation, she pushed onward. "Rosemary truly believes the bishop got salvation that day—and she did, too, she says . . . all thanks to Lavina's prayin' over them."

"Could be," Ben said.

"She's a true and brave soul, Lavina."

Ben nodded, his eyes beginning to glisten. "Maybe more than us all."

Whatever that meant, Susanna didn't much know. But she had a feelin' that her husband had made up his mind—had formed an honest opinion—of what went on at the Fishers' place. She was almost sure of it.

Benjamin looked weary from the long day, so she must leave off bein' overbearing. Quickly, Susanna dropped the matter with nary another word. Later, when her husband was well rested, she'd fish some more.

❖ ❖ ❖

Philip was right about his hunch. Rachel *was* discouraged, and it was a wise move to invite her on a short walk to Mill Creek beyond the house. The same location where he had first realized that Rachel could not see. He'd gone that day to soak up some sun. In the midst of flaming autumn colors, he had crouched near the stream that ran across the Zooks' property, tossing twigs into the water. He hadn't forgotten how beautiful the young woman was, standing there on the footbridge that spanned the banks, with little Annie guiding her mother's every step.

Now it was *his* turn to lead the gentle lady whose cheeks were already pink from the cold, even though she was wrapped in a long black shawl and wearing her winter bonnet. "We won't be gone too long," he said, his eyes on the snowy path ahead. "I thought a short walk would do us both good." He didn't go on to say, "After your ordeal today." Instead, he added, "Actually, it's a nice excuse for us to have some time alone."

Philip noticed that she smiled at his comment, and it gave him the nerve to continue. The weather also served to brighten things a bit, though he knew Rachel could not see the brilliance of the sun as they walked, her arm in his.

"I've been thinking . . . I want to offer to make arrangements for you to see a doctor. There are several I know in New York, and with some help from my brother-in-law, I think we could pull some strings and get you in quickly."

She didn't respond or react to his gesture.

"I'm willing to do anything to help you. I could even take you back to New York with me, but you'll want to think about it, no doubt. And pray."

"I don't hafta think *or* pray," she said softly as they made the turn toward the footbridge. "New York City is your world. I have no desire to leave here."

He had assumed that she might turn him down, and no wonder. How would an Amishwoman—blind at that—manage in the middle of bustling Manhattan? He could hardly imagine her there.

"It was just a thought" was all he said.

"I appreciate the offer, Philip. It's awful kind of you."

Awful kind . . .

Was he? If he were truly kind, he might tell her how wonderful he thought she was. How very lovely. That her sweet and joyful spirit shone through her every action, word, and deed.

Yet if he said those things, he was unsure as to where they might lead. The truth of the matter was he did not know how to make the leap "back in time," so to speak, from modern life to the Plain. Even if he knew that he loved Rachel enough to marry her, even then he did not know if her feelings for him were the same.

They came to the highest point of the small bridge, and turning, they leaned on the railing. He peered down at the frozen layers of ice, though he could hear the current continuing its flow far beneath the surface.

"Tell me what you see," Rachel whispered near him.

"Sunlight and snow. And stark black tree trunks intermingled with tall evergreens."

"Are there birds?"

"A few crows here and there."

She sighed. "Come spring, this area is filled with birds, making nests and raisin' their young. . . ."

He allowed that thought to linger in the stillness between them, not daring to spoil the moment with a reply.

But Rachel had asked him to paint word pictures for her now. And so he continued. "The sky is as blue as a still clear pond. And the clouds are like cotton balls looming in the distance, which means it might be partly cloudy tomorrow."

She snickered. "You ain't a weather forecaster, are you?"

"That's one thing I'm not. Ask me about deadlines, political interviews, assigned columns, and revisions, but don't ask me about the weather."

"Funniest thing."

He glanced at her and saw that she was grinning. Rachel Yoder had a subtle sense of humor, and he laughed right out loud. "I'm going to miss this place," he declared, thinking that he could've gone one step further and said that he would miss her, too.

Everything had been going along just fine—even the weather was holdin' out—until Philip said what he did 'bout missing "this place." Once again, she wondered if he was trying to dodge the strong undercurrent between them. After all, if she felt it, surely he did, too. Yet, she couldn't be sure how such things worked between a man and woman, really. She'd been courted by only one man in her life. And that man was now with Jesus.

She wouldn't allow Philip's aloof comment to get her down. Fact was, he'd invited her to go walking. Just the two of them. And sometime here soon, it was up to her to give him an answer 'bout whether or not they should have dinner together. Uncertain how she should go about bringing the subject up, she let him keep describing the sky, the fields, and the neighbor's barn.

"You know, Rachel," he was saying, "I believe it was Esther's letter that spared your life the day of the accident . . . by blowing out of the wagon."

"I guess you're right, though I've never quite thought of it that way."

"God kept you alive for a reason, I believe."

She smiled. "Esther's always said that. So has Mam.

But back then, it was much easier for me to wish the Lord had seen fit to take me to heaven, too."

"I understand why you might've felt that way," Philip replied. "But now that you've come this far, I pray that you'll accept the fact that God continues to be at work in your life."

That was the dearest thing he might've said to her. 'Specially today. "I fully intend to see again," she told him.

"I believe you will, too, and I won't stop praying for your healing till you do."

She thought it was interesting—him sayin' such a thing. Did he mean to keep in touch with her?

"Regaining your sight is very important to me."

There, he'd said it again. So . . . his interest in her as a person, sighted or not, had *not* brought him back to Bird-in-Hand. For sure and for certain, he had come out of sympathy. Pure and simple.

"I gave my heart to Jesus a long time ago," she said, feeling the need to say so. "It was right before Jacob and I married, and since then I've been learnin' that we can't always understand God's timing. So when you say that my sight is important, well, I know it's ever so much more important to God."

It was one of the most courageous statements she'd ever made. In fact, she actually believed she was becoming a mighty confident woman, the way she'd always wanted to be.

❖ ❖ ❖

Susanna was fully aware that her daughter had gone out for a walk with Philip, but she wondered what on earth was taking them so long. Goodness' sake, they'd been gone twenty minutes or more. Still, the idea of the two of them together didn't get her goat near like it might've when Philip had first come here.

No, she was thinkin' more and more that she just might be able to turn him till he came 'round right, smack dab into their Plain community. 'Course, she had no idea what Benjamin would think of such a thing, havin' a fancy-turned-Plain son-in-law and all. But it wouldn't hurt none to ask him. Then again, she guessed she'd best wait to find out from Rachel if there was any hint of romance in the air.

Besides, she wanted to hear more from Ben 'bout the bishop's soul-savin' experience. Seemed to her if it was gut enough for the old bishop, maybe she—*they*— oughta consider it, too. She could hardly wait for her husband to wake up from his afternoon nap.

❖ ❖ ❖

Their walk to the creek was coming to an end. Rachel could hear the sounds of the house—Copper yippin' in the yard, people moving 'round inside.

"Have you given any thought to having dinner with me?" Philip asked.

"When must you leave?" she asked, holding tight to his arm as they walked back toward the house.

"Tomorrow morning. I have several assignments due

for the magazine, and some aren't even under way." He paused, and they strolled in silence for a moment. "I was thinking we could go somewhere quiet this evening, if you'd like."

She didn't really want to prolong the agony of parting, yet how on earth could she turn this wonderful man away? "That would be real nice, havin' dinner with you," she said at last.

"I'll call for reservations." There was genuine relief in his voice.

Still, she wished he didn't have to leave tomorrow. Or at all.

Twenty-Two

$\diamond \diamond \diamond$

Their dinner was a quiet affair at the historic Strasburg Inn in the colonial-style Washington House Restaurant. Elegantly appointed, the dining room was warm and inviting, resplendent in soft candlelight. Philip had requested a private table upon calling in the reservation and was pleased when he and Rachel were shown to a table in front of a draped window, made even more intimate by the crackling flames in the fireplace across the room.

"It's perfect," he told the hostess. "Thank you."

"Enjoy your evening," she said with a professional air and a smile. No impolite sidelong glances here.

"Lancaster County is one of the friendliest places I've visited," Philip said as they were seated.

Rachel smiled and nodded across the starched white tablecloth. "I'm not surprised. Lots of us here are God-fearin' folk. Maybe that's the reason. Pennsylvania got its start with people lookin' for a place to settle and worship God in their own way."

He hadn't thought of that. "I remember studying about William Penn in school. He was a devout Quaker who founded this state and made a colony for his fellow church members."

"And anyone else who wanted to join. You have a gut memory, I must say."

"Well, you know how it is. Certain things seem to stand out." Looking into her innocent face, sweetly aglow with candlelight, he realized anew that coming to Lancaster County and meeting Rachel would always be high on *his* list of "certain things."

Rachel was ever so curious. Halfway through dinner, Philip began asking repeated questions 'bout the Plain life. Was he actually thinkin' of joining conservative circles? Oh, she couldn't permit herself to think such thoughts, even if they were true. Couldn't let herself be hurt by hopin' for a future with Philip.

Still, she listened intently, then answered to the best of her ability, all the while enjoying the wonderful-gut dinner, as delicious as any she'd ever eaten in any restaurant. Her only regret was that she wasn't able to see the lovely surroundings, which Philip described so carefully, or . . . Philip himself.

What if she could see his face, smiling at her across the table? What then? Would she see God's Spirit shinin' out through his eyes?

Just then, he reached for her hand. "I really do want to keep in touch with you, Rachel."

Philip's voice and the caress of his hand made her heart leap up, and she knew she cared far too much. Oh my, ever so much! Tomorrow Philip would be leaving for New York. His home. She daresn't let on how she felt. Wouldn't be wise.

Rachel knew well the feeling of apprehension, and

she was experiencing it now. "Wouldja mind orderin' me some coffee?" she said in a wisp of a voice, gently pulling her hand away.

❖ ❖ ❖

Susanna stood outside the door to her daughter's room, deciding if she should knock or not. It was nearly too late to bother Rachel. She might even wake up Annie. Still, she *had* to talk to Rachel before she retired for the night.

"I hafta confess somethin' to ya," she whispered when Rachel opened the door a crack.

"What is it, Mam?"

"Please, will ya come downstairs?" Susanna stood in the hallway, waiting for Rachel to put on her slippers. Then she shone the lantern on the stairs as they made their way to the parlor.

"Is everything all right?" Rachel asked, frowning as she sat on the sofa.

"Oh, jah, everything's just fine . . . now 'tis." She wanted to cry and laugh all at once. But first she had to tell her daughter what had happened. "Your pop and I had ourselves a long, long talk tonight—with Esther and Levi. Right after you and Philip left, Dat opened up and told 'bout Bishop Seth's salvation. How he'd seen God's power reach down and deliver our leader on the bishop's sick bed."

"Dat said all that?"

Susanna put her hand on her chest, taking a deep

breath before going on. "Seth was one of the main reasons the powwow doctoring has been goin' so strong in
the community all these years. But I ain't telling you
nothin' new."

"Mam, you sound awful excited," Rachel blurted.
"How can this be?"

"I'll tell ya how." Susanna stopped to catch her
breath again, so caught up with emotion was she. "Ach,
I feel so wonderful-gut just now—washed clean
through. I've been waitin' for you to come home so I
could tell you what Dat said."

Rachel seemed eager to hear, sitting quietly with her
hands folded in her lap.

"You know how you've been tellin' me, off and on,
that the sins of the fathers are passed down to the third
and fourth generation?"

"The Bible says so . . . wasn't me, so much."

"No . . . no, and that's all right. Dat and I talked
things out right gut, and I hafta say that several days
ago, I listened to one of them tapes Esther sent you. Bor-
rowed it from your room and played it . . . several times
over." She didn't wait for Rachel to reply, just kept a-
goin' forward with what she had to get out before she
might burst. "I wanna be ready for heaven like Bishop
Seth. I wanna know my sins are forgiven, too . . . here
on earth."

"Mamma?"

"Jah, you heard me right. I wanna be ready when
Jesus comes back to catch His Bride away. Want my
heart pure and clean, without any spot of sin."

"Oh, Mam, what are ya tellin' me?"

"That Dat said, 'We've been hearing 'bout salvation full and free our whole life long—from either Gabriel Esh or some Mennonite somewheres. So we ain't gettin' any younger, Susie. We should've turned our lives 'round back when we shunned young Gabe.'"

"Dat said that?"

"Every word. Then we prayed with Esther and Levi, followin' all the things they said to do—repenting of the known sins of powwowing and enchantment amongst our ancestors on both sides. Our *own* sins, too. Then we renounced the sins, and, ach, what rejoicing came over us both."

"Oh, thank the good Lord," Rachel whispered, leaning toward her, reaching for her hand. "Mamma, this is one of the happiest days of my life."

Susanna scooted over next to her daughter, and they fell into each other's arms, weeping for joy.

Rachel wanted to let the beautiful reality of the moment sink in. She certainly didn't want to think 'bout what lay ahead for her parents. They'd be shunned, sure as anything, if they spoke out, revealing to the People the things that had happened this night. 'Course, it would depend on the new bishop and the church membership, too. But the fact that Rosemary—the bishop's widow—had also received the gift of salvation, along with her husband, stood for quite a lot.

Here Rachel had hoped to be able to have her sight back by day's end. Instead, she was hearin' of the Light of God's truth shining into the very lives of her Old Order parents. *This* healing miracle, in the light of eternity, was far more important than her longed-for sight.

Many thoughts whirled through her mind as she stood near her bed. Too wide awake to sleep, she relived the evening with Philip, how he'd held her hand across the table, offered to "keep in touch," asked almost too many questions 'bout life in Amish country, and reminded her that "faith takes courage."

She realized anew how Philip's coming—Esther's too—had shown her just how much God must love her in spite of her blind state, that He invites each and every person to "see" through salvation by grace.

She pondered the divine work begun in her life, and her family's, on account of both Esther's tapes and Adele Herr's story of Gabe Esh. And her thoughts flew back to the very moment this afternoon when she recalled dear Jacob dying in her arms. How full of God's love he had been. How very precious the death of God's children . . .

Moved to tears, Rachel knelt beside her bed and poured out her heart to her heavenly Father for all the amazing things He had accomplished in her life. Then she added, "Lord, you know I've struggled and strived. I've stood on your promises for healing, but now I'm gonna do what Lavina said days ago. I'm gonna lay my head on my pillow tonight and simply *rest in you*. If I remain blind all my life, then that's the way I'll be. I just want more of you, dear Lord."

Twenty-Three

❖ ❖ ❖

First thing next morning, Mam offered to pray for Rachel. "After all my fussin' over Blue Johnny, I think it's high time to beseech the Lord God heavenly Father for your healin'."

Rachel didn't quite know what to make of the suggestion, but she gladly bowed her head, allowing her mother to pray that her sight might return "in your will . . . and for your glory. Amen."

"Denki," she whispered, embracing Mam.

"I won't give up neither," her Mamma said, her arms strong against Rachel's back. "We'll keep on prayin' and believin'."

That morning, hearing Mam's prayer, it seemed as if everything between the two of them had been near out of focus for a gut many years, and now, gradually, ever so slowly—and in God's timing—the picture was growing clearer. 'Least it appeared to be so.

She and her mother had come a long way in just a few days. And Rachel knew she had the Lord to thank for that. Mam was no longer her adversary. No, they were sisters in the Spirit! She also knew that they would never go back to the way things had been before, that they would move forward. From now on.

After helpin' Mam serve their one and only breakfast guest, Rachel left Philip and Dat chatting in the dining room and went to give Nancy Beiler a quick call. Rachel was ever so glad to actually talk to the dear woman who'd always insisted on bein' called "Auntie Nancy," after such a long time, too.

"Do you remember me?" she asked when the woman answered.

"Why . . . little Rachel, 'course I do! How in the world are ya, anyways?"

"Oh, I'm thinkin' that we oughta sit down together and have hot chocolate and cookies here one of these days."

"Sounds like a gut idea to me."

They chatted 'bout some upcoming work frolics and such, then Nancy mentioned that she'd heard the "old bishop died . . . and on Christmas, too."

"His funeral's today."

"Is it true what we're hearin' . . . that Seth Fisher got the assurance of salvation before he died?"

"Lavina Troyer was there to see it, and so was Dat."

"Well, now, don't that beat all."

"It's wonderful-gut news, ain't so?"

Just then, Rachel heard Philip carrying down his luggage, so she said to Auntie Nancy, "Maybe I'll see ya at the bishop's funeral?"

"I'll try to come. Wonderful to hear your voice, Rachel."

"*Da Herr sei mit du*—the Lord be with you." Then she hung up, trying without success to quiet her heart. Philip was preparing to leave!

She'd learned long ago that it wasn't befittin' to let emotions rule you. 'Twas simply childish to get flustered over an Englischer leavin' town, for pity's sake! Rachel wasn't a child anymore. She'd been taught to "choke it down," if ever tears threatened to spill. 'Course, that was back when she was a little girl. Still, she'd "worn her feelin's on both sleeves" near all her life, as Mam often reminded. Wasn't because she wanted to; heaven knows, she didn't. It was just how she was by nature. The Lord knew her heart, and that was that.

As a child she had been told—by older sisters, and Mam too—that she could "squelch her emotions" by simply standing or sitting right still, putting her hands over her eyes, and shutting them "real tight." And if she did that and waited long enough, the lump in her throat would begin to go away, ever so slowly—but it *would* go away. "Sooner or later, your foolish tears'll dry up, too, never to fall," Lizzy had said.

But for Rachel to keep back the tears, she had to hold her breath a gut long time, too. Even then, sometimes that didn't much help.

This moment—here and now—had been a long time coming, really. For all the days and weeks she'd thought of Philip Bradley, dreamin' of him and sayin' a prayer for him—all that—only for him to be sayin' his good-byes. Again.

Yet she refused to let her tears be shed in front of him. Had to make them "dry up," 'cause Philip was here in the parlor with her just now. She had to say "so long" without lettin' on that she cared so awful much.

"I wanted to say how much I enjoyed getting to

know you better, Rachel," Philip was saying from across the room.

She nodded silently.

"I want you to know that I meant it when I said I'd be glad to set up an appointment for you with a doctor in New York City."

A psychiatrist, he means, she thought.

"If you decide differently, please let me know." He paused for a moment, and she felt the gloom hanging heavy. "I'll leave my business card here on the table for your parents . . . if they would be so kind as to give you the information. And . . . if ever you want to call . . . about that . . . I hope you will."

I hope you will. . . .

She heard his words, heartbreakingly distant, but what more could she expect? That he might rush to her side and take her in his arms? Tell her how much he loved her? That he wanted to be with her for always?

Just then, Annie came running into the room. "Oh, Mister Philip, you aren't leaving, are ya?"

Rachel couldn't bear to hear their exchange, their good-byes. As Annie scampered out of the room again, Rachel turned toward the latticed window she knew was there at the end of the private parlor. Her back to Philip, she shut her eyes "real tight" and squeezed her fist against her mouth. It was no use. The lump in her throat was enormous, overpowerin', really.

Amazingly, as she attempted to keep her emotions in check—the Amish way—she realized that she could make out the shapes of pine trees through the window, like seein' through the veiling of her prayer Kapp. Ever so slightly, the trees seemed more and more clear. And the longer she looked, the more distinct they became.

All the while, as Philip talked, she blinked, getting used to the light again, truly marvelin' at this wondrous thing that was happening. The murkiness, every bit of haze that had persisted since the accident, was beginning to fade away. It was as if a cloud or heavy film had been lifted slowly, gently from her eyes.

Little by little, colors were coming into view. She could see the forest green of the pines, the azure blue of the sky, the dazzling white of the snow—and shapes, edges, lines, shadows . . . all the many things she'd taken for granted before the light had dimmed.

Taking a deep breath, she focused on the grandeur of the sky, the texture of the underbrush along the creek, shadows made by the apple trees lined up in their orchard behind the house. Even the neighbor's silo and tobacco shed, more than a mile away, had become visible to her now. At long last, healing had come. She could see!

She wanted to turn and look into Philip's face—oh, with all her heart she struggled with the urge to behold him. She wanted to see for herself the fine features Annie had described, look for the sweet spirit shinin' out of his eyes. He was right there in the room—standin' ever so near.

But what if she did tell him, and then her sight failed her again? Like it had the night Blue Johnny tried to use his enchantments on her? Hadn't been long before her hazy vision was gone again, and the empty darkness was worse than before. And what if Philip pledged himself to her—thinkin' she could see—only to be shackled with a blind wife, after all?

"If it's all right with you, I'd like to call you sometime," Philip said.

"I . . . I just don't know," she managed, torn between giddy feelings over her renewed sight and sorrow over Philip's leaving. But she kept her gaze centered on the beautiful rich landscape beyond the window. She allowed her eyes to focus, ever so slowly, on closer objects: the windowsill, its white latticed frame—the center coming together in the shape of a cross. She looked with wonder at the Victorian marble-topped table—she'd gone with Mam to retrieve it from an estate auction years ago. She gazed fondly at the rose-colored hurricane lamp. Last of all, she stared down in complete astonishment at her own hands, folded tight across her waist.

Sighing, Rachel broke the silence. "Thank you for the offer, Philip—to help me get to a New York doctor. . . ." She paused, then, "Have a safe trip home. And may God bless you always," she said softly. Yet her heart longed to announce the remarkable miracle, cried out from the depths of her soul to let him know. She could see again!

All the months of waiting for this moment, and yet she knew it was ill-timed. She could not tell Philip the truth.

It was only after the front door closed that she allowed her tears to fall freely. Then she rose and went to stand in the gentle curve of the bay window—away from view—watching him walk to his car.

Rachel caught sight of his face, if only for an instant. "Dear . . . dear Philip," she whispered, thinking that Annie was surely right to say how good-lookin' he was. His chestnut brown hair shone in the winter sun. Taking a deep breath, she continued to watch as he started the car, backed it out slowly, and turned toward Olde Mill Road.

Now that he was gone, she began to second-guess her resolve. What had she done? Had she made the mistake of her life by not telling Philip what had happened? That her vision had returned? She was ever so sure he would've pledged his love if he knew she had her sight. Yet she had withheld the truth.

She heard footsteps just outside the parlor door. "Rachel?"

It was Mam.

"Oh, Mamma, I can see!" she exclaimed.

Mam frowned in disbelief. "You what?"

"My eyes are perfectly clear. I see your green choring dress and your old work apron. And you're scowlin' at me to beat the band."

"Well, praise be!" Mam rushed to hug her, then called for Dat and Annie. "Come, quick! The most wonderful-gut thing has happened!"

Rachel and Mam scurried out toward the hall as Annie came rushing in. "Annie, come here . . . let me look at you, my darling little one," Rachel called to her.

Annie blinked as the realization began to settle in. Her mouth dropped open ever so far. "Didja say . . . oh, Mamma, you can see?" Her daughter's eyes searched her own. "You *can*! You can!"

Rachel shed tears of great joy as she knelt down and let her baby girl hug her neck. "Oh, Annie, God made you ever so beautiful," she kept saying over and over. "Ach, you're the pertiest little girl I know."

"God answered our prayer," Mam said, all smiles as she stood over them.

Dat emerged from the front room, peering over his reading glasses. "Well, what's all the commotion 'bout?"

"It's 'cause of Mamma," Annie said, releasing Rachel and running over to her grandfather. She hugged him hard at the knees. "Mamma can see again. She can see me . . . and you, too!" Annie looked up at Susanna and then down at their little dog, who'd followed Benjamin into the hallway. "Ach, Mamma can see *everything!*"

"Well, bless the Lord God" was all he said, wearin' the downright biggest grin Rachel had ever witnessed on his face. "Bless the Lord."

Later, after the excitement began to dwindle some, Annie ran off to color, and Mam went to the kitchen, prob'ly to call Aunt Leah and Esther with the news. Dat headed back to reading *The Budget*, but Rachel turned toward the parlor, searching for the business card Philip had left.

She spotted it—a small white rectangular-shaped card—lying on Mam's cherry tea table. Picking it up, she was tempted to look at it, to see the name of his workplace, what address it might be. But unsure of herself, she turned it over and over in her hand. Then, refusing the temptation to look at it, she began to tear it into tiny pieces. Scurrying outside, she threw the pieces into the trash can. Best not to be dwellin' on either Philip Bradley or his little card anymore.

Standing on the back patio, with her shawl wrapped tightly around her, she looked beyond the apple orchard, now stark against the blue, blue sky. Her gaze drifted to the snowy pathway leading to Mill Creek, where she and Philip had walked just yesterday. What had he said—that the walk was an excuse for them to have some time alone? Why had he said such a thing? Did he need an excuse? What had he really and truly intended to say there as they stood on the crest of the footbridge? Something important, something lovely . . . she was ever so sure of it.

She allowed her eyes to follow the outline of the oval gazebo, closer to the house, where ivy and morning glory vines adorned it clear up to the capped roof with greenery and splashes of color in early summer.

"So long, Philip," she whispered into the crisp cold air. "So long . . . forever."

Twenty-Four

❖ ❖ ❖

*L*ove? Could this feeling for Rachel Yoder be *love*? What was it anyway? Could *genuine* love make you feel this way—confused and troubled? And if so, how was a person ever to know if he or she had found the real thing—the one person with whom to spend the rest of one's life?

Philip pondered these thoughts as he traveled east on Route 340, then south on Harvest Road, to Emma's Antique Shop. Getting out of the car, he picked his way over the snow-packed walkway. Eager to see what was available in the way of an antique desk, he peered in the front window and was surprised to find a cherry wood rolltop desk, slightly smaller than the desk at the Zooks' B&B. Intent on getting Rachel off his mind, he opened the door and immediately spied the young Mennonite owner.

"Well, hullo . . . didn't expect to see you so soon again." She smiled so big her grin spread across her face. "And you just about missed me, too. I come real close to puttin' up my sign and goin' home to fix lunch for my hubby. I usually only stay open a couple hours in the deep of winter. But today, well, I had a feeling someone might drop by, lookin' to spend their Christmas money, maybe."

"Then it's good timing on my part."

She nodded. "What can I help you with?"

He motioned toward the antique desk. "I've been looking for a piece like that."

"Yes, I remembered what you'd said last time, so my husband and I went poking around at several different auctions in Massachusetts," she explained, leading the way to the desk, made in the late 1800s. "You didn't call back, so it's been sittin' here in the window since last September." She chuckled. "Must have your name on it."

"But is it in my price range?" he humored her.

"Well, I wouldn't be surprised if I came close to matchin' my price up with your pocketbook." She brushed a piece of lint off the top of it, patting the wood.

Philip liked Emma's jovial spirit. She was vivacious and cheerful, and her modest floral print dress seemed to emulate the meek and gentle spirit within. He thought if ever he was to make a lifestyle change, that honoring God by dressing more simply—conservatively, too—would be the least of his concerns. The more difficult thing, possibly: to embrace the Plain church as a covenant community, especially because he was a "secular" Christian in their eyes. Not so much from his own viewpoint, but from Plain church members who might be wary of his convictions. He would have to prove himself.

Catching himself again, he wondered why he was thinking this way. Was his subconscious working overtime? And if so, why?

Inspecting the desk, he noticed it had similar compartments to the old desk at the B&B—dovetail drawers and plenty of pigeonholes. "Nooks and crannies," Grandma Bradley liked to call them. But thinking of his grandmother sent his mind spinning back to Rachel and her quaint old-fashioned way of expressing herself. How was he ever to go on with his life if every time he turned around, he was thinking of the lovely and sweet young Amishwoman?

"What's your best price?" he asked, running his hand across the smooth surface.

"Since you traveled so far to look, I'll say $750."

The desk was in excellent condition, so he knew it was a good deal. Only slightly higher than what *she* must have paid. "I'll take it," he said impulsively, easily visualizing the piece in his apartment. His writing studio would be the perfect location. And a good thing, too; an excuse to rid himself of the useless computer desk he presently owned.

An excuse . . .

In his mind, he was back with Rachel, enjoying the invigorating walk through the snow, out to the frozen creek. There, he'd stood on the arched bridge with her, close enough to smell her hair, the fragrance of her beauty.

So why *was* he purchasing a desk and hauling it back to New York when his heart was here in Bird-in-Hand? Quickly, he dismissed the irrational thought that he ought to consider staying. He would return to New York. No need to labor over that decision!

Having finalized the transaction, he told Emma he'd

have to rent a small trailer to pull behind his car.

"Just as well," she replied. "Shipping costs are sky-high."

"Everything's high these days, but thanks for the excellent price. I appreciate it." He offered a smile. She had done him a favor.

It was as he was heading west toward Lancaster that he contemplated his own parents' long-lasting love affair, how workable and happy their marriage had been. Janice and Ken came to mind, as well, for he viewed his sister and her husband as a model couple. One of the essential ingredients for a good marriage was similarity of background and interests. He had read that tidbit any number of places.

Yet his and Rachel's backgrounds seemed foreign. How could their union possibly thrive and be blessed in the eyes of God . . . and man? And their interests? Other than eagerness to own land and farm, what else did they have in common?

Then the image of a precocious child came to mind. Blond, blue-eyed Annie. He had always wanted a houseful of little girls and boys for as long as he could remember. So he and Rachel shared a love for children. And they enjoyed talking together, spending time sharing openly. Most important, they had a strong desire to serve and honor the Lord in all things, and they both wanted to share the Good News, too. Now, thinking about it, he guessed they *did* have a number of mutual interests.

But what was he to do about it? Call Rachel when he arrived back in New York? Perhaps have a cordial chat on New Year's Eve? Start a letter-writing relationship? What?

All of us, at one time or another, must make a choice. The words Adele had written to him nipped his memory.

Turning on the radio, he was grateful for a Christian music station, hoping to drown out speculation. Wasn't it enough that he'd gone out of his way to demonstrate his caring—his keen interest in her well-being, wanting to help her see again? How many modern men would offer to take an Amishwoman to New York City, of all places? He'd stuck his neck out in making a ridiculous overture. The fact that she'd turned him down flat was probably a very good thing. And sensible.

Sure, he could admit that he cared for Rachel. This far removed from the Orchard Guest House B&B, he could. Safely en route to rent a trailer and journey home, he could. Philip knew, too, that she just assumed she'd never see him again, most likely. And rightly so. After all, he had refrained from declaring his love. Had not even made an attempt. Yet he had thought of her— missed her—nearly every waking minute from their first encounter until the present visit.

So . . . what significant things had kept him from proclaiming his love? His writing career, his parents, his sister and family—all these had definitely played a part in holding him back. Yet as he contemplated his mental list, he knew big city life was not consequential to him; rather, the contrary. His parents and Janice, Ken, and Kari would expect him to marry at some point. Possibly move away, as well. So they were not a hindrance.

New York had always been home. It represented all that he really knew. Haggling over who would snag the next cover story or feature piece. Flying in and out of foreign countries to interview ambassadors and political leaders. Frantically sketching out rough drafts, rewriting, revising—all to meet some crucial deadline. Climbing the corporate ladder to yet another level of stress and strain. Never having time to stop and breathe in the sweet fragrance of life. Worst of all, regularly lamenting the time spent in jockeying to achieve what *society* deemed success.

Sighing, he thought again of Adele and Gabe, how they had belonged together, yet sadly missed each other. Due to what? Adele's reluctance? Perhaps. But there was more to it, and he knew precisely what that was. Adele had been unwilling to face her need of Gabe, that he was the only man who could occupy that cherished place in her life. The only one. And she had been too reticent to make the leap.

Fear is the opposite of faith, Levi Glick had said on more than one occasion.

Philip turned up the volume on the dash radio, listening to a choral rendition of the old hymn—"I Surrender All." He had always enjoyed the pure, uncomplicated melody, even as a boy, but today the lyrics caught his attention most of all.

By song's end, he found himself humming . . . then singing, even after the music had ended. "All to Jesus I surrender, humbly at His feet I bow, Worldly pleasures all forsaken. . . ."

In the quietude, hearing his lone baritone voice fill

the car, he sang out the words of joyous inspiration and surrender. And as he sang, he knew that he was in love with—*dearly* loved—Rachel Yoder. Without a shred of doubt. She was the woman in his life, the one woman who could complete him, fill his heart with the kind of simple joy he longed for. She was his heart-mate, and he longed to tell her so.

Slowing the car at Anderson's Bakery, he turned around and headed east again, past the sleepy hamlets of Witmer and Smoketown, away from Lancaster City to Bird-in-Hand. And he felt truly happy. Never so blessed with a realization in all his life.

❖ ❖ ❖

The bishop's funeral wasn't such a sorrowful thing, really. Not for Rachel and her family. Many of the Plain folk in attendance had known Seth Fisher for well over fifty years—from the time he'd begun his leadership work in the area. Many, too, had already heard of his so-called transformation . . . at life's end, of all things.

Because she was so jubilant about her healing, Rachel had gone along with her parents to the funeral to pay her respects to the man whose death, in all likelihood, would bring change to the Amish church. On the way, they passed the intersection of the Crossroad, and she took in all the sights without a single qualm or jitter. In the future, they would save much time on buggy trips to Intercourse, Gordonville, and farther east to see friends and distant relatives. She had much to be thankful for.

Well over five hundred Amish mourners attended the funeral, held at the bishop's old farmhouse. Lasting three hours, the service was steeped in tradition and form. But it was the talk afterward among the People that encouraged Rachel most, just knowin' how fast the word was spreading 'bout Seth's salvation experience, as well as her sight regained!

Rachel spied Blue Johnny in the throng and was somewhat startled to see him. Still, he had every right to be here, and it made sense that he would come, really. After all, Seth Fisher had chosen *him* when Gabe rejected the status of powwow doctor more than forty years ago.

She excused herself from Mam and Annie, as they stood outside bundled up in layers against the elements, waiting for the coffin to be moved from the front room of the bishop's farmhouse to the long white porch—for viewing purposes. Dat and Levi stood nearby, giving her even more confidence.

Working her way through the crowd of mourners, she soon found herself standing near enough to whisper to the man who'd repeatedly pursued her to pass on his healin' gifts. "Excuse me."

Blue Johnny turned and looked at her, his face not recording surprise, but rather glee. "Well, if it's not Rachel Yoder. Now . . . didn't I say you'd come lookin' for me someday?"

"You may have said it, but that ain't why I'm here." Rachel looked him straight in the face, praying silently for wisdom. "I've been healed by the power of God. I don't need evil powers to make me see. And I believe you, too, must surely be searchin' deep down in your heart for the truth . . . just like most everybody else I know 'round here." She inhaled, holding her breath for a second, then pressing on. "Seth Fisher got delivered of the devil's gift before he died. And if you don't believe it, you can talk to Rosemary, his widow." She stopped and pointed toward the house, to Seth's frail wife just now coming out onto the porch. "Just ask Rosie what God told the bishop on his deathbed."

His dark eyes grew more serious. "I've heard tell— bits and pieces—of what went on. Hard to believe a simpleton could influence a mighty man like that, I daresay."

"Well, the Lord says in His Word, 'A little child shall lead them.' So I s'pose then you hafta have that kind of childlike faith to enter the kingdom of heaven."

His head tilted a bit to one side, and by the somber look on his haggard face, she wondered if he might be paying some heed to what she was sayin'. "Jesus can set you free of powwowing, too. You don't hafta die in your sins, Blue Johnny. You can turn your back on what the devil's been after you to do all these years."

He blinked his eyes like he was right nervous now. "Been hearin' this all my life from one Bible-thumper or another. Thing is, most folk look on me and my black box as a powerful-good miracle-worker." He lifted his hand to scratch under his hat. "But never has an Amishwoman talked to me the way you are."

Rachel shook her head. "I'm not a preacher, if that's

what you're thinkin', but I'm servin' the Lord in whatever way I can. If talking to you 'bout God and His Word is part of that callin', well, then, I'm ever so glad to do it."

Blue Johnny grimaced, saying nothing.

The bishop's body was being brought out in a long poplar coffin, wider at the shoulders and tapered on the lid. Time for the final viewing.

"I'll be prayin' for you, Blue Johnny."

"Praying . . . for me?" His eyes were pools of wonder.

Rachel nodded. "Jah, I will."

He didn't offer a smile but gave yet another dip of his bushy-haired head.

❖ ❖ ❖

No one was home when Philip returned to the Amish B&B. And though he tried the door and found it to be open, he nevertheless chose to remain outside until the Zooks and Rachel returned. He sat on the front porch for nearly thirty minutes, his feet and hands growing numb with cold, so he returned to his car, waiting with great anticipation.

Glancing at the digital dash clock, he decided to give Rachel and her family another half hour. If they didn't arrive home by then, he would leave a note for Rachel. *I must talk to you, my dearest*, it might say. He would post it in plain sight on the storm door—so either Benjamin or Susanna would be sure to notice it as they entered. He would be taking a risk of such a note ever finding its way into Rachel's hands, though. She might not be told of his message at all.

Sitting in the luxury of his warm car, he thought back to various conversations with Rachel, especially their last dinner together, when they'd discussed their differences at length. He considered his life as a future Amishman. Would he miss the many technological conveniences he was accustomed to? Would the Plain life be stimulating enough for his active mind? And what if he tired of the simple ways—would he long to return to the big city, regretting his decision to join the Anabaptist community?

But no, there was only Rachel for him—she was the answer to his heart's cry. Plain or not, she was his sweetheart. And whatever it took, he would leap the chasm that had separated them.

Don't make my mistake, Adele had warned, referring to herself and Gabe Esh. So Philip had benefited greatly from Adele's story—not to err and miss out on his heartmate. He *was* ready to take the plunge to simplicity, tranquility, and devotion—the biblical aspects of a life "set apart," the very things that had called to him since coming to Lancaster County, where his heart had turned back to God in total abandon.

Philip breathed a prayer, all the while picturing himself settled in the Bird-in-Hand area, working the land, possibly; helping his neighbors harvest crops, assisting his beloved in her blindness, witnessing of God's grace and love, writing on assignment—a Christian publication would be a welcome change—and growing old gracefully and happily with Rachel by his side. And, the Lord willing, he would father many children and lead each of them to the foot of Calvary's cross.

Yes, there was no longer any mistake about it. He had come home.

❖ ❖ ❖

Tables had been laid with plates and utensils for the shared meal—cold cuts of beef, hot mashed potatoes and gravy, various kinds of fruit, and coffee—following the burial service. After they served the men and teenage boys first, as was their custom, Rachel made sure there was room for Lavina to sit next to her. Women and children ate last, while the men stood 'round outside in the barn and outbuildings, comparin' notes on mules and upcoming auctions and whatnot.

"Looks to me like God answered your prayer," Lavina said, clasping Rachel's hand.

"Jah, He truly did."

Lavina's head was bobbin' up and down. "He's ever faithful, as Adele would say."

Leaning over, Rachel hugged Annie and noticed her missing front tooth. "Ach, when's the new tooth comin' in, do ya think?" She pointed to the tiny gap.

Annie's tongue did a gut job of feelin' for the new tooth. Suddenly, her eyes grew big as can be. "I feel it, Mamma! My big-girl tooth is on its way down."

Lavina and two of Rachel's sisters, Lizzy and Mary, laughed out loud at Annie's cute comment about the "big-girl tooth." Her sisters' tittering, especially, encouraged Rachel and gave her hope that a mended relationship might be forthcoming. Now that her sight had returned, maybe her siblings and their families wouldn't stay so far away. Maybe they'd understand, too, that she wasn't *narrisch*—crazy—or under the sway of some spell. She had faith—jah, even confidence!—that in time, her companionship with all her siblings would steadily improve. All eleven of them!

Meanwhile, she would pray and ask the Lord how to minister to dear Lizzy, first of all. Trust the Lord to show her older sister His grace and forgiveness, how He had brought Rachel to a clear understanding of the powwow "gifting" and its false belief system. In turn, Lizzy might pass on the knowledge to her youngest, the rambunctious and often impulsive Joshua. For now, Rachel would believe the Lord for divine wisdom to know what to say—and when.

"Did your New York guest leave already?" Lavina whispered during dessert.

"Right away this mornin'."

"Before your sight returned to you?"

"No . . . after."

Lavina's mouth dropped open. "Then . . . he *knows* 'bout your healing?"

She shook her head slowly, glancing 'round the table, hoping no one was paying them any mind. "I just couldn't tell him, Lavina."

"Well, why not?"

" 'Cause I thought I was doin' the right thing not to let on. I . . . oh, Lavina, I wanted him to care for me whether I was blind or not."

"So you didn't learn nothin' from Adele and Gabe, I guess."

Heart aching, Rachel felt her confidence dwindling. When did Lavina come to be so outspoken? She just didn't know if she could abide this sad, lost feelin' that had come upon her at the older woman's reproach.

"You love him, I know ya do, Rachel. It's all over your face."

"But it's best this way" was all she could bring herself to say.

Twenty-Five

The sky was beginning to streak bright golds and reds due to a myriad of clouds. Rachel watched from her vantage point in the buggy, enjoying the ride home. Never again would she allow herself to take her eyesight for granted. God did a wonderful-gut thing, giving it back. She couldn't keep from looking—no, starin'—at clouds, trees, farmland, neighbors' houses, even color-less plank fences.

Winter had always had a feel of silence to it, the cold seemin' to gobble up near all the sounds, 'cept for boots gnawin' away at crusty blankets of snow and horse hooves clapping against hardened roads. And there were the occasional shouts of glee from children playin' "Crack the Whip" on the pond. All of it, Rachel felt she was seeing and hearing for the very first time.

"We had a right gut turnout for the bishop's ser-vices," Dat spoke up in the front seat.

Mam nodded. "I think lotsa folk came out of curi-osity, in a way."

"What do ya mean?" Dat sounded awful serious.

"Well, you know, all the talk of Seth's salvation going 'round. Some might've thought one of the preachers would stand up and give an account of the bishop's final words or suchlike."

"Seems to me they should've."

Mam sighed and Rachel could hear it from the back-seat. "Word's travelin' faster than ever these days."

"Jah, and a few had heard of *my* news," Rachel chimed in. "I have a feelin' somebody must've gotten on the phone and called around."

Mam craned her neck and smiled real big at her. "Couldn't keep such a thing as my daughter's recovery to myself, now, could I?"

She hoped Mam felt the same 'bout the bishop's change of heart, wantin' to spread the word. 'Cause far as she was concerned, that was the best miracle of all.

"Well, what the world!" Dat said as they came down Olde Mill Road toward the house.

Rachel had been taking in the view on the opposite side of the carriage, gazing at just 'bout anything she laid eyes on, while Annie kept a-huggin' her. But when she turned, she was shocked to see Philip's car parked in the designated guest area, with Philip himself inside! She remained silent, though her heart beat so hard, she was perty sure Mam would hear it up front.

Annie jumped out of the carriage as soon as the horse stopped. "It's Mister Philip!" she said, running through the snow. "He's back . . . again!"

"Looks like we might be gettin' ourselves an Englischer son-in-law, Mam," Dat joked.

"Now, Benjamin, don't jump to conclusions." Mam turned 'round again, but this time she reached for Rachel's hand. "Your pop and I wouldn't be opposed to such a thing . . . in case you wondered. We'll help him turn 'round right . . . Plain and all."

Still, Rachel remained speechless. Philip had said good-bye already. Why on earth had he come back?

Walking hand in hand with Annie, he hurried over to the buggy. "I've been waiting for you, Rachel," he said, the biggest smile on his handsome face.

"Mamma . . . look who's here!" Annie said, grinning and showing her missing tooth.

Rachel set her gaze on his countenance, the first she'd seen him up close. Her eyes followed his hairline, took in the rich hues of his thick, light brown hair, his cheekbones and fine nose, his mouth. Philip was a treat for the eyes, all right, but it was his spirit that had attracted her first of all. She would never forget that.

"We'll be goin' inside now," Mam said loud enough for all to hear, 'specially Annie, who didn't take too kindly to the idea. But she went anyway.

Dat dallied a few seconds longer, tying up the horse. Then he skedaddled off, without so much as a glance over his shoulder.

"Rachel?" Philip's eyes searched hers, narrowing as in disbelief. "Can it be . . . that you can see?"

She nodded. "I didn't know if it was wise to tell you before."

Not waiting a second longer, he climbed into the buggy and found his way to her seat. "When did your sight return?" he asked, sitting next to her.

"While you were saying good-bye. It took me by surprise, I must say . . . that's why I kept my back to you . . . didn't tell you."

His smile was warm and earnest. "I wondered why, but I understand now."

"Why did you come back?"

"Because . . . I love you, Rachel. I couldn't leave without telling you." He reached for her mittened hands. "I've loved you ever since our first day together . . . in Reading."

She gazed on him, beginning to tremble, not with fear but emotion. "But how can this ever be?"

"I want to be Amish, Rachel. I want to live the simple life . . . with you and Annie."

She knew if she tried to speak, the words would come out too squeaky . . . too high. She fought back the tears—swallowing hard over the lump in her throat— her heart overjoyed.

"All my life," Philip continued, "I've felt something was missing, Rachel. It was your lifestyle—your Lord— I was searching for." His smile said more than a thousand words. "And I was looking for *you*."

"Oh, Philip . . ." Rachel's heart knew the answer before he ever posed the question here, under the covering of the winter sky and the carriage top. "*Ich liebe dich*, Philip—I love you, too!" She fell into his warm embrace, tears of happiness clouding her sight.

"I want to do things properly, according to your ways . . . should I ask your father for your hand?" Philip asked, all seriouslike, as they gazed on each other's faces.

She smiled at the notion. "The People don't do that sort of thing, but if you want to, that's just right fine." And the more she thought on it, the more she realized Dat might honestly like the idea.

So Philip did just that, and Dat took to it with ever such delight, followed by Mam's jovial well-wishing. Her father explained the rules of courtship, and when they told Annie the news, she jumped up and down for the longest time. But nobody seemed much annoyed by it, least of all Rachel and Philip.

Twenty-Six

$\mathscr{P}$hilip could hardly keep up with Adele's many questions when he called her on his cell phone. She wanted to know when all this "excitement" had taken place, when he and Rachel were to be married, where they would live, and had he told his family yet. Most of all, she was delighted "beyond words."

"I have money stashed away for a down payment on a farmhouse," he told her. "Rachel and I haven't set a wedding date yet, but you'll be one of the first to know when we do. As for my family, I'll tell them on New Year's Eve. We plan to 'pray in' the year together at our—*their*—church."

"Now . . . how on earth will you make the transition to Plain life?"

She was being the Adele he'd come to know and love, asking pointed questions, sounding like an interviewer! Yet the dear lady had his best interests at heart, he knew that.

"I believe I've weighed every possible aspect of Amish life over the past three months. How hard can it be for a man who despises big-city life? Besides, I won't have to give up my car, Rachel says." He paused, more sober now. "I've longed for this sort of change since my first visit to Grandpap's cottage in Vermont. And Rachel, well . . . you know how very precious *she* is!"

Adele's laughter was warm and reassuring. "You're going to have a wonderful life, Philip. May the Lord bless you both."

They chatted a little longer. Then he said he would keep in touch. "You'll hear from me again soon. About the wedding, especially."

"You call when you can, and please tell Rachel I send all my best. May God give you lots of little Bradleys. Oh, and if you wouldn't mind, tell Rachel to pass on the word to Lavina that I received her color copies of Gabe's artwork."

"Gabe was an artist?"

"Evidently. The drawings Lavina sent are from his childhood," she told him. "Remember, his name means 'God is my strength,' so we should have expected him to be multi-talented, right?"

Philip liked that. Adele had a terrific perspective on life these days. So much had changed for the dear woman who had lost so much, only to help Philip and Rachel find their way. "I'll talk to you soon."

"Happy New Year, Philip. Remember, God is ever faithful."

Ever faithful . . .

Rachel went to the kitchen phone and dialed up Uncle Amos—his business phone in the woodworking shed. 'Course, he'd hafta run into the house and get

Esther on the line. But it was worth the inconvenience, for sure and for certain.

At long last, she heard Esther's voice. "Can you and Levi come over tonight?" she asked.

"For goodness' sake, Rachel. You sound nearly breathless. Are ya all right?"

She took a slow, deep breath so she could get out the words without faltering. "Philip Bradley came back. He loves me, Esther. And I love him. Ach, I'm ever so happy!"

"Well, what do you know 'bout that!" There was no hesitation. "We'll be right over."

Rachel hung up, gettin' that awful giddy feeling. But mixed in with the giddiness was a prevailing peace. She thought of a favorite verse in Philippians: "And the peace of God, which passeth all understanding, shall keep your hearts and minds through Christ Jesus."

Rachel returned to the front room and stood near the fireplace, rubbing her hands together, thankful that Dat had a blazing fire goin'. When she was warmer, she moved to the windows and looked out at the gathering dusk, rising amidst snow-powdered pines, truly thankful for God's goodness and grace.

Philip went to stand with her at the window. "Our friend Adele approves."

"I had a feelin' she might."

"And she sends her blessing." He reached for Rachel's delicate hand, looking deep into her beautiful brown eyes. "Do you remember how Gabe signed his illustrious postcard?"

Rachel nodded cheerfully. " 'Soon we'll be together, my love.' That's how he signed off."

"You remembered."

"How could I *forget?*"

Happily, they embraced, then turned to peer out at the sky, now dotted with stars and a near-full silver moon. Winter's wind had blown away the imposing buildup of clouds, making way for a clear and radiant twilight. The future was just as bright.

Epilogue

❖ ❖ ❖

I've begun to think our life theme must surely be God's faithfulness. My dear Philip refers to Adele's words often, even 'round the farm, in the seemingly incidental things. Jah, God's hand is ever so evident in our lives.

Of all things, just days before our wedding, Lavina offered to rent us her big farmhouse. She said she never needed such a large place. Well, it's three times bigger than *we* really needed. But that's just fine, 'cause not too long after we were settled in, Adele's doctor said she didn't need to be in a nursing home anymore. "Come make a home with us," we told her. So Philip, Dat, and I went up to Reading and moved her and her few belongings to our place.

We're one happy family, and Adele and Lavina live in the Dawdi Haus, built onto the southeast side of the main house. They look after each other like cheerful older sisters, and they tend to us like two doting *Grossmutters*.

Lavina's decided she wants to will over her house and part of the land to us before she dies. 'Course, we ain't lookin' forward to it anytime soon, but till that day comes, Philip's workin' the soil with Lavina's older brother and cousin. And he seems to love every minute of it.

Our baby's due in a few weeks, and Philip's first choice in a name for a boy is Gabriel. Adele thinks that would be "just lovely." Lavina too. Annie's counting the days till she's no longer an "only-lonely" child, as she puts it. I keep myself busy cooking, canning, and crocheting infant clothes and cradle afghans for our first little Bradley.

My sight is just as clear as ever, and the nightmares are less frequent now. I am grateful for the dark valley the Lord allowed me to walk through. Now I can truly empathize with other hurting souls. Believe me, I've had a gut many opportunities to talk to folk 'bout the Lord. It just seems one door after another keeps opening up for me.

For Philip, too. He's writing a short story collection, set in Amish country—puttin' all his new experiences as a Plain farmer into it. Honestly, he sold his computer, printer, and whatnot and seems ever so content to write longhand on the antique rolltop desk he bought at Emma's. The desk reminds us all of Gabe's postcard to Adele, which she still happily displays in her room.

Philip's parents and sister have already come to visit. They're always welcome here, and his young niece, Kari, is so attentive to Annie. There's just too many bedrooms in this great big house. One day, I believe, we'll have them all full up with children, though. Lord willin'.

Thou shalt see thy children's children. . . . Ach, Jacob surely must be smilin' down on us.

Last I heard, Smithy Lapp's courting a widow lady over in his own township. Seems to me that makes better sense. 'Course, who am *I* to be talking 'bout staying in home territory for a life-mate! Thing is, Philip and I know God put us together. Plain and simple.

At day's end, no matter the weather, we take long walks and watch the sunset, or at least the sky and the farmland stretching out on either side of us. Philip calls it the "best relaxation therapy" he's ever known.

We've had gut fellowship with several young couples at our Beachy Church. A group of the men have come alongside Philip and taken him under their wing. Hardest thing for me to get used to, at first, was Philip's coarse whiskers. Now his beard's nearly as soft as goose down. He fits right in 'round here, too. Perty soon, no one'll ever know he was "fancy" at all.

The Crossroad will forever serve as a reminder of God's grace and mercy in our lives. Every time we pass through, we think of how God has blessed us.

Esther and I have joyfully returned to writing letters the old-fashioned way. It's a nice change, even though I did enjoy hearing her voice on the tapes. When we get really homesick for each other, we just pick up the telephone. She, too, is expecting again—possibly twins this time!

As for the new bishop, Mam says he's much more open to the People reading their Bibles, even encourages them to buy the newly translated Pennsylvania Dutch New Testament. I rejoice daily at the things we see God doing here.

Another wonderful-gut thing is happening. Not

only do Lizzy's and Mary's families come to visit—even show some interest in having a Bible study—my brothers, Noah, Joseph, and Matthew, are beginning to warm up to us, too. Still, I'm hoping for the day when *all* us Zooks can have a big get-together. Maybe Philip and I will have it here at Lavina's place. . . .

Annie's a busy bee at school her first year, and she's lookin' ahead to helping Philip—she calls him Pop—gather pumpkins here right soon. We'll hafta show him how to make apple cider, too, while we're at it.

Powwow doctoring continues in the area, though people are beginning to associate it with voodoo and black magic. So the word's getting out, thanks to our pastors, as well. And, of course, Gabe Esh who got all this started so long ago. It seems that God has allowed us to stand on the shoulders of those who've gone before us—those who've been godly examples.

A few months back, Blue Johnny moved away, we heard, and so far no one's stepped forward to take his place. We pray daily for our community, that the People will be willing to walk the road to Calvary's cross and find healing for body, mind, and spirit.

Yesterday, Mam dropped by with some patterns for crib quilts. I liked the Lone Star best. So she and I, along with Lavina and Adele, are gonna have us a little quiltin' bee next week. Annie will sew her very first stitches in this coverlet for her new brother or sister.

After years of enduring darkness and pain in a co-coon of my own making, it's ever so gut to gnaw out of the protective covering—through the scars—and open my new wings. Some days they're a bit fragile, even doddering, but one thing I know for sure and for certain, the Lord has daily granted me a "speckle of pluck." Not a full measure of confidence just yet, but I'm trusting for that as I take one flitter of my new wings, a day at a time.

Author's Note

✧ ✧ ✧

Divine protection—"underneath are the everlasting arms"—and Spirit-directed intercessors, who prayed even in the wee hours, made it possible for me to complete this, my most recent journey of faith.

I am also grateful to the Lancaster County residents who assisted me with research for this book and its prequel, *The Postcard*. Graciously, they reject any acknowledgment, as is their Plain custom, yet I appreciate their willingness to share.

My study of the life of Helen Keller ignited the inspiration for my character Rachel Yoder and her reaction to suffering a conversion disorder, causing blindness. In addition, I owe a debt of gratitude to the research assistance of Amy Watson, manager of Library Information Resources for the Helen Keller Archival Collection.

On some small scale, I was able to understand the world of the visually impaired due to my study, as well as incorporating information from the American Foundation for the Blind.

As always, my husband, Dave, shared equally in the joys and sorrows of this venture into Amish tradition, and I am delighted to call him "first editor."

Much appreciation to Gary and Carol Johnson of Bethany House Publishers, as well as my faithful editors, Barb Lilland, Anne Severance, and the entire BHP team. Special thanks to Jane Jones and Barbara Birch who read the manuscript for accuracy. I also wish to thank two of Jacob J. Hershberger's former students who shared their recollections of the late Amish Mennonite bishop, whose devotional columns in *The Sugarcreek Budget* of Ohio ("Lynnhaven Gleanings") inspired the subplot for this book, as well as *The Postcard*.

Big thank-yous to Auntie Em's Antiques & Gifts of Monument, Colorado!

The book *Gifts of Darkness* is purely fictitious, though based on actual writings by Amish church members and clergy.

Many blessings to my readers, who inspire me daily with letters and cards. I pray your hearts have been made receptive to God's redemptive love—lives set free—by the message of this book.

WELCOME TO LANCASTER COUNTY

Torn From Her Family and Home, Katie Must Search Her Past to Find Answers to Her Future

THE HERITAGE OF LANCASTER COUNTY · 1
SHE ONLY KNEW THE AMISH WAYS, BUT WITH ONE VISIT TO THE ATTIC, HER WORLD BEGAN TO CRUMBLE

THE HERITAGE OF LANCASTER COUNTY · 2
SHE LEFT BEHIND THE AMISH WAYS TO PURSUE A LIFE SHE'D NEVER KNOWN....

THE HERITAGE OF LANCASTER COUNTY · 3
E LIFE SHE'S ALWAYS DREAMED OF, YET HER AMISH ROOTS ARE CALLING HE R HOME.

BEVERLY LEWIS — THE SHUNNING

BEVERLY LEWIS — THE CONFESSION

VERLY LEWIS — THE CKONING

In the quiet Amish community of Hickory Hollow, time has stood still while cherished traditions and heartfelt beliefs have flourished. But the moment Katie Lapp finds a satin baby gown hidden in a trunk, she uncovers a secret that could shatter the tranquil lives of everyone involved.

Following Katie Lapp from the eve of her wedding, through her banishment from the close-knit community, and into her search for a mother she never knew, THE HERITAGE OF LANCASTER COUNTY provides a dramatic and powerful look into a life of faith, a search for truth, and a promise of peace.

Through vivid characters and heart-warming prose, author Beverly Lewis recreates the simple life of the Amish in this trilogy of hope and reconciliation that shows us that even when we think we are far away, God's love is always present.

THE HERITAGE OF LANCASTER COUNTY
The Shunning
The Confession
The Reckoning